P9-CLS-982

WATCHED

CJ LYONS

WITHDRAWN

sourcebooks
fire

Fitchburg Public Library
5530 Lacy Road
Fitchburg, WI 53711

Copyright © 2014 by CJ Lyons
Cover and internal design © 2014 by Sourcebooks, Inc.
Cover design by Christian Fuenfhausen
Cover image © Dewayne Flowers/Shutterstock; Tonkovic/Thinkstock

Sourcebooks and the colophon are registered trademarks of Sourcebooks, Inc.

All rights reserved. No part of this book may be reproduced in any form or by any electronic or mechanical means including information storage and retrieval systems—except in the case of brief quotations embodied in critical articles or reviews—without permission in writing from its publisher, Sourcebooks, Inc.

The characters and events portrayed in this book are fictitious or are used fictitiously. Any similarity to real persons, living or dead, is purely coincidental and not intended by the author.

Published by Sourcebooks Fire, an imprint of Sourcebooks, Inc.
P.O. Box 4410, Naperville, Illinois 60567-4410
(630) 961-3900
Fax: (630) 961-2168
www.sourcebooks.com

Library of Congress Cataloging-in-Publication data is on file with the publisher.

Printed and bound in the United States of America.
WOZ 10 9 8 7 6 5 4 3 2 1

To my patients who suffered in silence before finding the courage to speak out. Thank you for teaching me that heroes are indeed born every day.

"It is not light that we need, but fire; it is not the gentle shower, but thunder. We need the storm, the whirlwind, and the earthquake."

—Frederick Douglass

cap·ping [kap-ing] *Verb, Slang:*
1. The act of shooting or killing someone with a gun.
2. The practice of capturing covert screenshots, usually of underage girls and boys, and then using them to coerce the subjects into performing sexual acts on video. (See also: *capper*, noun, slang)

cap·per [kap-er] *Noun, Slang:*
1. An informer.
2. A person who captures covert screenshots for the purpose of blackmail, bullying, sexual gratification, or to trade among online communities.

PROLOGUE

You don't know what it feels like to hold a life in your hands, but I do.

There's nothing like it. Better than sex, it's a rush that leaves you panting, wanting more. And more is so easy to get. You, all of you, you're just waiting for me.

And I'm coming for you.

You won't know I control your life, your future, your every waking moment…not until it's too late.

Best thing of all? Even once you know who I am and what I've done to you, there's nothing you can do about it. You are mine. Forever.

Your life will never be the same— you might die or you might keep living, but your life will always be mine. Ants squirming under a magnifying glass, no matter where you run, no matter how you fight, no matter if you give up and kill yourself…I win.

The law can't stop me. You can't stop me. No one can.

—Confessions of an anonymous capper

1

Some guys think fire is sexy.

Watching the abandoned house burn, I spot a few of those in the crowd. While firefighters like my uncle are hard at work, these guys are hanging out, staring, licking their lips, one hand shoved deep down the front pocket of their jeans. Pyros.

That's not me. I don't love fire. I hate it. I envy it.

I *need* it.

I didn't start this fire, but I understand whoever did: the joy of creating something so beautiful. The temptation to give it freedom, let it take control, destroying everything in its path.

One spark is all it takes.

You think you can control it. You know it's wrong, but you don't know what else to do. You're trapped, a flame dancing along a match, running out of time, nowhere to go.

You figure you can stop. That you only need it just this once. Then everything will be okay and you won't ever, ever do it again. You won't have to, because you're in control.

At least that's what you think.

But sparks breathe and grow into flames. Flames surge into a full-blown blaze. You try to smother them, but it burns, hurts so bad you pull back. Lose control.

If you ever even had it to begin with.

That's life. My life.

Some days I want to burn the world to ashes. Let the flames loose to scour the filth and dirt, devour the pain—my pain—and start fresh and new again.

But fire never keeps its promise. You can never give it its freedom—just like I can never let my feelings escape, never tell anyone the truth.

If I did, my whole world would burn like the house in front of me.

It's mesmerizing, watching the well-rehearsed movements of the firemen attacking the flames. There's no one inside the two-story frame house on Pine Street, so they're coordinating an exterior attack. A few of the guys nod or wave at me. Most of them are grinning as they lean against the water gushing through their hoses—and they don't even know it. In their own way, they love fire as much as the pyros do.

I wish I could love anything that much. Most days I just feel numb. Other times, there's this rage burning inside me, consuming me, until it takes all my energy to keep it from escaping like the flames curling through the house's busted windows.

Dave, the engineer, checks the gauges on the side of the pumper truck—lime green, emblazoned with the Smithfield, PA, Fire Department insignia—then joins me.

"You guys need anything?" I yell over the riotous clamor of water, engines, men shouting, the house groaning and moaning. Fires are noisy places. Most people don't realize that.

Or appreciate the stench. Not like a wood fire you build on a cold winter's night, safe at home. House fires mean all sorts of shit going up in smoke: carpet and plastic and clothing and insulation. The smell is the main reason the crowd stays back, not heat or fear.

It always amazes me how little fear civilians have—if they could get close, they would. Their faces light up, eyes reflecting the flames, and if it weren't for guys like my uncle and Dave keeping them back at a safe distance, they'd walk right into danger, like they're in a trance or something.

I guess we all have a love-hate relationship with fire. Some more than others.

"I can make a run to Sheetz, grab some sodas," I tell Dave. Fighting fire is thirsty work. And these guys will be here for a while, long after the last flame is doused. Putting out the fire is the fun part; the real work comes during the cleanup.

"Thanks, Jesse," he says. "But we're covered." We stand side by side in front of the pumper, arms crossed over our chests, and watch the fire's dying throes. "No signs of a meth lab or any hazmat shit, thank God. She was a bitch, but your uncle, he grabbed her by the throat and throttled her good."

Firemen talk like that, like fires are women, like conquering a fire is better than sex.

It's not PC, but if you've ever been inside a building, smoke so black even the strongest light can't penetrate it, thick with poisonous chemicals that would kill you if you weren't breathing through a mask, your heart pounding in your head as you

5

inch your way forward, desperate not to get lost or fall through the floor and drown in the water your brothers-in-arms are pouring into the flames…if you've ever been there, you'd talk like that too.

I've never told my uncle or any of the other guys at the station, but fire isn't a "she" to me. Fire *is* me, like the blood in my veins or the electricity that jump-starts my nerves.

It's the fury that wakes me with its acid burn every morning, the pain that curdles my insides until I clench every muscle, trying to regain control. Fire is the part of me I can never show the rest of the world, but sometimes I have to let it out or I'll spontaneously combust.

We watched a video in health class last year. It was about not hurting yourself—drinking and driving, eating disorders, killing yourself, whatever. In it, a girl talked about cutting.

She said seeing her blood was like wrapping a chain around her heart, anchoring her to the real world. Without the blood, she'd just float away into nothing. Only by tearing into her own flesh, allowing the blood to escape, could she release the pain building up inside.

I'll never forget that girl. She's me—before they locked her up and fed her drugs and turned her into a zombie telling other kids, *don't worry; be happy.*

Yeah right. Sometimes adults are so clueless, I wonder if they even live in the same universe as me. There are so many things going on right in front of them, inside their own homes even, and they're so damn oblivious. Wandering around in the dark, never seeing—or maybe they choose not to see. Which, in my book, is even worse.

Doesn't matter. All you can do is figure out what works for you. For that girl, it was cutting. For me, it's keeping my mouth shut and lighting my fires.

"Come summer, it'll be you," Dave says, giving the dying blaze a nod. I turned sixteen a few months ago; now I can join the department as a junior firefighter. Everyone assumes I'll follow in my uncle's footsteps, so I guess that's what will happen. No one ever asks me.

"Was it our guy?" We're far enough away from the civilians I don't have to worry about being overheard. Few outside the fire department and the cops know there's a serial arsonist at work in Smithfield.

"Yeah. Sixth one. Same signature."

"You think he's a bug?" Firefighters call people like me, who start fires out of compulsion, firebugs. I hate the term, although I have to admit that when the need strikes, I do feel like a worm, unable to crawl away from it—lower than low, belly rubbing the dirt.

Then I light a fire, bring it to life, and I feel almost human again.

"No. This guy's a pro. Cops are trying to follow the money trail, but it'll take time." Dave shrugs. Catching the guy isn't his job—putting out the fires left in his wake is.

"They came around last night, talked to my uncle. At the house." My uncle is assistant chief, in charge of personnel. Smithfield's a small city made smaller by the recession, and firefighters don't make much despite the risks they take to protect civilians. The temptation to earn extra money burning down empty buildings so owners can cash out puts even firefighting heroes at the top of the cops' suspect list.

"I'll bet he gave them an earful."

"Kicked them out. Said to get a court record for the personnel files, they want them so bad."

He looks at me, frowning. The lights flash across his face, red, white, red, white. "Jesse, you know anything about these fires?"

I shake my head. "No."

It's the truth. I can never lose control, let my fires enjoy a taste of freedom like this guy's. If I did, I'd destroy everything: my life, my family, everything. "I'm just worried about my uncle, is all." That part's also true, but not the way he takes it.

"Don't worry. He can take care of himself. Now you'd best get out of here before he sees you. He won't like you out this late on a school night."

I nod and head down the block toward my pickup truck, making my way through the lookie-loos. Like most of Smithfield, this street is a roller coaster of steep hills, old-fashioned cobblestones poking through worn-out macadam.

Sometimes it feels like Smithfield never left the first Great Depression behind. With its coal-stained frame and brick houses huddled against the wind whipping down from the Allegheny mountains that surround it, it hasn't changed much since my mom and uncle grew up here. Except the problems Smithfield faces today are a lot different than they were in the last century.

Meth, heroin, oxy—infecting both parents and their kids. And plenty more bad things going on in the dark behind closed doors. The lousy economy isn't helping any. Smithfield is set in some of the most beautiful countryside imaginable, but you tend to forget that when you live here and all you see is the broken-down concrete at your feet.

It's past ten on a Sunday night, but the block is crowded with men slouched against the shadows, using the spectacle of the fire as a chance to make a few bucks selling drugs. Dark hoodies hide their faces, but their hands give them away: fast moving, hand to pocket, money to hand, hands meet in exchange, nod of the head, hands back in pockets, saunter away.

I don't know why they even bother hiding in the shadows; anyone can tell what they're doing. No one seems to care. It's that kind of neighborhood…becoming that kind of city if things don't pick up soon.

Women gather with babies and young children, holding them tightly, talking to each other as they watch the destruction. One more drug house gone. No thanks to the city. They seem to think the arsonist is some kind of modern-day Robin Hood. They chat about planting a garden or having a new place for the kids to play since the house was on a large corner lot.

Wait until they see how long it takes the city to clean away the debris. Until then, the blackened, skeletonized remains of the house will beckon to their kids, daring them to risk falling into the gaping basement filled with soot and mud and water, climbing cracked timbers, combing through the ashes searching for treasure. Just last month my uncle's crew had to rescue a little boy from an old coal chute he'd fallen through after a similar fire buried it from sight.

I stop as the roof on the burning house falls in, releasing black smoke and flames to swirl into the night. The crowd pulls back with a cry of terror followed by cheers. My uncle and his men lunge forward, their grins wider than ever. This is the final battle, the last of the fun part. Then comes cleanup—smoking cigarettes while raking through the ashes, dousing any smoldering embers.

The crowd applauds the firefighters as the blaze surrenders. They don't understand what's really going on inside the fire or the kind of men who run toward an inferno instead of away from it.

They don't know fire like I do.

They don't want to.

Lighting a blaze, breathing life into the sparks, watching the flames come alive then die, leaving behind ashes of despair... Every fire I start is a new beginning, a second chance—a way to release the pain and find the courage to go on living.

Without my fires, I would have killed myself long ago.

With my fires, I can imagine hope.

———

Sunday, five hours later...

Miranda's fingers flew over her keyboards—both of them—as she followed the boy's trail from the streaming video. Looked like the kid in front of the webcam was in a normal bedroom in a normal house—no one would ever believe what he was doing at three in the morning. She was certain none of it was his idea. Just like her being here watching wasn't exactly how she wanted to spend a Sunday night, either.

She couldn't believe her luck, finally tracking down one of the Creep's private live feeds. She couldn't close in on the Creep himself; he was much too careful. But his client, the perv from Tokyo, was an amateur at covering his tracks, giving Miranda the chance to trace the kid back to his home ISP.

If she could pull this off, the kid would be okay—they'd all be okay. At least that's what she kept telling herself, typing furiously, seeing lines of code glowing against the back of her eyelids with each blink. She was exhausted, but it was worth it. She'd seen the kid before in the Creep's glitzy teaser ads—movie trailers aimed at an audience with sick and twisted minds—but this was her first chance to track him to where he lived in the real world.

Occasionally she had to glance at the other screen—the one with the live action—to check the time code. 3:18 a.m. EST, 4:18 p.m. Tokyo. If they logged off before she finished, she'd lose the kid. Maybe forever.

She tried hard not to notice what was actually happening, what the Tokyo perv was making the kid do, but then realized it was important that she pay attention. Not to the action playing out but to the kid. His face.

JohnBoy was his screen name. Not his real one, of course. Just like Miranda wasn't hers.

He could be any of them—he could be her. She had to bear

witness, not treat him as a disposable commodity, used and tossed away, like the Creep and his clients did.

It was important. It was why she did what she did.

Except now she was running out of time. In a few days, the Creep would win. Everything. Unless…JohnBoy…maybe he was the one. Magic Thirteen.

He was a year or two older than her, sixteen or seventeen. He looked strong enough, nice muscles, tall—as tall as her dad, even. So many of the others she'd found, they'd already been broken, damaged beyond repair. You could tell it by their eyes: dead and dull, staring at nothing.

Not JohnBoy. Despite the fake smile for the perv halfway around the world, she caught a spark of defiance in his eyes, hidden behind each blink. More than defiance. Hope.

As if he knew she was there, searching for him. As if he needed her as much as she needed him.

Shoulders tight, carrying a burden much too heavy for a skinny fourteen-year-old girl barely five feet tall, she hunched over her keyboard, fingers pounding the keys so hard shock waves raced up her arms.

Hang on, JohnBoy. I'll find you. I promise.

2

Who the hell was William the Conqueror? I stare so hard at my exam paper my vision blurs. I know he's important, but was he before or after all those Henrys? Somewhere in the middle? I can't think, I'm so exhausted. After I got home from another fire last night, King woke me for a live-streaming session with one of his clients.

Some days I get home from school and stand inside the door, unable to remember if I'm coming or going or anything about the day or if I even went to school. So much for education being the path to freedom.

Maybe some of us never find a way out. We end up trapped forever—like all those peasants and serfs used as cannon fodder by William and the Henrys and every egomaniacal dictator who came after them.

My phone buzzes in my pocket. Talk about your egomaniacal dictators. No phones in school, definitely not while taking a test. Those are the rules. But this is the phone King gave me. The one I must never, ever turn off or not answer.

I stretch to cover my movement as I slide it under the desk, typing with one hand.

JB: Can't talk.

King: Client wants JohnBoy. Now.

JB: Can't. Test. Gotta go.

King: Get out of it.

JB: Can't. Teacher.

King: I don't care. Five minutes. Live feed or else.

I stare down at my hand, at the words filling the screen. My mouth is dry; I can't get enough spit together to swallow. *Or else.*

Two words more frightening than anything the teacher can throw at me. I glance up at her. She's marking papers, clueless.

Not me. I know too much—learned it all when I was twelve, real-world stuff, true shit, not lies written by the conquerors for the history books. I know what King's "or else" can mean. The Spanish Inquisition has nothing on him when it comes to devising new and cruel ways to torture. King's torture doesn't leave a mark or bruise—his weapon of choice is the Internet and he uses it to reach anyone, anywhere, anytime he chooses.

I accidentally pissed him off a while back when the battery died in my cell and I missed his call. He punished me by setting my mom up on a blind date with a psycho she thought was a guy from the church choir. She was so excited, changed her dress three times—it was her first date since my dad walked out on us. Mom juggles two part-time jobs plus taking care of my little sister, Janey, so she doesn't have time or energy to meet nice guys, much less date. I'll never forget the smile she had as she ran to answer the door when he rang—I hadn't seen that smile in years, not since my dad. It lit up her entire being, like she'd swallowed a piece of heaven.

I haven't seen her smile like that since, either. Her "choirboy" cornered me after he brought her home and told me exactly what he'd do to her if I ever kept King waiting again. Then he walked out of Mom's life, and she went back to being overworked, underpaid, and overwhelmed.

That's King's idea of "or else." Hard to care about a history test when your life is already over.

Pocketing the phone, I turn my paper over, lay my pencil on top, and walk up to the teacher. She glances up, startled. "What is it, Jesse?"

"Can I please use the boys' room, Mrs. Henderson?" I'm always extra polite with teachers. Best way to get them to do what I need them to do.

She looks disappointed in me. It's a look I get a lot. I'm used to it. Before King, it would have bothered me. I was always one of those kids who tried hard to be the best at everything. But that was a long, long time ago. Long before Mrs. Henderson ever met me. But every now and then, an adult like Mrs. Henderson realizes I'm not fulfilling my potential. Some kind of instinct makes them wonder why I'm such a loser.

Can't they see? I'm not a loser. I'm the Energizer Bunny, running a triple-A life fueled by anger, adrenaline, and anxiety.

But they can't see it. They don't *want* to see it. No one does.

"You know the rules, Jesse. You can't leave during a test."

Class only started ten minutes ago, so no way will she believe I'm already finished. But no way can I finish, not with worrying about the price I'll pay if I keep King waiting.

"I feel sick." It's the truth. Nothing new. I've felt sick, worse than sick—a dirty, queasy, constant burning in the pit of my belly—ever since I met King. Or rather, when he met me. I was twelve then. I'm sixteen now. The feeling hasn't gone away, gets worse every day.

Her frown deepens. I've used the sick excuse too often with her. Shame, really, since I love history. All those stories of far-off lands and adventure. It's the last class I'd ever skip if I had a say. But of course I don't. I have no say in anything. My life doesn't belong to me. It belongs to King.

"I'm sorry, Jesse. If you think you need to go down to the nurse, you'll get a zero for your test grade unless she can confirm that you're really sick."

I look down at my size twelves, then up at the clock above her head, ticking away my precious five minutes. I nod. "I understand."

She scratches out a hall pass to take to the nurse. I grab my backpack and leave. As soon as the door closes behind me, I slide my phone free.

"Why aren't you live?" King answers.

"On my way—" The phone is yanked from my grasp. It's Mr.

Walker, the vice principal. He's always sneaking around the halls when class is in session.

Stupid. I should've been more careful.

"I'll take that, Mr. Alexander," he says triumphantly, as if he'd just single-handedly disarmed a suicide bomber.

Little does he know he actually does hold my life in his hands.

"Please, Mr. Walker—" I slouch, trying to make myself smaller than my six one. Don't want to intimidate Walker, who's only five eight with lifts in his shoes. He has short-man syndrome big-time.

He arches an eyebrow at me, then hangs up the phone. Hangs up on King.

Shit, shit, shit, shit. The acid churning through my gut makes it all the way up to the back of my throat. Tastes like burning rubber. King is going to be furious. And I'll be the one to pay the price.

"That's my emergency phone. I was calling to let my mom know I'm sick and headed to the nurse's office." Over the past three years, I've learned how to act better than any of those pretty boys in Hollywood. I can see he's wavering, hold up the hall pass to convince him.

Unfortunately, Mrs. Henderson chooses that moment to come out and see what's going on. Two minutes later, my phone's confiscated after Walker sees I wasn't really talking to my mom, I'm back at my desk scratching doodles on my test paper (because who can think when they're imagining things far worse than any atrocities good ole Willie the Conqueror ever could have performed?), and I'm ordered to detention after school.

Most kids would be whining about how life sucks or how unfair it all is. Not me. I couldn't care less about my grade or detention or graduating.

If I had my way, I'd be gone already. Enlist in the Marines or Army, get my GED, have Uncle Sam pay for college. Wouldn't even care if they sent me to a battlefield, shit getting blown up, bullets flying.

That kind of war would be heaven. At least I'd have a fighting chance.

Not like now. Now, with King in my life, I don't have a chance in hell.

I stare at the closed classroom door. My phone is down the hall with Walker, waiting for me to pick it up after detention. By then it will be too late.

King is going to kill me.

3

The rest of the day passes by me like I'm in a fog, trapped by smoke so thick I can barely choke it down. I make it through history and English. Then as the school empties for the day, it's just me and the other losers sitting with Walker in detention.

All I can think about is what King will do to me—or worse, my mom or sister. I'm the man of the house; I'm the one who's supposed to be taking care of them. Yet here I am, trapped at a desk. Watching the clock, my heart speeds faster than the hand clicking the seconds away.

Walker is working on his laptop, occasionally looking up to give us all the hairy eyeball. I'm stuck with the typical detention kids: stoners caught smoking pot or huffing in the janitor's closet, the token cool kids being made an example of for chatting and texting during class, two jocks, both with black eyes, who glare at the rest of us, and an emo chick who hides her face behind her hair the entire time.

Despite the worry turning my spit sour and the acid churning through my gut over King's retaliation, I stare out the window, trying hard not to imagine what he'll do to me.

There are a few kids milling out front, missed their bus or waiting for rides. A silver Camry pulls up, the horn honks twice, and a man jumps out of the driver's seat, leans across the roof, smiling right at me.

The car's nothing like my dad's—he always had different ones, old junkers we'd work on together and then he'd sell them and start over again—and the man doesn't look like him, but for a moment, a single moment, less time than it would take an atom to split, my heart beats faster, warming my entire body as I smile back. It's Dad. He's come to rescue me, to save Janey and my mom.

For the duration of one breath—not even a full breath, all I do is inhale, imagining Dad's scent of leather and grease and Lava soap—I'm free. King can't hurt me. No one can.

Then I blink and a kid races to the car, the man waving to him to hop in, and they drive off—leaving me with the same void in my heart that I've had since my dad left four years ago. I lower my head down onto my desk, closing my eyes against the rush of emptiness. I should be used to it by now. Besides, I can't afford the luxury of indulging in fantasies, like Dad ever coming back.

But if I did, my dream would go like this: I finish school and get a job, probably by joining the army. It's not a lot of money, but it's enough so I can afford a place for Janey and my mom. In my dream, they're sitting inside my truck, I'm loading the last suitcase into the back of the pickup, and my uncle comes running out to stop me.

I whirl and land one of those punches that only happen in the movies. *Smack* and my uncle goes down...and he stays down, staring up at me with a mix of fear and respect.

Janey and Mom cheer. I hop into the truck and drive us off into the sunset and our new lives. Away from him. Away from King.

That's my dream, what keeps me sane. I might even be able to make it come true if I work hard enough, focus. Just have to make it through high school, just have to survive that long…

Our phones are lined up in front of Walker's laptop like trophies. One of the girls' cells—pink and all bedazzled in rhinestones—keeps vibrating, bouncing against the desktop, *buzz, buzz, buzz…buzz, buzz, buzz…*until it finally skitters all the way across the desk and falls to the floor between the desk and the wall.

A blond girl wearing more makeup than my mom ever has bounces up. "Mr. Walker," she calls. "My phone!"

Walker looks up, irritated. He rolls his eyes, but it's obvious she's one of the rich kids whose folks could hassle him for destruction of property or the like, because he gets down on his hands and knees behind the desk to scramble for the phone. It's still buzzing and skids under the radiator. He curses and I see my chance.

Before I can think twice, I race past the desk, grab my phone, and rush out the door and down the hall. I spin around a corner and plow into the girls' room, figuring they'll never look for me here.

Footsteps pass by outside in the hall. I lean panting against the sink, thinking I might be sick. My eyes are wide, like a wild animal's, and I barely even notice the fruity perfume smell of the pink soap or how much cleaner the girls' room is compared to the guys'. All I care about is a few moments of privacy so I can call King and beg his forgiveness.

The hall is silent. I risk moving into the farthest stall—the handicapped one with its own sink and a tiny window. My fingers tremble so bad they bounce off the phone's keyboard. We use an Internet calling app—less traceable, King says, plus we can do video. One-way, of course. He sees me. I've never seen him.

It rings four times, each ring ratcheting up my pulse, until finally King answers with a gruff, "What the hell do you think you're doing?"

"It wasn't me. I didn't turn off my phone. The vice principal confiscated it." I plead my case in a rush, not bothering to breathe between words.

"You know the rules."

"It wasn't my fault. The teacher—"

"I can't help it if you're too stupid to outwit some dumb teacher. There are consequences when you don't listen to me. You know that by now."

I scramble, trying to come up with a solution. I have nothing. Finally I say, "What do you want?"

There's a pause and I know the bastard is smiling. Like always, he has me exactly where he wants me—no way out.

You think I'd be used to it by now, but every time I surrender to him, I lose a piece of myself. Like those zombie movies where they reach inside your chest and tear out your heart or intestines or liver. That's me, walking around with half my insides torn out—half boy, half zombie, all of me belonging to King.

"It's not what I want," King says. "It's what my friend wants. He's kinda like your uncle, only he likes girls. Watch."

The phone's screen cuts to a video feed. From the date and time stamp, I know it's live. At first all I see is a car dash and steering wheel. Then the camera jerks up, and I see a school bus pull up to let some little kids out on a country road with no sidewalks. *My* road.

"No. You can't." My pulse throttles my voice until only a whisper escapes.

I swallow hard as the kids climb down the bus steps and scatter in all directions. The camera focuses on one little girl walking with two others, a bright pink backpack making her an easy target.

Janey.

"Please. Tell him to stop. I'll do anything." Sweat cements my shirt to my flesh as I search for a way out. I can't go through the school—too many teachers and guards. I'll have to risk going out the window. I try to force it open. Locked.

"Tell him to stop!" I scream as the car door opens. The camera jerks up and down when the man holding it crosses the street to follow the girls. Follow Janey.

King says nothing.

"Answer me, you son of a bitch!" Anger and panic fuel my punch as I swing my fist into the window. Hurts like hell but bounces right off. Damn safety glass. I spin for the door; I'll just have to make it past whoever might be searching for me outside.

"Is that the tone of voice you use with me?" King demands, his voice flat.

I pause, my hand on the door. My entire body vibrates with the need to get to Janey, the urge to hit something—someone. I force myself to swallow my rage, close my eyes, and whisper, tasting every word as vomit: putrid, rancid remnants of my soul. "I'm sorry. Please stop him. Please. Don't hurt my baby sister. She's only seven. I said I was sorry."

Silence.

"Please." I'm begging for her life—not that King cares. "I'll do anything. Just stop him."

The man in the video keeps walking. Janey can't wait for King's answer.

I open the door and speed out into the hall, sideswiping a janitor, sending his bucket across the linoleum to crash into the lockers. He yells but I don't hear it. All I hear is the silence on the phone. I race down the hall, take a corner so fast my sneakers squeak as I skid, bounce off the wall, and aim for the side doors, praying they're still unlocked. Someone shouts my name from behind me, but I ignore them.

As I run, I dare a glance down at the video. Janey's at our door, fumbling for her key.

"You're supposed to be there with her, aren't you?" King says. "Little girl like that, it's not safe for her to be alone with no one at home."

The man with the camera starts up our driveway.

"No, please." I'm sobbing now, don't care. Any pride I had has long since been ripped away. "Please, make him stop."

"It's all your fault. It's your job to protect her. Your job to do as I say. You failed on both counts, JohnBoy."

I reach the door at full speed, prepared to crash through it headfirst if it's locked. My hand hits the push bar. Thankfully it slams open and I'm free.

The man reaches our front steps.

I was running late this morning, so my truck is parked at the far end of the lot. The world goes red around the edges as I run faster than I ever have in my life.

It will take me eight minutes to drive home, even if I speed. I try not to think about what could happen in eight minutes, but of course that's all I can think about, visions of blood and Janey's screams filling my mind.

Then the man looks down. I can see his shoes: polished black leather, little tassels with brass horseshoes holding them in place. Crisply creased charcoal colored slacks. Much too nice for the cracked pavement of our concrete stoop. The camera gives a little shiver and his hand appears. In it is a large folding knife—the kind hunters use to skin their kills.

"No!" I yell, my voice hoarse. "Please, King. No!"

"You knew the consequences. I'm a man of my word, JohnBoy."

The man flicks the knife open with one hand.

The screen goes black.

4

This is all my fault. The thought echoes through my brain and I can't stop it. Just like I can't stop King's man from hurting Janey.

As I drive, wrestling with the old Ford F-150's propensity to spin out on sharp curves taken fifteen miles an hour too fast, I keep trying to call King.

He doesn't answer.

Finally, I turn down the lane my uncle lives on. There are only four houses, clustered together at the end, with big, wide yards carved into the forest that surrounds them. My uncle's house is the second one in, a redbrick ranch with a small barn out back. He keeps saying he wants to get a horse—Janey would love a horse—but it's too expensive. He's got six acres, most of it gone wild. Behind his house are some woods and past them another small clearing with an abandoned single-wide trailer.

The truck skids as I twist the wheel to turn into his driveway and slam on the brakes. I heave the driver's door open and almost trip and fall in my hurry to get inside. There's no sign of the man from the video. No sign of anyone.

I barge through the front door. "Janey!"

The house is silent. I run past the living room on the right—the

TV's on, PBS, but no Janey. Dining room on the left—empty. Kitchen—empty. "Janey!" Now I'm screaming, all my fear and anger exploding into my voice.

I hear footsteps from the hall leading to the bedrooms. There are three bedrooms. Janey shares one with my mom; I get my own and so does my uncle, since it's his house. I turn down the hall, my hand in a fist, ready to hit someone. Ready to kill.

"I'm sorry, Jesse," Janey says as she comes out of my room. She's carrying a padded envelope the size of a school binder. "I was just gonna leave this—"

"Janey," I gasp, rolling her into my arms and hugging her so tight she makes a squeaking noise. We fall to the floor—mainly because my legs can't support my weight—and I pull her down with me. "You're okay."

She pushes away. "What's wrong, Jesse?"

I heave in a breath, then another. Reach out to hug her again, gentler this time. "Nothing."

She hands me the envelope. "I know I'm not supposed to go in your room, but—"

She has no idea that I don't want her in my room because King is always watching everything that goes on in there. He can control any camera, maybe even any computer, that's connected to the Internet—that's how powerful he is.

I can't stand the idea of him ever, ever catching sight of her. Too late for that now, I guess.

"That's right," I say with mock sternness as I take the envelope. Inside there's something small and heavy with squishy stuff wrapped around it. I shove it into my backpack, drop the pack to the floor. "Don't go in my room. Or else."

I make her favorite oggly-woogly-scary monster face and she squeals in delight, running past me to the living room. I chase after her, taking care to never force her to run too fast, but I know she loves it, being treated like any normal seven-year-old. I let her tackle me and clobber me with pillows, until I see her getting congested and the slightest bit wheezy, then I beg for surrender.

She spins around, hoisting the pillow with triumph as I climb to my feet, acting like it's me who's out of breath.

"Get your vest and I'll fix you a snack," I tell her, handing her the special vest that vibrates all the mucus out of her lungs before it gets too thick for her to cough up. She hates the damn thing, but the rule is no TV unless she does her chest PT.

Janey has cystic fibrosis, which means living with a lot of rules. Thanks to my mom's constant vigilance, Janey is doing great, but between worrying about her and paying all the doctors' bills and getting her to her appointments at Children's Hospital three hours away in Pittsburgh and working two part-time jobs, one cleaning a nursing home, the other cleaning a hospital in Altoona, my mom barely has time to breathe, much less worry about me.

Used to be my dad helped out a lot—especially with me, since all the medical stuff, measuring and timing and shit pretty much freaked him out—but since he's been gone, it's down to me to be the man of the family. Mom tells me not to worry, that my uncle will always take care of us, that he'll always give us a roof over our head, but of course that only makes things worse.

So many secrets, so many lies—is it any wonder that some days it feels like I'm sleepwalking through my life, numb to the world?

Not today. Today King's threats and the visit from his goon squad have me wide-awake. As I slice an apple for Janey, I peer out the kitchen window, searching for any signs of the man with the fancy shoes and sharp knife. My own knife feels small and flimsy—should I get a gun? How can I protect Janey?

I grab Janey's enzymes and take her the snack. I zip her into her vest as she looks past me, mesmerized by the TV, and start the chest PT machine. She swallows her enzymes without me even needing to prod her and settles back as the vest hums and whirls, gently pounding her chest wall. I squat beside her. "You good to go?"

She nods, her chin quivering in time with the vibrations. "Turn up the sound."

I adjust the volume on the TV, kiss her on the head, but she's already gone, following Dora the Explorer on a trip into the jungle.

I know the answer of how to protect her, but it doesn't make it any easier. I spin away, unable to look at her anymore—she's such a sweet kid, the thought of anyone hurting her…it's too damn painful—and finally I go to my room and the laptop that sits on the desk facing my bed. King is waiting.

But he doesn't use the computer—he's like that, enjoys keeping me off balance. Instead he calls on the phone.

"Where is he?" I demand.

"Waiting. Watching. He likes your baby sister." King laughs.

"No. Get rid of him. No one comes near Janey. Not ever again."

I sound strong. Defiant. Like I might actually stand up to him this time. We both know better.

"There's a price to pay," he says. As if I could forget. "You'll owe me."

"What do you want?"

He pauses. I have no idea what King really looks like—I've only ever seen what he wants me to see. Hell, I'm not even sure if the voice I hear is really his.

Three years and seven months we've been at this. In my mind, he's a cross between Heath Ledger's Joker and Ted Bundy. As the silence lengthens while I wait to hear what my punishment will be, I imagine him licking his lips, tasting victory.

"It's time you made some new friends. And then introduce me to them," he finally says, his voice sounding just like my uncle's when he calls me down to help him in his basement workshop. A tone that makes my bowels go loose.

I grab my stomach, clenching it as I force the panic from my voice. "What do you mean?"

"You're getting too old for most of my clients. Unless they see you with other boys. Younger boys."

"You want me to—" I can't even finish the thought. The phone almost slips free from my grasp. I stare at it. It's in my hand. But I can't feel it. My fingers have gone numb. My entire body is a block of wood—except for the acid burning inside me. I reach for my Zippo in my back pocket. I need fire, flame, a spark of life.

"I want you to have some fun. Like your uncle does with you."

31

I flip the lighter open. Inhale the rush of butane. Stare, mesmerized by the dancing flames caught in my hand. So many colors, so much power.

My life is dull, dead, gray. I have no colors. I have no power. All I have is anger, simmering like the flames before me, buzzing through my veins where no one can see it. Where I won't—can't—let anyone see it.

"What's it going to be, JohnBoy?" King asks in a businesslike voice. *Paper or plastic? Do you want fries with that? Diet or regular?* "You or your little sister?"

I can't answer—no words can make it past my clenched jaws.

King knows just how far to push to get me where he wants me. "Take the weekend," he says magnanimously. "I want your decision by Monday."

He hangs up.

The flame cradled in my palm weaves its magic, moving in time with my breathing. Fury burns through me. I snap the lighter shut, killing the fire.

That's when I decide I no longer have any choice. I'm going to hunt King down. Find him. And kill him.

It's the only way to save Janey and Mom. My uncle I couldn't care less about—this was all his fault to start with.

And me? Who cares what happens to me? I sure as hell don't.

5

Miranda had just finished revising her suicide note when her mom knocked on her bedroom door and came in.

"Mom." The single syllable carried the aggrieved righteous annoyance of an entire generation.

They both knew it was a poor attempt at normalcy. *Fake it until you make it,* Miranda's first therapist had said. *Smile until it kills you,* Miranda had heard. It about did. Shortly after was the first time she tried to kill herself.

"I just saw the mailman leave." Her mom stood in the open doorway, trying not to stare as Miranda carefully closed her journal and tucked it under her pillow. She'd earned that much privacy, and her parents always honored their part of the contract. Even if Miranda cheated. It was for their own good. "Let's go out and get it."

Miranda rolled her eyes at her mom's falsely cheerful tone. She bounced up from her bed, a twin-sized mattress and box spring on a basic frame, covered in a simple bed-in-a-bag set of sheets and comforter. On their budget they couldn't afford better, not that Miranda cared. She rarely slept anyway. Too much work to do, too little time left. "Oh goody, let's."

Mom laughed and shook her head so her short, dark curls

bounced. She knew Miranda was mocking herself more than anyone. After a beat, Miranda allowed herself to laugh as well. Why not? Her entire life was some kind of Orwellian farce. It would be funny if it wasn't happening to her—to them. Mom and Dad had lost as much as she had, had paid the price for Miranda's mistakes.

A single moment of carefree fun, captured by the wrong screen at the wrong time. And now all their lives were forever changed for the worse. Yet, her parents never gave up on her, no matter how bad things got.

Things would be so much easier if they had—then Miranda could just give up, surrender. But they stood by her, so she had to find the energy to keep trying. She owed them that much—and so much more.

She snagged her mom's hand and squeezed, laid her head on her shoulder—their shorthand for a full-body hug. Together they walked down the hallway of their tiny two-bedroom apartment to the front door.

Her mom waited, letting Miranda take the lead, just like Dr. Patterson said to. Miranda reached a hand for the dead bolt but didn't touch it. She wanted to turn it. Not just once, but three times, magic three. Three was safe—just like funny five and lucky seven. Not two, never two—two wasn't company, two was a crowd, a dangerous, chaotic, people-get-hurt crowd.

Miranda froze, her hand hanging there like she'd forgotten it belonged to her. She could turn the lock, but then what?

"Go ahead," Mom coaxed.

Miranda closed her fingers around the cold nickel. Flip-flap-flip, one-two-three, open-closed-open sesame. The door was unlocked. Miranda stared at the lower knob, the one that would open the door to the outside world. Instead of touching it, she stepped to the door and pressed her eye against the peephole.

The hallway outside their apartment was empty—at least as far as she could tell. What if someone came as soon as she opened the door? Or worse, when she'd already stepped outside and the door was closed behind her and it was too late to get back inside? Or maybe they'd be waiting for her on the elevator down to the lobby mailboxes, or if she took the stairs, they'd be coming up while she was going down, and they'd trap her on the steps, with nowhere to run or hide?

And what if they followed her back home, came inside, found her parents, hurt them? Hadn't her mom and dad been hurt enough already?

Miranda slumped against the door, eyes closed, shutting out the world beyond. This was why it'd be so much easier for everyone if she did go ahead and kill herself. It really was the safest thing. Why couldn't her parents or Dr. Patterson see that? It made sense; was logical, practical, cheap, efficient…and third time was a charm—three, a safe, magic number.

Her mom rubbed her back, between her shoulder blades, just like she had when Miranda was a little girl and had the flu. Disappointing Mom and Dad was almost as painful as facing the world outside. Almost.

"Maybe tomorrow." Miranda sighed. It was so hard turning

around and seeing the look on Mom's face. The unshed tears, the way her shoulders slumped.

"We don't have to go all the way," Mom said. "Remember your contract, Miranda. One step at a time, but you need to keep moving forward."

Anxiety buzzed along Miranda's nerve endings when she realized her mom wasn't going to let her slink back to her room and hide in safety. "Please, not today, Mom. I'm working on a really important project."

Liar. All her projects had failed miserably. Oh sure, she'd been able to help a few kids who'd fallen victim to cybercappers and other bullies, but none of them knew the capper she searched for: the man who'd destroyed her and her family's lives. The Creep.

Unlike other cappers who used their stolen videos and photos for a quick buck or to bully people their own age, the Creep specialized in blackmailing kids, young kids. It was as if he delighted in tormenting them, and by catching them young, he'd have plenty of opportunity to devise new ways to torture and compel them to do what he wanted.

Over the past few months, once the Creep started the countdown to her birthday, posting ugly messages hinting at his plans, Miranda had sent more than a dozen letters accompanied by old cell phones her dad found when he moonlit as a security guard at the Smithfield Telenet Arena.

Thirteen messages, in fact—a safe number she'd thought, although maybe it really was unlucky, but how could it be when it was created by two of the best numbers of all, one and three?

Thirteen lifelines offered. Thirteen attempts to save others from the fate she suffered. Thirteen times she'd let herself hope that this was it, that this would be the one, the path to finally finding the Creep and finishing him before he could hurt her family again. Lucky thirteen—the boy called JohnBoy. She'd really thought he might be the one to save her.

But he hadn't answered. Just like the twelve before him. Thirteen failures.

She didn't have the energy to hope anymore. Or the time. Her fifteenth birthday was Sunday. She shuddered, hugging herself to hide it from her mom, who still watched, although her eyes had gone dull with disappointment. The Creep would strike again—a birthday surprise, his last post had promised—and she couldn't be here to see what torture he devised for her family this time.

That's why Dr. Patterson's one step at a time didn't matter. By Sunday, Miranda would either have beaten the Creep or she'd be out of steps. Permanently.

"Just open the door," Mom said. "You can do it."

Miranda stood still. The clock on the living room wall clicked away the seconds. Mom stood still as well, acting like she could outwait Miranda. But they both knew she had to get to work.

"Ariel—" Mom's voice wasn't angry or upset, no longer disappointed even. Just flat-out sad.

"Don't call me that!" Miranda spun on her mom. Her mom, once upon a time, had been an MFA student, studying literature. A published and critically acclaimed poet, she had named her daughter after a beautiful spirit in one of Shakespeare's plays, not some silly Disney mermaid. But Ariel was dead, buried these past two years thanks to the Creep. "Never call me that!"

Mom just sighed, turned, and walked back down the hall to get ready for work. Miranda stared after her for a long moment. Then she yanked the front door open so fast a wave of air from the hall flew at her face. Quickly she slammed the door shut again. One. But three was a better number. Three held magic and luck—she needed all she could get.

She held her breath, fear knotting her stomach as she opened and closed, opened and closed the door. Finally, her body covered with a fever sweat, she locked it. Clack-click-clack.

Shame burned her, tangled so deep with her terror that she couldn't unravel the two. She knew these feelings, these thoughts she couldn't control were crazy—hey, it's okay to use the word when you're living it—but she was powerless against them. Which left her vulnerable to the real threat.

Not stranger danger lurking in the hall of her apartment building. Not the fear that if she didn't find good, safe numbers her family would suffer.

The real danger was out there, waiting and watching. The Creep.

She ran back to her room, her sanctuary, and threw herself facedown on the bed. The only sound in the room was her strangled breathing from under the pillow, each breath counting down to her birthday in three days. The day the Creep had promised to return.

6

As I stare at my lighter, I contemplate the one huge problem with my plan: I know nothing about King. Especially where to start looking for him.

For obvious reasons, I don't like computers, never use them except for homework. The one that's in my room, always on, that was a gift from King via my uncle. Some gift: a twenty-four/seven peephole into my life.

I'm a pen-and-paper kind of guy—especially after King came into my world. I grab my backpack and retreat to the kitchen, trying to look like I'm getting ready to do my homework instead of plotting a murder.

I grab my notebook, my personal one, smaller and more compact than my one for school. It's bent and warped because half the time I carry it folded in my back pocket or my coat. I always have it with me for notes and ideas and just to doodle thoughts in private. I can sketch and write and do whatever, then burn the pages before anyone sees them. I like holding the pages over the flames, watching them catch fire, then fall to ash. Closest thing to privacy I have.

Now I sit down and open it to a blank page. In the center of the page, I write *King* in big letters. I sketch flames around them as I ponder. What do I really know about the man who controls my life?

Not much. I know he knows my uncle. That's what started all this. My uncle owes him a debt of some kind. One that I'll never be able to pay off.

I'm pretty sure King really is a man—he could be disguising his voice, but we've talked so many times that I don't think so. The way he talks makes me think he's older than my uncle, who's twenty-eight. My mom's thirty-four and King sounds older than her as well.

He sounds like he went to college, likes to use big words.

He lives on the East Coast—somewhere in my same time zone from the times he calls, but has clients all over the world, hence the middle-of-the-night private shows.

I wonder if he has kids of his own. Could a father do what he does to me and other kids? He's mentioned others, ones who tried to renege on their deals with him, has sent me videos and pictures. Some he cybersmashes, others pay the price in real life—one kid, he looked about my age, was badly beat up when King outed him as being gay. Two more killed themselves, sent notes apologizing to King, saying they should never have tried to double-cross him.

At the time I half thought they were all fake, King's way of keeping me in line. But the man on the "date" with my mom and this other guy who followed Janey home, they weren't fake.

King has the dirt on a lot of people, kids and grownups. I circle his name with a line of faceless stick figures, his army of scumbags, ready to do his bidding. If I did what King asked, that's what I'd be signing up for. He'd never let me loose after that, could have me do anything…even kill someone.

Maybe those kids who killed themselves had help, someone who made their deaths look like suicide.

I shiver and slip into my jacket. It was my dad's, left behind with the rest of his stuff after he ran off to start a new life four years ago. I'm not sure why I kept it after Mom boxed up everything else. Sometimes I get so angry at Dad for ditching us, leaving me to clean up the pieces. So many times I've thought of burning it, imagining what the cracked leather will smell like as the flames devour the last bit of my father.

But I never actually do it. I've grown into the jacket. It's become a part of me, heavy across my shoulders, reminding me I'm the one responsible for Mom and Janey now.

I wonder if that's why Dad left it behind—too heavy. Too much to carry.

Maybe for him. Not for me. I'll never let Mom and Janey down.

I glance at my paper. I've drawn a shadowy sketch of a man, my best memory of my dad. I stare at it for a moment, then cover it in flames, black as my pencil skids across the page, devouring his face.

Back to King. Surely after almost four years I know something more about him.

He's good with computers—but anyone is compared to me.

He doesn't like boys—not like my uncle does. I have no proof, but from King's tone when he's dissecting my performance or coaching me for one of his clients, he seems bored, more interested in getting paid than anything. Definitely not like the tone of his clients. Those pervs don't bother to hide their interest.

Power, control—that's what King loves. Even more than the money, I think. The way he gets so creative when he wants to punish me or put me in my place. The things he's done to other kids even when they do everything he asks. This is all a game to him—one he'll win at any cost.

Over the years I've seen how twisted his mind is. It scares me because even before today, I knew he'd stop at nothing to get what he wants.

He really will kill Janey or Mom, just to prove to me that he can—and he'll get away with it. That's how smart he is.

How the hell am I ever going to stop him?

I scribble over King's name, pushing harder and harder on the pencil until it snaps. Even then he's not totally erased from sight.

As I reach into my pack for another pencil, I find the envelope Janey gave me when I got home. I look at it suspiciously. Sometimes King sends me stuff: new phones or props or clothes he wants me to wear. But his stuff always comes addressed to my uncle in boxes with return addresses to make it look like it was ordered online.

This one is addressed to me. The name on the return address is the radio station I listen to: a hard rock, heavy metal station, the only one not country or oldies around here. But the address can't be right: One Hope Lane. I know most of the county, riding out to fires, and I've never heard of it. Besides, I've gone past the radio station; it's on Broad Avenue.

I look over my shoulder even though the kitchen is empty. Janey's still watching her after-school shows, Mom's not due home from her shift at the nursing home for another hour, and my uncle won't be home until after that, unless there's another fire. Then he'll be even later.

The kitchen is in the back of the house, faces the yard and, beyond it, the meadow and forest. No neighbors on this side; no one can see me. I'm alone.

But I don't feel that way.

I should be creeped out like I was when I first realized King could watch me through the laptop anytime he wanted—he controls that computer, can power it up remotely, and he knows if I try to shut him out by closing it. I've learned to accept that I have no privacy, but it still grates on me.

One Hope Lane. What if it's one of King's clients, tracked me down somehow in real life? It could be King, playing a trick. He loves anything that will keep me off balance, keep me easy to trip up.

I get up and go into the family room to check on Janey. Her chest PT is about done, so I unhook the vest even though it's a few minutes early. As I set up her afternoon breathing treatment, I ask, "Where'd you get that envelope? The one addressed to me?"

She finishes coughing and spitting out mucus, handing me her wet, slimy tissues. They don't gross me out; I'm used to it. Even glad that everything she's coughed up is white, no hint of the green that means infection. She's scheduled for a tune-up at Children's tomorrow—she and Mom will be gone all day, making the rounds of the specialists who keep Janey healthy.

"It was in the mailbox," she finally answers, making a face like I'm trying to trick her.

"No one gave it to you?" I cringe at the thought of the man with the knife getting close enough to give her anything.

"Nope." Her eyes grow wide. "What's in it? Are you trying to sneak something past Mom?"

Typical little sister, always looking for a chance to insert herself in my life. She has no idea how hard I work to keep her out of it.

I laugh and hand her the nebulizer mask. "Not past Mom, past you, you nosy brat. Maybe it's your birthday present. Maybe I'll just have to send it back if you peeked."

She knows I'm only teasing but squeals anyway. "No, don't send it back, Jesse. What is it? Whatcha get me?"

Her birthday is a few weeks away and I've been working on a hand-drawn graphic novel starring her. Not many words—I suck at words—but tons of fun pictures. I start her nebulizer machine and smile. "You'll just have to wait and see."

She flumps down into her chair, wrinkling her nose at me as the mist swirls around her face, then motions me out of the way so she can see the TV. I return to my spot in the kitchen and examine the envelope again.

The postmark is two days ago, Altoona—the post office where all our mail, even local Smithfield stuff, goes through. No answers there. Finally I grab a steak knife and slice the end open.

A black cotton T-shirt falls out. Lands on the table with a very un-T-shirt *thunk*. I open the folded shirt, finding a cell phone and charger wrapped inside. Along with a carefully folded note. The

T-shirt advertises the big car show this weekend at the Telenet Arena at Smithfield College. I've been listening to the ads on the radio; my uncle's been talking about us going. They're going to have all sorts of drawings and giveaways—even a new car. I am starting to think this is all some weird promotion, and open the note, expecting to find free tickets or a chance to win.

Instead I find a phone number. And the words: *I can help.* Printed on a screen capture of my face.

I freeze, terrified. It's a trick. It has to be. A trap set by King.

Hands trembling, I shove everything back inside the envelope and bury it at the bottom of my backpack. I'll burn it all later tonight.

But I can't stop thinking about it. How does King do that? Read my mind, know my vulnerabilities? It's like he's in my head, knows exactly when I'm desperate enough to think of fighting back, to risk the consequences.

I sink into a chair and fold my arms on the table, resting my head on them, my face hidden in the darkness I've created. It's hard to breathe, like someone's choking me. There's no way I can take on King by myself. He's too smart, too strong.

There's only one person who can help me stop King: my uncle.

I take a deep breath and raise my face, squinting at the sun that's low in the sky, hanging just above the trees at the edge of the property. Even though it's April, most of the trees are barely budding, their naked limbs clawing at the fading flame-colored light.

My uncle. I almost laugh at the irony—my English teacher would love it, I should write an essay or something. The one man I can't trust is the only man who can save me, save my family.

It makes sense in a warped kind of way. After all, my uncle is a firefighter, a hero. He saves lives, helps people every day.

And I need help. Like I never have before. I can't go to Mom—if I tell her about King, I'd have to tell her about my uncle. After Dad walking out on us—on her—she's so vulnerable, blames herself, tries so hard to be both mother and father to me and Janey. How can I ever tell her what her own brother does to me? It would kill her.

Forget the cops or teachers or anyone else—no one would believe me about my uncle, the hero firefighter, and if they don't believe that, they'd never believe there's some creepy guy online who has been controlling my life for the past three years. Besides, King would find out—he always does—and he'd hurt Janey or Mom.

I don't trust my uncle, but surely he'll help—for Janey and his own sister, my mom. He loves being a hero. Plus, he hates King—refuses to talk about him, even though I know King tells my uncle sometimes what he wants him to do with me. Special events, King calls them.

But now King's raised the stakes, now it's life or death.

My uncle. He has to help now.

7

After my mom comes home from work, I wait outside on the front stoop, picking at the crumbling concrete along the edge of the top step until a shiny, new, black Ram hemi grumbles its way up the driveway.

A man my height only with dark brown hair instead of my dingy blond climbs down. He's got plenty of muscles and walks like he knows where he's going today, tomorrow, next year.

When I was little, younger than Janey, before I knew better, I adored my uncle, his confidence and strength. Loved it that he took extra time with me, treated me special.

Now I despise him. But I don't dare ever let him see that, because we have nowhere else to go. My mom and Janey wouldn't last long out on the street. It's my job to keep them safe. That means keeping my uncle happy—and King, his invisible not-so-silent partner.

"What's up, Jesse?" my uncle asks, strolling up the front walk and staring down at me like I'm a little kid with a skinned knee. Like next to him, I'm nothing, a klutz who can't even keep from tripping over his own two feet.

He wants me to think that. To remember my place. After almost four years of living in his home, eating the food he puts on the table, he doesn't have to say anything. I know what we owe him.

What *I* owe him, for taking care of my family when my dad walked out. But sometimes, between him and King, I wonder if there'll be anything left of me when they finish taking what they want.

Today, finally, I know the answer. If I give in to King's demands, there won't be anything left. He'll own me, body and soul. If I give in to him, I'm as good as killing myself—only I have no choice but to stay alive in order to protect my family from King and my uncle.

Who am I kidding? I'm screwed. Totally, completely screwed. In every damn sense of the word.

All's that left is to save Mom and Janey.

My uncle nods his head, passing me by, and I know he wants me to follow. Wordlessly, he leads me inside, shedding his coat in the front foyer, calling "Hi!" to Janey and telling my mom that we'll be working out in the basement. He speeds down the wooden steps, barely touching them.

I close the heavy door behind me and trudge down. The basement is partially finished with cheap paneling and linoleum flooring. There's a weight bench and heavy bag, along with a scruffy old recliner, TV, workbench, and shelves with tools and half-finished projects.

By the time I reach the bottom, he's taken his flannel and T-shirt off and is straddling the weight bench, doing bicep curls with a dumbbell. I know he probably already spent time at the gym at the firehouse this morning before coming home to catch a few hours' sleep and then leaving again. He's a people person, hates being alone in the house. So when he gets up in the middle of the day after a shift, he likes to go and "hang out." Janey's seen him stop by her school, watching the kids out playing, but she thinks he's checking up on her, thinks it's cool to have an uncle who cares so much.

When I was a kid like her, I used to think that too.

He raises the weight slowly, gaze fixed on me watching him, veins popping along his muscles. He likes it when I watch. I indulge him, sinking into the recliner across from him. He smiles and lowers the weight, then repeats the motion.

"You going to tell me what's wrong?" he asks. "If not, get over here and we'll pump iron."

He's not talking about lifting weights.

I shift uncomfortably in the recliner, but it's so old and worn the movement makes me sink in deeper. I remind myself that my last hope, my only hope, is my uncle. I need to smother my anger and convince him to help me.

So I tell him what happened today. About Janey and the man with the knife. About what King wants me to do next.

"Wow." He finishes his set, lowers the dumbbell, and wipes his chest with his T-shirt. "That's a tough one. What are you going to do?"

"Whatever King has over you, it can't be worth Janey's life." All my frustration and fear flash over into my voice before I can stop it.

Without using his hands, he pushes to his feet, standing over me. I edge back in my chair.

"King has nothing on me." His voice has flared from polite "don't care, but I'll listen" to "don't you dare go there" edgy. His hands bunch into fists that make the muscles he just worked bulge even more. "You think I'd ever take that kind of shit from anyone? Let a creep like him blackmail me?"

"Then why—" I trail off, my world teetering, making me feel seasick as the pieces finally fall into place. I thought my uncle hated King because King was using him just like he used me. But no. "He pays you. You do this for money."

"Not only money." He yanks his T-shirt over his head, shoving his arms through the sleeves. "I love you. And I love my sister and Janey. A firefighter doesn't make shit—especially not when three more mouths to feed show up uninvited on my doorstep. And you, you were so lost. You needed a man in your life, someone you could look up to. Everything I do, I do for you, Jesse."

I'm silent, trying to swallow my anger, but it's not going down easy. Then the logic behind his words catches up with me. "Wait. You're saying I'm to blame for all this?"

He shrugs. "I don't know what arrangements you made with King—it's none of my business—but a man has to take responsibility for his own actions. I never did anything with you that you didn't want, Jesse. You never said no. And look at the good that's come from it. Your mom and sister have a safe place to stay; they're not homeless out on the street. You've got food, clothing, hell, I even gave you my old truck. How many sixteen-year-old kids have it as good as you? I sure as hell didn't when I was your age."

I blink. The world fractures into puzzle pieces as my eyelids close and open and close and open. Each time, I expect to see it go together in a way that makes sense, but it doesn't. I open my eyes and my uncle is still standing there, truly believing I wanted everything that's happened to me these past few years, that I asked for, that I even…liked it.

I taste burning in the back of my mouth and don't have enough spit to wash it away. I hang my head, try one last time. "What are we going to do about Janey? I can't let King hurt her or Mom."

"Of course you can't. They're your responsibility. You have to follow through with whatever you promised King. Man up, Jesse." He's impatient, as if we're talking about me backing down from a scary leap off the high dive, like when I was six and he climbed up, jumped with me, holding me safe.

Maybe not so safe. After, alone in the changing room, was the first time he insisted we shower together. I was so young and dumb. I didn't tell anyone, scared no one would ever love me or think I was special the way my uncle did.

"I-I can't…" My voice shakes away the rest of my words.

He doesn't hear. He's pacing back and forth, full of energy. "I'll help you. We'll go over to the car show this weekend, start looking."

"Looking?"

"Sure. For your new friend. A kid who needs a role model, some-one who can show him the ropes, let him know he's not alone." He stops behind me. My shoulders tense, but all he does is ruffle his fingers through my hair and kiss the top of my head. "Don't worry, Jesse. It's still you and me. I'll be with you every step of the way."

His phone rings and he grabs it. "Gotta take this." He runs up the steps, leaving me alone in the basement.

The door slams shut behind him and I'm still sitting there. Frozen. Like the coward I am. The light from the naked bulb overhead burns against my eyes. I close them but they still sting. Warm, salty tears escape. All I can think is: *this is my fault.*

I deserve whatever happens to me—I'm weak and sick and stupid and every name King or his clients ever called me. I can handle that. Can handle anything King—or my uncle—wants to do to me.

Standing, I rub my face against my shoulder, leaving a wet, gray trail on the white cotton of my tee. What I can't handle is something bad happening to Janey or my mom or some other poor kid because of me.

I sniff hard and move to unlock my uncle's toolbox. Not the big one on wheels. This one is a heavy, red steel one that sits on the lowest shelf along the back wall, hidden in the shadows. He doesn't know I know the combination, but I saw him open it last time we came home from the shooting range. He has a few guns, but the one I take is the smallest: a snub-nosed .38 revolver. So small, I can hide it in the palm of my hand or slide it into my pocket.

King and my uncle are right about one thing: It's time for me to man up. Time for me to accept responsibility for my actions and deal with the consequences—even if it means ruining the rest of my life.

What other choice do I have?

8

Miranda's only luxuries were her computers. One clean, protected with the highest security a civilian could create, almost never online. The other dirty—vulnerable. This was the one Miranda used to stalk her stalker. The Creep.

She'd tracked him back to the company he worked for, thought she had an idea about where he might live, but she'd never gotten close to his real name—that's why she was reaching out to his other victims. Surely she wasn't the only one who'd ever stood up to his cyberblackmail and bullying. But two years of hunting, and she'd never had a nibble. Two—a bad number, dangerous.

But thirteen was a good number. She'd been so very certain that thirteen would be lucky, would break the curse and lead her to her prey. She had a plan, a trap set—if she didn't run out of time.

All she needed was a little help. Just one person willing to answer her call. She'd never be able to re-create her life—her real life, *Ariel's* life, the one that was meant to be—or rebuild her parents' lives. But if she could catch him, stop him, bring him to justice…well, that'd be something worth living for.

Except she'd failed. Thirteen wasn't lucky at all—despite her sleeping with the envelope under her pillow for three days and nights (three was the best, the most magical number; she loved three; three was family: Mom, Dad, Daughter), despite all that, thirteen had failed her just like the twelve before.

She lay on her bed, covers over her head, and in the darkness, re-created lucky thirteen's face. Especially the expression in his eyes, the way the skin beneath tightened and the corners creased. She'd thought it was defiance, a sign of strength, resolve—all the things she needed so desperately. Wistful thinking. Lucky thirteen had let her down.

Nothing to live for now. And only three days left until the Creep's birthday surprise torment.

Three was magic, third time a charm, so why not end it now? Why torture herself by waiting?

She threw off the quilt and reached for her journal with her suicide note nestled inside. If she was going to end it, it would be on her terms, not the Creep's. She'd be heard in death—even if he'd silenced her in life. Her fingers brushed the suede cover of her journal, the words inside calling to her like an aching need.

Maybe she should just do it now—foil the Creep's plans before he ever had a chance, go quietly into the dark like the poets talked about...except that wasn't really what they said, was it? And it wasn't how she felt; it was just she was so exhausted. She wasn't sure she had the strength to "rage, rage against the dying of the light" not even for three more days.

Three long, dark, dismal, hopeless days.

She opened the journal, her note falling into her hands. It was written with her favorite pen, a purple felt-tip her mom used to use when she composed her poems, back in the good old days: BC, Before Creep.

The paper was perfect as well—thick, creamy like parchment, with marbling that hid the stains left behind by her tears.

9

After dinner, I take advantage of the fact that King has given me time off—even if it is to think about something so vile that I couldn't manage to eat any of the Salisbury steak Mom made. I can't believe I'll be free of him until Monday when I have to tell him my decision. Time to myself is something that almost never happens in my world where King can pretty much see and hear everything I say and do twenty-four/seven. I'm so used to being tethered by him, it's hard to remember a time when I was free to just be a regular kid. I guess it was when I was twelve, before my uncle took that first video and gave it to King. Amazing what fallout a few minutes captured on a cell phone could have: my life, in ashes.

I grab my coat and backpack and leave the laptop and King's phone behind as I escape to my favorite thinking spot: the abandoned single-wide in the field behind the trees at the back of my uncle's property. No one except me has been in the trailer for years. It's too far from the road for casual partiers, too dilapidated to attract homeless folks, especially with all sorts of nicer empty houses sitting around, waiting for foreclosure. So I have it all to myself.

This is where I come to start my fires.

Like I said, I'm no pyro. I don't want to burn the place down. I start fires as a way of purging the pain. Fire is my only chance to be in control.

And let's face it, my life? Definitely not in control of anything there. Not even what happens to my own body.

A large steel wok on the middle of the kitchen floor is my fire pit. I keep a coffee can filled with sand beside it since there's no running water here in the trailer. I've collected a bunch of different fuels and fire starters—some burn longer, some hotter, some make tiny explosions or bright colors. Thanks to my uncle and his firefighting textbooks, I've learned a lot of ways to start fires using stuff from around the house and garage.

But my favorite is to simply use my lighter. I enjoy holding fire in my hand. Enjoy feeling in control, able to keep it contained like I do my fury.

Moving in the dark, not needing any light beyond my Zippo, I gather tinder, picking and choosing the perfect mix of slender pieces of dried grass and twigs, and paper shredded to just the right size.

I create the spark.

I breathe life into the glowing red embers.

To the rest of the world, I'm out of control—of my body, my time, my actions…but not this. This is mine.

The flames grow, rejoicing in their freedom. They don't know they're prisoners in a cage I've created. They don't know me at all.

But I know them. I am their God, their Creator, their Master.

They swirl, blue-gold-red-purple-gold-again, stretching and bobbing, begging for more, more, more. They are at my mercy.

Heat surges through me and I feel my heartbeat in my fingertips as I feed the flames dancing in the dark. I decide their fate. I control how long they live.

Although I'm always tempted to let them escape, wild and furious, devouring everything in their path, in the end, I will kill them.

I have the power here. And no one—not my uncle, not King—can ever take that from me.

I almost add the strange note and envelope to the flames. Something makes me stop.

I know the letter is King trying to screw with me. He's always playing mind games like that, pushing to see how far I'll go. Has to be a trick.

Except…what if it's not? What if there really is someone out there, someone who can help?

The phone is old, just buttons to dial and a tiny screen. No keyboard, no web, no camera. Anonymous.

God, how I would love to be anonymous. Leave JohnBoy and Jesse far behind. Not to mention the choice I have until Monday to make.

Running won't help. King would find me sooner or later. And before he did, he'd find Janey and Mom. Let that man with the knife loose on them.

He'd blast my name and face all over the Net. Make sure I'm on my own, an outcast, labeled a perv or worse. I've seen him do it to others—by now I can read his fingerprints all over a cybersmash. He blitzes every media outlet, social media site, until every corner of the web is plastered with his lies, twisting his victim's most intimate secrets as he reveals them to the world.

So running isn't an option. Going to the police is just as bad. Either one would end with Janey or Mom dead.

Could I do it? Do what King wants? Do that to a little kid? No. Never.

What's left? I rip a page from my notebook, the one with my earlier scribblings, my daydreams on how to find King and kill him. My fingers tremble as I hold it over the hungry flames. I make them fight for it until fire surges over the paper, singeing the hair on the back of my hand before I finally release the page. The fire devours it, wants more.

I haven't burned the mysterious letter. I reach for it but instead pick up the phone again, weigh it in my hand. The flames won't like it, too much work for such a small fire.

I look down and realize my fingers are dialing, like the tiny part of me brave enough to try to fight back against King has to go into stealth mode while the rest of me sits there, a quivering mass of cowardice.

"Hello?" To my surprise it's a girl's voice. She sounds as startled by my call as I am. "Hello?"

I don't know what to say. My finger hovers over the End button, ready to hang up. But something holds me back.

"Is this Jesse?" she asks.

Five words and I'm holding my breath, hanging on to her voice like it's a lifeline out of the dark. She has a beautiful voice—not breathy or high-pitched or giggly like so many girls. Low, clear, warm. It's the voice of an angel.

"Who is this?" I cover my mouth with my hand and spin

around the trailer, searching for someone spying on me. What if King finds out? I'm ready to end the call before she answers, but I can't resist learning her name.

"Miranda. I'm Miranda. I can help you."

"Liar. No one can help me. This is a trick." I don't want to say any of that—especially not to her, not in this vile, hateful tone—but I can't help myself. It's too damn dangerous. If this is a trick, if she works for King…Fool. Idiot. He'll kill Janey, kill Mom.

I throw the phone across the room. It slams against the wall and bounces back, skidding up against the hot wok. I snatch it away from danger. Then jerk my hand back. Can't have it both ways. Either burn the damn thing or call her back.

Either way, at least *I* will have made the decision. Not King.

I hunker down and stare at the fire. The flames are hungry. They need me. Without me, they'll die.

Janey or King? The words flicker through my mind as I shred the envelope and serve it to the fire. The flames like it, the inner lining popping and bursting into bright colors, although the plastic gives off a stink. The flames are happy again—thanks to me.

The phone rings and I jump, knocking the coffee can of sand onto the fire, killing it. The trailer goes dark except for the green glow of the phone's keypad.

A second ring. My palms are wet with sweat. I wipe them on my jeans.

It rings again.

Janey or King? King or Janey?

My insides feel hollowed out. I don't know what to do. All I know is that I can't do this anymore, can't handle this. Not alone.

I need to take a chance on someone.

I grab the phone and answer. "He's going to kill my baby sister."

10

He's going to kill my baby sister."

I can't believe I actually said the words out loud. Immediately, I pace in the darkness, searching between the bent and crooked blinds hanging from the windows as if my words could conjure King or one of his minions. All I see is black, nothing alive in the dark.

Dead silence on the phone. Maybe I imagined it—maybe I imagined her. Then a voice, so close it's as if she's inside me.

"We won't let him do that." Another moment of silence, but this one is okay. Like she's giving me time to accept the fact that finally there's someone on my side in all of this—someone I can trust.

Can I trust Miranda?

"Who are you?" I ask.

"Before we say anything else," she answers, her tone all business, older than the kid she sounded like before, "I need to know. Are you anywhere near a computer or cell phone—I mean other than this phone, the one I sent? We need to be careful."

"No. I'm alone. In a deserted trailer. There's nothing here." I consider her words. "I know King can spy through webcams and computers, but he can use phones as well?"

"King? That's what you call him?"

"That's his handle—at least his latest one."

She makes a grunting noise as if making a note. "He uses spyware downloaded to computers and phones. Turns their microphones and cameras on remotely without you knowing. He can see or hear anything going on near them, plus use their GPS to track you."

I stop pacing. That means King knew I was taking a test when he called today. He heard the vice principal confiscate my phone, knew everything.

Today, Janey—it was just another one of his games. Bastard! I want to lash out, hit something. I snap my lighter to life. Stare at the hungry flame. It would be so easy to set it free. Unleash its fury—my fury. But I don't. I kill it.

I'm alone again. Except I'm not. I have this strange girl, Miranda. Or at least her voice in the dark. Curiosity tinged with uncertainty along with the tiniest breath of hope seeps past my defenses. "He set me up."

"What?"

"Nothing. Just something I should have figured out a long time ago. How are we going to stop him?" Another thought occurs to me. "How did you find me?"

"I've been tracing his victims, reaching out."

"Traced? How?" The thought of her—of anyone, especially a girl—seeing the things King makes me do...I almost hang up.

She seems to understand. "I know how he works. The blackmail, the threats."

"Like sending someone to hurt my baby sister."

"Or posting naked pictures of you all over your school's website, sending them to your dad's boss and your mom's thesis committee. Yeah, like that." She sounds bitter—in fact, her voice sounds a lot like my own voice inside my head when I'm pissed off and confused and want to kill King or stand up to him or run away from all this.

"He's done it to you." My breath rattles through the phone.

She's silent for a long moment. "Two years ago."

"So—how did you stop him? How did you get away?" Her breathing quickens, like she's frightened—or trying to hold back tears. I want to be there with her, not talking in the dark like this. But most of all, I want her not to be crying and not to be scared. I want her to be brave and smart and bold enough to show me a way out of this before Janey or my mom get hurt.

"I didn't." Her voice is hushed. "I stood up to him. Refused to do what he asked. And he—he's destroyed my life. Not just mine. My parents'. And he's not done yet. I have to stop him. I have to. Will you help me?"

She wants *me* to help *her*? How can I do that? I don't know anything.

I think about what she said about King ruining her and her parents' lives. If I help her, he could do that to me and Janey and Mom. Hell, he might do it just for me talking with her. Maybe this is another one of his games, and as soon as I get home, there will be a message from him wanting even more from me in retaliation.

"I can't risk it," I answer, feeling empty inside as my last sliver of hope is doused. "I wish I could, but I can't."

11

Miranda was almost in tears. He couldn't say no—Jesse was her lucky thirteen. And she was out of time. When he finally called, she'd dared to hope...But maybe thirteen wasn't lucky, not for her. After all, one plus three added up to four. A bad number.

"Please," she said, sniffing back her tears and hoping he didn't notice. "Please, Jesse. Don't hang up yet. Would you just listen? Just for a few minutes? You're the only one I can talk to, the only one who would understand."

There was dead silence. Then the sound of a metallic snap. "What's that?" she asked. "Are you still there?"

"I'm here." His voice sounded resigned. "Just lighting a fire. It's cold and dark where I am."

She pressed her free hand against her own dark windowpane, the cold racing up her arm, down into her heart. "Where I am too."

"Are you okay?" he asked, his voice hushed but with a spark of defiance in it. She remembered the look in his eyes and knew he wanted to rush to her rescue; he sounded like that kind of guy. A knight in shining armor. Or he would have been if the Creep—King, Jesse called him—hadn't beaten him down.

Miranda couldn't be angry with him for saying no. He had his little sister and mother to think about.

"I'm not okay," she admitted. "But I'm safe, if that's what you mean. There's no pervert holding me hostage or anything. At least not physically."

"Where are you?"

"Tyrone."

"That's not too far. I'm just outside of Smithfield."

She knew that; it was why she'd chosen him. But she didn't dare tell him that, not now. It was too soon.

Another pause but it didn't feel awkward. Then he asked, "What you said about your folks losing their jobs and moving because of what King did to you, was that true? They really did that?"

"He found us the first time we moved, when we were still in Pittsburgh." Being bullied out of one school had been bad enough, but then to have the Creep cybersmash her again—this time with a fake porn video that went viral—that had been too much.

But she'd survived, which only gave the Creep another chance to destroy her family. "After that I left school; my folks gave up their jobs so we could move here, but I guess that wasn't enough fun for him. So last year for my birthday, he posted an ad online. Used my mom's picture and all her info along with a rape fantasy. Five thousand dollars to the man who made it come true and posted a video of it."

Dr. Patterson would be proud of her, talking about that night so calmly. When the Creep contacted her, let her know it was all her fault and that he'd never stop hounding her and her family… They'd said she was lucky they found her before all the pills had gotten into her system. Miranda had decided adults had a warped idea of what lucky really was.

Jesse made a noise like he was ready to hit someone. "What happened? Was she okay?"

"My dad's a Pittsburgh cop—well, he used to be. Before... all this. But he's taught me and Mom how to take care of ourselves. When my mom walked out to her car that night and two guys tried to jump her, she pepper sprayed the hell out of them, kicked them in the balls, and when they ran, used the phone they'd dropped to video their license plate. Cops nailed them."

"But not King."

"No. And their lawyers got them off." It'd been months later when they went to trial. She'd been so scared, testifying about why her mom was targeted, then when the judge dismissed the case on a technicality, her dad had gone after the men in the hallway, almost got arrested.

The thought of losing him—or her mom—had reduced her to a screaming, crumpled mess collapsed in the hallway of the courthouse. That night was the second time she'd tried to end it all. A razor blade that time. The ambulance ride was the last time she'd left their apartment.

"Your mom sounds pretty cool."

"She is." Miranda couldn't help but smile. Somehow he knew exactly the right thing to say. "She wants to be a poet—was in grad school and everything." She sighed. "Now she works nights at the post office. They have a good health plan." They needed every penny of it with the counselors and hospital and doctors. "And she teaches a few days a week, English as a second language classes, to bring in extra money. When I think of how perfect their lives would be without me—"

"Don't say that! You did the right thing. You stood up to King and his blackmail. How old were you?"

"Thirteen. It was my birthday and he grabbed video—well, you know as well as I do how he works." King and the others like him. Hiding in cybershadows, waiting for people to make a mistake, a single slipup, trust the wrong person, get too close to the wrong camera, cell, or computer. Damn cappers. Made them harder to catch than the child predators who trolled, actively looking for victims. Those guys the FBI and cops were good at reeling in. But cappers? They were shadows, hiding in the dark crevices of the Internet, invisible until after they already had their prey trapped.

"Thirteen? And you went up against King all by yourself? And now you're trying to track him down, stop him?"

She thrilled to the awe in his voice. It was almost as good as when her folks told her how proud they were of her…something that hadn't happened lately, mainly because she hadn't done anything to make them proud. Instead, she'd retreated farther and farther away from the outside world. If she could just find the Creep and stop him once and for all, then she maybe she could face her folks again.

As it was, it was getting harder and harder to look at them—so tired and beaten down, their dreams destroyed, because of her—without wanting to die.

"Trying," she said, her voice bitter. "Two years trying. And failing. You're the first who has even answered my message."

"How many have you sent?"

"You're number thirteen."

"How many kids do you think King has—"

"Tormented? Blackmailed? Bullied? Who knows…I've found kids stalked by other creeps online, been able to help a few, but he's the worst. His victims are too scared to do anything about him, and I can't do it alone."

He was quiet again. She liked that about him: he didn't just jump in with false promises. Jesse thought before he spoke. She had the feeling he wouldn't make a promise he couldn't keep. Just like her folks.

All victims of King. Good people, their lives torn apart.

"If I helped you," Jesse said, his voice dropping to a whisper, "what would you need from me?"

12

Really?" Miranda's voice chimes out like a birdsong. Musical. Magical the way it trills through my veins, warming me despite the chill inside the dark trailer. "You'll help?"

I hear the happiness in her voice, can't believe I'm the one who put it there. After everything she's been through, how can I say no?

"First," she goes on, as if she's worried I'll back out, "we have to make sure King doesn't know we're talking. We need to use secure communications like these old cells that don't even have GPS. And we can't use your real name," she says, sounding much older and more confident than fifteen. "We have to create a persona for you to hide behind."

Fine with me. Thanks to my uncle, I stopped being Jesse years ago—sometimes my mom has to shout my name over and over again before I realize she's even talking to me. And I hate being JohnBoy, wish I could leave him behind forever.

Maybe with Miranda's help I can.

A whisper of hope sighs through my body. I quickly douse it. Hope is too painful. It's all I can deal with handling what's right in front of me. I can't take thinking about the future. Instead, I focus on Miranda. "A persona. You mean like knights when they leave on a quest and get new names."

"Exactly. Richard the Lion Heart."

I shudder and crouch closer to the flames in the fire ring. "No. Not Richard."

That's my uncle's name.

"But you have the heart of a lion."

I do? Really? Miranda thinks that? I sit up straight, grip the phone tighter.

"How about Hawkeye?" I suggest. "It's from *Last of the Mohicans*." One of my favorite books—most kids think it's boring, stop reading before all the juicy stuff happens. But not me. I love those old books, have even read all six of the Musketeer novels.

"Oh, that was a great book," she says in unison with my thoughts. Did I really hear her? Or was it a trick of that pesky glimmer of hope?

My chest does a weird thumpity-thump. My entire body feels light, and I look down at the floor to make sure I'm still all in one piece. I see the chunk of cinderblock I'm sitting on that's making my butt go numb. I should be cold, huddled here inside the unheated trailer, but I'm not. I feel very warm, like I have a fever or something. And it's not coming from the tiny fire I've built on top of the ashes of the first.

Miranda's still talking. "Hawkeye's not quite right. And not Athos or D'Artagnan," she says without me even mentioning the musketeers. She pauses. "How about Griffin?"

"Griffin?" I try it on for size. I like the way the syllables roll off my tongue. If Miranda likes it, no way in hell am I gonna argue. Besides, at this point, I'm not even sure if I'm awake.

Maybe I'm imagining this entire conversation. It sure as hell doesn't feel real. I hold my hand over the tiny blaze I started. The warmth feels good—but Miranda's enthusiasm and faith in me feel a whole lot better.

"It's perfect. Heart of a lion and eyes of an eagle, wings to fly with and claws to fight with. Did you know the ancient Greeks considered the griffin their protector against evil? That's you."

Again with that crazy flip-flop in my chest. I'm none of that, which sooner or later Miranda will discover. She'll hate me then, I know. But right now I'm overwhelmed and chickenshit and all I can say is, "Griffin it is."

There's the sound of keys clicking faster than I've ever heard anyone type. "Okay, I've got you an account set up for email and IM. Don't use it from any of your home computers or your cell phone, otherwise King could track you. You don't need to actually send the emails—too easy to trace. Instead just create a draft. We can both access the account and see each other's drafts. The IM should be safe enough if you delete them and clear your history each time."

"Okay." I pause. "But what are we going to use it for? You do have a plan, right?"

"Before we talk about that, there's a guy," Miranda says, sounding hesitant—so different from the confident girl I've been talking to. "In the videos. Looks like the same one in all of them—"

Right. She's seen the videos. I turn away, facing a corner even though I know she can't see me, wishing I could curl up in a ball and hide. It's hard enough to force myself to go through the motions with my uncle or when King has me do a solo show. Then it's almost like I'm not even there at all. I'm not sure where I go, exactly. Just away. I try hard never to think of anyone actually seeing the end product.

"I'm sorry," she says quickly. "I shouldn't have asked. I just had to be sure—"

"Is that how you found me? Through the videos?" I'd thought King sold them to individuals, had hoped they'd be private—one perv at a time easier to handle than millions. But of course people have seen them—knowing King, he's sold them to every perv on the World Wide Web.

"No, no. The Creep—King—has clips out there, like a movie trailer. Nothing dirty, but you can tell there's the promise of more. Advertising, I guess. They're how I found you."

"If you could find me, who else can?" I pace the trailer, the fire neglected. A sudden urge to run home takes over me. A need to make sure Janey and Mom are safe. Then I stop. "If you could find me, why haven't the cops?"

"I don't know. It wasn't easy to find you—like I said, I've only found thirteen of his victims and it's taken me two years to figure out how."

"But you're just a kid—"

"I'm almost fifteen," she says, obviously insulted. "And I'm really good with computers. I mean I was even before—but now I've had two years to learn so much more. I'm probably as good as the cops." I smile at the pride in her voice, liking that Confident Miranda has returned. "And there are tens of thousands of videos like yours out there. Hundreds of thousands of still pictures. Maybe even millions. I guess the cops just haven't been able to get to all of them."

"You said your dad was a cop, but he couldn't do anything about King."

"Computers and my dad don't exactly mix. He's a patrol officer, likes working with people, taking care of the neighborhood. He had the detectives working on it, but there was no way to find King. He covered his trail too well. Even spoofed my ISP so for a while they thought I'd done it myself, to get attention. I had to prove my own innocence. How sick is that? Then we took everything to the FBI—they have a whole bunch of people working child pornography and cybercrime."

"The FBI? And they couldn't find King? How the hell can we find him if the FBI can't?"

Her voice returns, stronger than ever. "The FBI doesn't care much about King bigger fish in the sea, they told my dad. Oh, they'll try. But the stuff King and guys like him do, it's hit and run—they post something anonymously and it goes viral, passed device to device. Tracking it is like trying to track a flu bug back to the very first sneeze halfway around the world. Plus, since the victims help to create the content, they don't see it as a big problem, just a little cyberbullying and capping—"

"Capping?"

"Taking a screenshot capture of a photo or video without your permission, then posting it online."

"There's so many other guys like King out there, they have a name for it?" I'm not sure if the burning in my veins is anger or disgust. Both.

"Are you kidding? They have societies and awards and entire websites devoted to these pervs grabbing photos and video. Guys vote on the hottest or cruelest or most disgusting. The adult ones aren't even illegal. It's called revenge porn. You trust the wrong person for one second, just long enough for them to snap a photo, and your life is ruined. Anyway, the cops have to focus on the really, really bad ones. Like the snuff porn and the baby porn and the torture porn—"

A stray flame leaps high and singes my palm. I jerk away. Doubt floods me. If King has that many partners in addition to all the people he can manipulate through blackmail… "We can't risk it. There's too many of them."

Disappointment fills the silence between us.

"I mean, if even the FBI can't—"

"We're better than the FBI, Griffin."

I can't help it. I love the way I feel when she calls me that, like I'm not even me, I'm someone bigger, better, smarter, stronger. But I can't waste time worrying about myself. "How can we keep Janey and my mom safe?"

"Are they safe now? I mean, the man in the videos, is he your father?"

Now I see what she's getting at. God, it's been so long since someone cared enough to ask the tough questions—myself included—that it takes me a while to realize she isn't curious; she's concerned. That should have felt good, I guess, but instead I feel like I've been sucker punched.

All these people in my life—my mom, teachers, the guys at the firehouse, the cops and paramedics my uncle hangs out with and who are always over at the house for cookouts and stuff—none of them ever cared enough to think twice about what my life is like.

But this girl, younger than me, a total stranger, she's risking everything. To help. Me.

I choke back my feelings as I squat in front of the fire and feed it more tinder. In return, it leaps and dances for me. I imagine I see Miranda's face smiling out at me from its soothing gold waves. For the first time ever, fire isn't pain and fury—it's hope.

"He's my uncle," I say, my voice sounding like it's coming from somewhere else. "He took us in after my dad left us four years ago."

She doesn't say anything, just listens as I pour out the whole story. About my mom and dad both losing their jobs, about him taking off to find work, leaving us and never coming back. About us getting kicked out of our apartment and my uncle taking us in.

"Without him, we'd have nothing." My uncle is constantly saying that to me; my words emerge scorched with bitterness. I realize my hand is wrapped around the phone so tightly my fingers have gone numb.

"He uses that against you," Miranda finally says. "He's as bad as King."

Yes, yes, yes! I want to shout the words. A spark flares to life at the thought that I'm not crazy, that this wasn't all my fault, that I didn't invite my uncle to do what he does. But I can't say anything, not without losing it. And I can't lose it in front of Miranda. I want—no, I need—her to like me.

"Jesse—Griffin," she corrects herself. Griffin. It's a strange name, but she chose it and it feels right. And Jesse—he belongs to my uncle, like JohnBoy belongs to King. "Do you want me to try to find your dad?"

"Yes," I say but immediately want to take the word back.

For four years, I've imagined my dad's life. Maybe he's got a new family, one that he'd never, ever abandon. One that he loves more than us.

He and Mom seemed in love. They fought, sure, but they were always kissing and hugging and holding hands. And Janey, Dad would always find time to play with her even when she was a little kid and whiny and sick all the time. Which left me... was I the one he didn't want to come home to? I loved being with him, the way he'd take time to teach me things, like how to bait a hook or what spark plugs were or why falling stars weren't really stars.

Maybe I was too much work, always asking questions, always wanting to hang out with him. Maybe I drove him away?

That's the nightmare scenario. Along with others, like him lying dead on the side of the road or him in prison or hit on the head and wandering around with amnesia. But after four years and no word from anyone, I've come to realize that the answer is probably the simple truth: he found a better life without us.

It's the same answer Mom finally accepted after the cops found no trace of him. The reason why she cries all the time and is so happy to see my uncle willing to spend time with me.

Funny how it all comes back to me. That's the real nightmare, that the life I'm living now is my own damn fault.

I shake away my thoughts as I realize Miranda is asking me questions. She sounds so excited to help that I answer automatically, giving her his name, James Timothy Alexander, date of birth, hometown, and everything I can remember. I'm surprised at how much I can't remember—like my life before my uncle was a dream that's slipped away.

A dream I'd give anything to get back.

"Okay," she finally says. "I can work with this. But we still need a safety plan for your mom and Janey. In case your uncle—well, what if he—"

"He'd never hurt them," I jump in. "He loves them." Then I remember earlier. The way he said King's threat against them was my problem to solve.

"Love isn't always enough, Griffin," she says like she's reading my mind. Again. "Some people only have enough love for themselves. I think your uncle might be like that."

"And my father as well? That's why he left?"

She hesitates. "Maybe. I don't know. But we do know your uncle is willing to hurt you. And he's working with King."

She's right.

"I can't trust him." Which means I'm in this all alone. With Janey and my mom's lives in my hands. God, could they have found a worse person for the job?

"Griffin." Miranda's voice is clear, like the flames stretching toward my hand—bold and bright despite the surrounding darkness. "You're not in this alone. Not anymore. We can do it."

13

Miranda hated making promises she couldn't keep. And she really, really wanted Jesse—Griffin—to get his life back. She hated that she had to lie to him. Although she'd help as best she could, he really was on his own when it came to facing King.

That's why she'd chosen him, why she needed him: to be her arms and legs, to go where she couldn't—to face King for her.

Maybe even kill him. An evil whisper circled through her brain. Griffin sounded like he might be the kind of guy who would do that, especially if he thought it was the only way to keep his family safe.

No. Catching King, exposing him for the creep he was, that was vengeance enough. There didn't have to be bloodshed.

But there could be. She remembered the wild-animal expression her dad had had when he went after the two men who'd attacked her mom. That was why she couldn't risk letting him know what she was doing—fear that he'd do something he couldn't live with.

Yet, she was willing to risk Jesse.

She forced the awful truth back into the shadows, where it hid with the others: the black heaviness that made her feel helpless and alone, to the point where she didn't even have the strength to climb out of bed. The clanging that rattled through her veins and compelled her to count and do things she knew made no sense, like flicking the light switch three times or circling her bed five laps before going to sleep. The pain she felt every time she saw the scars on her wrists and thought of freedom for herself and her parents. And the most evil four-letter word of all: hope. Hope that she could actually someday have a life again.

Griffin, despite everything that had happened to him, sounded, well, nice. A four-letter word. Okay, not nice. Normal. She could work with that. She hated to manipulate him, but she was out of time. This weekend was all she had left.

For almost a year she'd been planning for this, ever since her mom was attacked on Miranda's last birthday. That's when she'd realized the Creep would never stop.

The trap was set, now she needed to get Griffin there as bait.

———

"I have a plan," Miranda says.

Of course she does. Just like King has a plan and my uncle has a plan. Everyone has plans for my life. Except me.

Miranda's plan is simple: I ditch school tomorrow, pick up supplies she's going to order online, prepay, and have ready for me. She says not to worry about the money and that she'll walk me through how to use everything.

"Use how?" I ask.

I should be terrified, letting a total stranger—a girl even younger than me—take control of my life, involve me in a plan to take down King. Instead I feel stunned. Numb. Except for a warm spot buried deep in my gut—she treats me like I actually have what it takes to stop King. I don't want to lose this feeling and the only way to keep it is to deny the fact that she's wrong in trusting me. So very, very wrong. "What kind of equipment are we talking about?"

"Nothing fancy. A digital recorder. Audio and video. I found one that looks like a pen, you can stick it in your pocket and no one will ever know."

"You want me to go undercover? Face King in person?" I shake my head even though I know she can't see me. "Are you nuts? Besides, he could be anywhere in the world."

I can hear her breathing; a little hoarse, like she's got a cold or is scared herself. "I think I know where King lives, Griffin. It's not far from you."

"How do you know that?" She said she was good with computers, but no one can be as good as King. The way he's everywhere, knows everything. I glance around as if expecting him to lunge from the shadows. The fire is dying. I feed it more kindling, wanting its light as much as I need to regain control over something, anything.

"He's not perfect. If one of his so-called projects isn't getting the attention he wants, especially if it's someone he's cybersmashing, he'll assume an identity and go trolling, leaving nasty comments to jump-start the conversation. I've been collecting those identities, tracing them. Two came from the same IP address: Smithfield Telenet."

"If you traced his email address, do you know his name?"

"No. Both email addresses were dead ends. One belonged to a guy who retired and moved to Florida years ago. The other belonged to a guy who died a while back. But it can't be a coincidence that he used two from the same company. He must work there."

"So do hundreds of people." I know Smithfield Telenet. They're the main employer in the valley—in fact, they're sponsoring the car show Miranda sent me the T-shirt for. "Wait. You think he'll be at the arena. At the car show."

"Telenet employees and their families get in free on Saturday."

"That gives us less than two days to figure out who he is. How are we going to do that?" I don't want to argue with her, but the idea of coming face-to-face with King in less than forty-eight hours? I'm not ready for that.

"I'm collecting more of his possible online IDs. With your help, I can narrow them down. Trust me. We can do this."

I'm shaking my head again. No, no, no. How can she be asking me to face King? Doesn't she know what I'd be risking? "Why do I have to meet him in person? If we figure out who he is, why can't we just return the favor, cybersmash him ourselves? Or better yet, send everything to your dad's police buddies or the FBI?"

"It won't be enough evidence, not for the police or a court. He's covered his tracks too well. We need to get him on tape, confessing."

"To me?" Suddenly I have the urge to smother the fire, hide in the dark. I've exposed too much of myself. But not half as much as I'd be exposing—and risking—if I went through with her plan. "No. I can't. There has to be another way. Why can't you confront him? He's hurt you as much as he's hurt me."

There is a long silence and I think maybe she's hung up on me. "I wish I could, Griffin. But I can't be there. I can guide you over the phone—you can send the recording to my computer, I can take it from there. I'll be your eyes, watch your back. I promise. I won't let him hurt you or your family. Can you trust me?"

There's a knot in my throat as I fight to say yes. But of course, I can't.

"I want to. I really do, Miranda. I just can't. There's too much at stake." I'm ashamed of the words as soon as I say them. But I can't risk Mom and Janey. I remember the man with the knife. On our doorstep. Only a few feet away from Janey. This isn't some kid's game, running around playing spies. This is life or death.

"I know that," she says as if she's inside my head, knows all my thoughts and fears. "But isn't that why we're doing this? To save your family? And mine?"

Silence. The fire dies to sorry embers begging for fuel. I let it wither. Darkness gathers around me, bringing with it a cold that feels like it's coming from somewhere inside me, not from the temperature outside.

Miranda waits. Sensing she's pushed me as far as I can go tonight. I appreciate that. I pace the trailer, arms wrapped tightly around my chest, as if I need to hold on to something before I lose it. I feel the gun inside my jacket pocket. Hate its weight, the way it nudges me like it wants me to do something I don't want to do.

Something I can't do. It was stupid to take the damn gun in the first place. Not like I'd ever have the courage to pull the trigger. Even if we find King.

Finally her voice breaks the silence. "Would you at least think about it? Call me tomorrow and let me know? Whatever you decide, Griffin, it's okay, really."

She hangs up. And I'm left alone in the dark.

She's wrong. It's not going to be okay. If I decide not to help her, my life goes on the way it has been—and that's not okay. If I decide to help her, King could destroy everything.

Or—my fingers go ice cold at the thought, too audacious to consider—we could win. Beat King. And I'd be free.

But at what price?

14

Sitting in the darkness of the cold trailer, it feels like my chest is being squeezed so hard my heart is about to burst. I can't breathe and my fingers and lips have gone dead.

I run out the door, letting it slam behind me. I feel in my pocket for Miranda's phone, but instead my hand emerges with my lighter. *Burn it,* is all I can think. *Burn it all. It's the only way you'll feel better, feel less like a coward and more like a man. Do it! Take control. You have the power. Burn the world!*

Racing through the trees between the trailer and my uncle's property, I'm not sure what I'm running away from, but I think it's myself.

Fury and fear dance through my insides like the flames I created earlier. My heart pounds so hard I practically collapse against the barn behind my uncle's house. I slide down the splintered gray wood and end up sitting in the dirt, leaning against the scene of my first fire.

I hate the barn. It's old and full of cobwebs and mouse turds and something must have crawled under it and died long ago, leaving behind a stink that makes you gag just opening the door.

That's not why I hate it, not why I tried to burn it down.

Right around my thirteenth birthday, I'd stolen my uncle's

lighter—the same Zippo I carry now with its fire department emblem ruby red against the silver—and came out here to think, to cry, to feel sorry for myself, to escape, to make a plan, to die…I had no clue. But something about the lighter, the way it never surrendered, never betrayed, always had a flame…and those flames, so bright yet deadly. They mesmerized me.

Cowering in the barn on that summer day, about ready to pass out from the heat and stench of dead possum, I built my first fire. For tinder I used my uncle's favorite T-shirt, some softball championship his department won. Soaked it in a bottle of his favorite booze—Old Grand-Dad, it tasted awful, burned all the way down—added my uncle's tickets to an upcoming baseball game and a pile of his mail—hoped there was a check for a million dollars in there—and lit it all with his favorite lighter.

The booze must have been high test because the whole thing went up, *whoosh*, Aladdin's genie roaring out of his bottle, ready to wreak havoc.

At first the destruction was delightful. Fit my mood perfectly, the way the flames devoured everything. They didn't care who owned it. They just ate and ate and ate. And I controlled them.

Or thought I did. They quickly turned on me, spreading across the wood planks, seeking more fuel. I panicked and doused them, or at least thought I did, then ran, locking the door behind me to hide the evidence of my crime.

Only I hadn't realized I wasn't alone. Janey, just turned five, had followed me into the barn while I was gathering all my uncle's stuff to burn. Hidden in one of the stalls, I hadn't known she was there until I heard her screaming.

I ran back, smoke seeping between the cracks in the barn's siding, panic making me want to vomit as I pried at the door until my mind caught up with my fingers and remembered how to undo the latch. I ran inside. There were no flames, only a few smoldering embers in a pile of straw, but the smoke was thick enough to choke me. Janey stopped screaming and that's when I got scared, battling blind through the smoke, her racking coughs and wheezes guiding me. Finally, I found her, carried her out.

If I'd been a few seconds slower in getting the door open, a few seconds faster running back inside the house where I wouldn't have heard her screams, she could have died.

I'm her big brother. It's my job to protect her. No matter what.

As I lean against the barn, remembering that awful day, tears slip past my guard. I can't feel them. My face is numb and so are my hands, so I wipe them dry on my shoulder. Despite the memories, all I see are flames. All I want is to burn, burn, burn…

Maybe that's my way out, not trusting some girl I've never met who calls out of the blue with a crazy scheme.

I could burn it down, tell them I was responsible for the other fires plaguing Smithfield as well. Haul me away, lock me up, keep me behind bars. I'd be safe. I could trade my silence for Janey and Mom's safety, and King could go to hell along with my uncle.

It takes me two tries with my numb fingers to flick the lighter open. Flame dances in my palm.

I could do it. End it all. Burn it down. Go out with a blaze of glory.

God, how I want to. I can't blink or look away, my entire world consumed by the flame in my hand. I have the power. I am in control.

Do it! A voice whispers in my head. *Set it free. Burn it all.*

The flame dances in time with my breath. My chest is tight, my heart beating so hard my vision spirals red.

Burn it all…I could, I should…I close my eyes, my hand flipping the cover onto the lighter, the flame winking away. Swallow hard, try to breathe, shove my hands, shaking uncontrollably, deep into my pockets.

Miranda's right. I've known it all along, just didn't want to face up to it. I climb to my feet and trudge through the darkness, past the barn to the house and the door at the rear of the garage. I reach it but don't open it. I can hear my uncle talking to someone on the other side.

"You've made out good on this deal. We can't push it."

I don't hear anyone answer; he must be on his cell. Is he talking to King? Maybe my uncle is telling King to stop pushing me so hard, to let me off the hook. I press my ear against the crack between the hinges and strain to hear more.

"No, I told you. Last night was the last time."

King had me do a private show last night. Hope surges through me, a bright flame. My uncle does care after all.

But then he says, "At least until things cool down."

Maybe he can't solve everything with King. But if he buys me some time, it would help. I hear his boots on the cement floor as he paces. The garage is filled with stuff from our old apartment and my dad's things plus everything my uncle has in there, so there's no room for a car, barely room to walk.

The light comes on. I press myself against the outside wall, so he can't see me through the window in the door. From my angle, I can see him. He has a bag open on the floor—a big canvas bag like the ones he carries his turnout gear in. Only it's not a coat or pants that he's taking out of this bag.

It's a Halligan—a pry bar firemen use to open doors and windows. Then he takes out some cans and bottles of chemicals. I recognize a few—have even used some of them to start fires. The last thing he pulls out is a container of the highly concentrated chlorine used in swimming pools.

We don't have a swimming pool. But now I know not to waste energy on hope. He's not helping me. He's not talking to King.

Because one of the best fire starters around is concentrated chlorine combined with petroleum. I often carry a small film container of the stuff myself—it's quick and easy, gives you a hot fire with a bit of a delay.

It's also what started all the fires in town. The arsonist's signature.

15

Miranda hung up with Griffin. She stared at the phone a long, long time. It wasn't that late, only nine o'clock or so, but it felt like 3 a.m., locked in her room in the hospital, walls crowding in as the drugs wore off, taking with them the gentle clouds that fogged her brain, leaving behind terror spiking her veins with broken glass and razor blades.

She closed her eyes. Focused on her breathing just like Dr. Patterson had taught her. Griffin was the one, he was the one, he had to be the one, he was her last chance, her final chance…and time was running out.

The sound of the apartment door opening interrupted her mantra. She leapt from her chair by the window and shoved the phone beneath her pillow, beside her suicide note.

"Sweetheart, I'm home!" her father called out.

Miranda couldn't help her smile as she ran from her room and leapt into his arms. He wasn't that tall—not quite six feet—but he was strong, strong enough to lift her off her feet with a hug.

Her dad was one of those guys born a couple of generations too late. He belonged in a different time, one where cops on the beat knew everyone and were greeted with homemade doughnuts and cupcakes when they stopped by. Back then, her dad would have been the kind of man that other men would tip their hats to as he strode past, and his kids would have called him "Pops" as they played catch with him on a manicured lawn beneath a sprawling maple tree.

That was the world and family and life her dad deserved. The life he'd built for himself, patrolling one of the worst zones in Pittsburgh. He hadn't minded, not with his beautiful, brilliant "girls" waiting for him at home and the chance to really make a difference for the people he lived to serve and protect.

But this—twelve-hour days working as a campus cop, ticketing parked cars and listening to whiny drunk college kids followed by more hours working overtime at the Telenet Arena, a job she'd convinced him to take a few months ago, supposedly to pay for her online classes, classes she hadn't even bothered to attend— this was hell for a man like him. And she saw it every day in the lines around his lips and eyes, the way he barely made eye contact with her mom anymore, as if he were the one who had let them all down.

It wasn't his fault. Every time she saw that look on his face, she wanted to cry out, *It was me! Blame me. Yell at me. Why do you even bother anyway?*

But she never gave the words a chance to escape. Instead, she'd just hug him even harder, hoping that was enough…even though she knew it wasn't.

"How was your day?" he asked, releasing her.

"Good," she lied. "I made spaghetti for you." With their conflicting schedules, her mom and dad never got to eat together, so

Miranda made it a point to sit and pretend to eat with both of them. It was the least she could do.

"Hmmm, hmmm good. My favorite." He went to change out of his uniform while she heated the food. Then he rejoined her in the tiny kitchen. "Need help with your homework?"

She shook her head. "It's trig." A lie. Carefully calculated to play to his one weak spot. Dad had an associate degree in criminal justice but never made it past high school algebra when it came to math.

He started eating. She watched. Spaghetti used to be her favorite as well, but somehow it seemed wrong to indulge herself. A small punishment for the lies and manipulations and the pain—past, present, and future.

"So"—he gathered noodles with his fork—"your mom said you didn't make it out today. Want to go for a walk with me after dinner? You and me together? Just like we used to."

She sat in stony silence, his words hanging in the air alongside the limp noodles dangling from his fork. He set the fork down with a clank. "Ariel—"

"Miranda," she snapped.

He hated her new name, even more than Mom. But she needed Miranda. It was her only armor between the life she had—the life she'd loved—and her new life. Without Miranda, she'd return to that weak, stupid, trusting little girl, clueless, sniveling victim that she was.

Miranda was strong. Ruthless. Miranda would get the job done, one way or the other.

His sigh rattled her. "Sweetheart, you know what the doctors said. We have a deal. You need to keep moving forward."

She drew her knees up to her chest and picked at her cuticles, trying to deflect his disappointment. Usually she could outwait him and he'd surrender.

Not tonight.

"Your birthday is coming up," he surprised her by saying.

She jerked her head up. Did he know? Had he read her journal?

No. His expression was one of hope and…happiness. A glimpse of her old dad, the one who whistled as he walked up their front steps, came out from behind the clouds. God how she missed him. "I thought—we thought, your mother and I, and Dr. Patterson said it would be okay, we thought maybe, well…" He gaze stumbled against her stare. "Anyway, I wanted to tell you before your birthday on Sunday. So if you don't like it, we can come up with something else. Not disappoint your mom—"

He slid three tickets across the table to her. Special passes to a private rehearsal of the Pittsburgh Ballet Theater's performance of *Giselle* in June.

"Dr. Patterson thinks a goal, a date, something to work toward might be helpful. There will only be a handful of people there. It will be a very, very safe environment. And your mom remembered it was your favorite."

Miranda couldn't look up, her gaze weighted down as if the tickets were made of lead. How could she face her father when she'd be forced to demolish the light in his voice? Because there was no way in hell she could promise come June that she'd even be alive.

"But," his voice faltered, "if you don't think—if you're not sure—it's okay. I know it's important for you to be in control, to have a choice, but…" His voice stumbled again. "I think we need to know there are options. You—we—need to have something to hang on to."

Hope. He was talking about hope. Nasty little four-letter word.

She couldn't lie to him. Not again. Instead, she unwound her body from the pretzel it had twisted itself into and stood up, embracing him with a hug that she poured every ounce of her body and soul into.

"Thanks, Daddy," she whispered. He reached his arms up to circle hers, squeezing her tight.

And then she let him lie to her—to both of them. "Everything will be okay, sweetheart," he said, his voice thick with tears. "I promise. I will never, ever let anything happen to you. We will make it through this. You'll see. Everything will be all right."

16

My uncle's still in the garage, so I sneak around to the front door and let myself in as quietly as possible. Maybe he's not the arsonist. Maybe he found all that stuff and kept it so he could dispose of it properly…except then why would he have brought dangerous chemicals home?

Maybe he was teaching some of the other guys about the arsonist's techniques. That way they could fight the fires better. In the middle of the night? If that was it, he would have left all that hazmat shit at the firehouse, not here where Janey could get into it.

I pull my boots off—the hardwood floors squeak—and tiptoe down the hall to my room. Keeping the lights out, I set my boots down and take off my jacket. Footsteps sound behind me. No way in hell can I face my uncle, not now, not with what I'm suspecting. I drop my jacket on the floor and dive under the covers, fully dressed. I pull them up over most of my head and pretend to be asleep, hoping my pulse racing up my neck won't give me away.

Could he really be the arsonist? Maybe he was helping the police, showing them how an arsonist works? I add up the dates of the fires and my uncle's work schedule he was on duty during all of them, had been there to put them out before they could hurt anyone.

My uncle comes in without knocking. He leaves the door ajar so there's a sliver of light. At first he just stands there. I can feel his stare. I hold my breath, my entire body clenched into a tight knot. Then there's a click—he's closed King's laptop so he can have privacy. He never cares that it's me who will pay the price for shutting out King.

Somehow I can wrap my head around my uncle's betrayal of me, his insistence that King is my problem, not his. But I can't accept that he'd ever betray the guys at the firehouse, that he'd betray his code of honor as a firefighter. He loves fighting fires, loves being the hero, leading his men into danger and then out again on the other side.

He picks my dad's jacket up from the floor. I tense, remembering Miranda's phone in the pocket, praying it doesn't fall out. Or the gun. Shit. I'd forgotten about the gun. I dare to open my eyes a slit. He doesn't go through the pockets. All he does is hang it on the back of the desk chair, gently, carefully, his hand lingering on the leather collar.

He sits down beside me in the dark. A strong smell of chlorine slides beneath the blankets to gag me. With it, the stench of petroleum. And I know he is the arsonist.

I hate it. I hate him. I blow my breath out in a fake snore as he lays his hand on my head, his fingers combing through my hair. Revulsion and disgust at his touch threaten to shatter my control.

He sits there for a long moment, sighs my name. Twists it into a sound so sad and filled with regret, it feels like I'm responsible for everything wrong in the world.

Then he leaves. I'm alone in the dark, face buried in my pillow, smothering my anger and fear.

Until I can find a way to move Mom and Janey out of here to someplace safe from both King and my uncle, his secrets are my secrets.

Punching him, pummeling him, pounding him into the ground would be so much easier and feel so much better. I fantasize about it, but I can never do it. I have to put my family first.

My uncle's right about one thing: I'm all they have.

I'm pretty much awake the whole night. When I do drift off, it's only a few minutes before dreams of facing King turn into nightmares of his retaliation. Those morph into dreams of fire, drowning in fire, burning, burning...and my uncle outside, shaking his head in regret, walking away.

Not exactly eager to face anyone, I get up early, grab my shower, shove what little cash I have into my pockets, wash a bagel and peanut butter down with a glass of milk. Back in my room, I stare at my desk. My dad's jacket hangs from the chair where my uncle placed it last night. King's phone is on the charger hidden below the desk and his laptop is still closed.

The closed laptop frightens me. I should have gotten up and opened it last night after my uncle left my room. King will put up with occasionally being locked out of my life, but not for long. And I'm already on his shit list.

Even though he gave me until Monday to make my decision, I know he'll want to be able to reach me—I'd taken a huge risk liberating myself from the shackle of his phone last night when I fled to the trailer. My hand raises, almost against my will, stretches toward the desk. King has trained me well. Even the thought of disobeying him has my stomach churning acid, and bile scratching at my throat.

My hand falls. On my dad's jacket. Before I can think twice or lose my nerve, I grab it and race from the room. Two minutes later, I'm hunched over the steering wheel of my truck headed God only knows where. But I'm free. For now.

The air smells crisp, like spring has decided to stay—always a risk here in central Pennsylvania where we often get Easter and Mother's Day blizzards. I roll down the windows, the bracing chill clearing my mind. There will be a price to pay for this morning's baby steps of rebellion. Was I ready to go all the way and trust Miranda?

I drive my truck toward school but keep going past it until I get to a road leading up into the woods. It's single lane, rutted, used by hunters and hikers to get up to the ridge where the State Game Lands start. The trees—oak and maple with tiny red-green smudges where they'll soon have leaves, tall hemlock, and pine—keep me in shadow until I emerge at the parking area on top. I get out of the truck and climb onto the hood, the engine ticking as it cools beneath me.

A large bird—a hawk or turkey vulture or eagle, it's too far away to tell—glides across the blue sky over the valley. There are no clouds, not even those fuzzy ones Janey always tries to blow away like they're dandelion puffs.

Just me and the sun. I can't remember the last time I was free of King like this. Filling my lungs with the sweet air, I sit there and do nothing. I don't think. I don't try to plan. I don't come up with lies to tell anyone who might discover me. I'm just me, alone for the first time in what feels like years.

Finally, I take Miranda's phone from my pocket and dial. "I'm in."

17

Miranda was ensnarled by code and almost didn't hear the phone ring when Griffin called. She grabbed her Bluetooth and answered, her gaze still blurred by streams of characters.

"I'm in," he said.

She swallowed hard, her breath catching with excitement.

"Okay, here's how it's going to work," she told him, knowing her voice was rushed and manic but feeling like she needed to talk fast to get this all out before she forgot something. "The button camera-recorder I ordered for you looks like an ordinary pen. Just clip it in your pocket, click the top once to start recording and again to stop—"

"A pen does all that?"

"Sure. I could have gotten one that streamed it wirelessly but it was too expensive, so this one uses a USB port, just take the cap off. But here's what I was up all night working on—how would you like it if we did this so you never have to confront King in person at all?"

"You mean get him to talk, confess, over the phone or computer?"

"No. I was thinking we could infiltrate his computer—well, I could, with this program. See, we'll use the USB drive on the pen to upload this program, once I finish it, into your computer, then once I gain access to your computer, I can follow him back to his."

"And then what? Copy all his files, send them to the FBI or something?"

"Well, if he's smart, there won't be anything on his computer. That's why he's so hard to catch—with the live streams he sets up between you and his clients, he's watching remotely. There's nothing on his hard drive."

"So there aren't copies out there all over the net? It's just King's clients who have seen me?" He sounded relieved. She hated to disillusion him.

"Sorry, no. If I were King, I'd screen capture the video feed from my client's computer and bury the file on their hard drive, then send new customers there to download it."

"And if the cops ever search his client's computer, they'd find the files and downloads but nothing would lead back to King?" His breath whistled over the airwaves into her ear via the Bluetooth. "Why do you want to risk using this program on my computer if we're not going to find evidence on his?"

"If we get control of his computer, we can turn the camera on and get a picture of him. And I can capture anything he does, like getting paid by a client or setting up a new kid by grabbing a screen capture of them."

"We'd just wait until some other kid gets screwed by him?" He did not like that. Neither did she. She didn't have time before King struck again on her birthday. Only two days left. But other than planting porn onto King's own computer, there wasn't much she could do.

The code on her screen blurred. God, she was so tired, so very, very tired. She needed this all to be over.

Then she saw the flaw in her plan.

"Wait," she told Griffin. She closed her eyes, thought everything through once more, twisting and turning the plan in her mind. "We might not be able to do it this way. King will know when you connect the USB drive to your machine."

"So?"

"So, he'll be able to see what files are on it."

"We're back to plan A? Finding him and me confronting him in person at the arena tomorrow during the car show?"

"Give me a second to think." She twirled in her chair, gaze spinning around her room. It was painted beige, like the rest of the apartment—her mom kept talking about repainting the whole place, but they hadn't found time. Miranda didn't have any framed photos—no glass allowed after she came home from the hospital. But she had filled one wall with a collage of images ripped out of magazines and catalogs.

The images were of things from Ariel's life: wishes and dreams and lace and rainbow stuff. Miranda had arranged them to create a larger picture of her own dream, a window that didn't look out over a parking lot and trio of Dumpsters but instead looked into the future. Or maybe it was the past, Ariel's past. Anyway, the small scraps of color and light and hope combined to create a large, single rosebud. Pictures hidden in a picture.

"Maybe I can rework this to hide the program in a file that would make sense for you to upload to your computer. Steganography," she told Griffin. "We'll use steganography."

"Sure, if I had a clue what that was."

109

"It's hiding data inside computer images. King asked you to find a kid, right? I'll grab some stock photos, embed the computer code inside them, so when he opens the file to view them, he'll also unleash the code onto his hard drive. And it would make sense for you to take photos and transfer them to your computer. You can tell him they're of Janey's friends and you want his help in picking out the right kid to approach."

There was a long pause. "I don't know if I can convince him. That's so…twisted."

"It's not like they're real kids. And better than you facing him in person, less dangerous."

"You can do that? Set it up so King never knows I'm the one who betrayed him?"

"We can do it. Together. Bring him down. For good."

18

Miranda has only been in my life for less than a day, but I love the way she makes me smile. She just never gives up, not on the crazy idea that we can take down King—not on me.

I can't remember the last time anyone had faith in me like she does. No. That's a lie. I can. I just don't want to. Dad used to talk to me just like Miranda does, like he somehow assumed that I could do anything I put my mind to. I remember the glow of pride I'd feel when we'd finish working on one of his cars and wash the grime off side by side, filling the sink with black suds, me basking in his presence.

I blink hard and fast, willing away memories of him. He's gone and he's never coming back and who needs him anyway? I can do this. I can handle King and my uncle, take care of my family. Even if he couldn't. Loser.

"Where to?" I ask her, surprised my voice sounds choked. I clear my throat to cover it.

"Altoona," she answers. She gives me an address. There's a clacking sound in the background and I know she's typing on her computer, working her cybermagic. "It should be open by the time you get there."

I turn the truck engine on, plug the phone in to charge as we talk—thankfully it fits the same adapter as the one for King's phone. I lean back in the driver's seat as I steer the truck down the mountain and have to adjust the rearview mirror because for once I'm sitting up straight and tall instead of hunched over the wheel.

Thanks to Miranda.

"I never had a chance to thank you," I say, feeling suddenly shy. "For finding me. For doing all this."

She stops typing and pauses. "You are very welcome, Griffin." It sounds like there might be a smile coloring her voice. I hope so. Like to think I can make her smile. "But you're the one doing all the hard work. We're in this together."

That makes me feel even better. I'm not used to being part of a team. "Are you sure this is safe? I mean, King won't be able to trace you, will he?"

"Not if I get this right," she mutters, determination lacing her voice. Silence except for the keys clicking in the background. "Hey, Griffin?"

"Yeah?"

"Could you just talk to me? Keep me awake while I work this out?" She sounds exhausted. "I know it's crazy. It's just that I'm not used to having anyone to talk to. It feels good."

"I'll bet you have tons of friends," I say, embarrassed about how my life must look to her. I mean, look at me, no friends, no life beyond what my uncle and King plan for me, no hopes or dreams or any of that normal high school shit. Right now the most I have to live for is crushing my mother when she learns the truth about my uncle.

I've just begun to realize the enormity of the price we will pay if we win. But the price of losing is even worse.

It's a few moments before I realize Miranda hasn't answered me. I'm so used to disappearing inside my own head that I can't even carry on a normal conversation. Doofus.

I wrack my brain trying to think of a neutral, nonloser topic when she says, "Griffin, what kind of life do you think I lead? Tell me what you think my normal day is."

That's a weird question. What kind of day did any fourteen-year-old girl have? "You mean like, tell you what I imagine? Kind of like a story?"

This is the strangest conversation I've ever had. With anyone. Much less a girl I like. A girl I want to like me.

The smile returns to her voice. "Yeah. Tell me a story. The story of my life."

I echo her smile. It feels strange, like I haven't done it in a long, long time. Not just rearranging the muscles of my face, but feeling it on the inside. That nagging corner of my brain, Mr. Reptile, urges me to be careful. Being happy, caring too much, daring to hope—these can all lead to disaster and pain.

Right now I don't care.

"Once upon a time," I start, and Miranda breaks out laughing.

"No, silly. The real story. I wake up in the morning and…"

I lean back, losing myself in fantasy. Used to be I was so good at this—ever since I was a kid, I've been a big reader, could lose myself in a story. Escaping to fantasy worlds where the imprisoned prince fought free of the ogres or a magic spell ended the nightmare…it was how I survived those first months with my uncle.

Until that weekend at the motel. Right before I turned thirteen. No amount of fantasizing provided an escape after that. I had to learn how to throw up a barrier, deny my feelings.

And now Miranda threatens to breach those walls. *Danger!* Mr. Reptile Brain is shouting.

I ignore the warning and start. "You wake up to music. Happy music, something that makes you feel like dancing. And birds singing outside your window. Your room is bright and cheerful, done all in—" I almost say pink but don't. Too predictable and that's not Miranda. She's much more sophisticated than that. "Shades of red and gold, like ribbons on a Christmas present. You hop out of bed, already smiling, because you know this day is going to be great."

"Really? What makes it so great?" she asks, not challenging the fantasy; instead, her voice sounds like she's half-asleep.

"You're going to meet me, of course," I ad-lib. Then I get nervous—have I pushed it too far?

"Cool. What are we going to do on this perfectly great day?"

"There's no school today."

"Of course. Never on a perfectly great day."

"So we'll—" A memory pops into my head—my own perfect day fantasy from when I was young, before my dad left us. It never happened; it was one of those grownup promises that parents make when they leave you to walk home from school in the rain because they were stuck in line waiting for an interview for a job they don't even get and couldn't come pick you up. But that doesn't matter because now it's even better, sharing it with Miranda. "We'll pack a picnic lunch and drive out into the country, over the mountains and past the farms until we reach a meadow that smells of hay rolled into bales—"

"Oh, I love that smell. And the way the hay bales shimmer gold against the green fields when the light hits them just right."

"That's where we are." My smile widens. I'm thrilled I've got something right, found a place where we could meet. Even if only in our imaginations. "Wait. It gets better. There's a hot air balloon lying on its side, filling up. We walk inside it and it's like being inside a beautiful stained-glass cathedral."

"Or a kaleidoscope," she whispers. "Color and light all around us."

"Exactly. We watch the colors change as the balloon fills and then it's time to go."

"Where?"

"Up in the air, of course. We'll have champagne and—"

"I don't drink." Suddenly she sounds very serious. Did I break the spell?

"Cider and strawberries," I quickly amend, "and chocolate and—" I stall, realizing I have no idea what her favorite food is.

"Chocolate truffles, the dark ones—and that chocolate cake with the frosting, what's it called…ganache. I love that."

I have no idea what she's talking about, but she makes it sound delicious. "Anything you want, it's there. At first there's the rushing noise of the hot air lifting us higher and higher, but then everything is silent. It's just us and the breeze, floating like a cloud across the countryside. We look down and we can see our shadow gliding over the fields."

"It's beautiful," she sighs. "So peaceful. So romantic," she adds and the glint of humor is back in her voice. "What do we do next?"

My entire body thrills with the idea that she wants more from me. Not like my uncle or King's demands. Miranda wants me, the real me. A flush of heat rushes over me and I want to be with her in real life, see her face, touch her hair, touch every part of her. Not the horny, hot and sweaty ready for sex kind of want that guys my age are supposed to feel…not sure if I can ever feel that way. I think maybe my wiring has been too damaged. But I want—no, need—to get close to her. I want that kind of connection. Not about sex, more about…trust is the best word I can think of.

I almost say the words, almost trust her with my true feelings, but the silence has gone on too long and I lose my nerve. "Next we float over to a carnival and we climb down from the balloon onto the top of the Ferris wheel and ride it around and around until we're dizzy."

There's a slight pause, and I know I've disappointed her. She wanted something else. So did I. But I don't tell her that.

"Thanks, Griffin. That was a spectacularly perfect perfect day."

I perk up even though I realize she's just being polite. "Next time maybe you can tell me what your real life is like."

Silence thuds between us. *Way to go, bozo*, I chide myself.

Our sweet little fantasy shattered, I drive on. Stupid to dream anyway, not with having to deal with King—and my uncle. What was I thinking, hoping to ever have a chance with a girl like Miranda?

19

The code on the screen in front of Miranda blurred as she choked back tears. Griffin was so very sweet. No one had ever treated her like he did, and here she was, getting ready to destroy his life. Her first friend in two years and she was betraying him.

Was it worth it? Stopping King?

It was wrong, her using him like this—he still didn't appreciate how much his life would change after he helped her. Even if King ended up in prison, Griffin's—no, Jesse's—life would never be the same.

And if King didn't go to jail…if they failed?

Miranda had an exit strategy, was ready and willing to escape this life if it meant her parents could reclaim theirs. But what about Jesse?

Guilt translated itself into her fingers, and she pounded the keyboard so hard she felt the vibrations echo all the way up to her elbows. She had to get this right. They had to win. They couldn't let King beat them.

"I think I have it," she finally said. "Now it's time for the dwarves to go to work."

"Dwarves?" he asked.

"Sorry. My nickname for a group of hackers I'm friends with."
Strange friends. They'd never met IRL, had never even shown
each other their faces. They shared one thing in common: they'd
all been burned by trolls and cappers like King. Trust most definitely was not their forte. But testing code, making sure it would
work without King detecting it—that was right up their alley.

"Why do you call them dwarves? Is that some kind of computer slang?"

She laughed. She loved that he could make her feel normal
enough to let down her guard. "No. There's seven of us and they
have screen names that are all kind of crazy like Misscreant—I
think she's with Anonymous—Topaz, XFactor3, and Dumpty, so
it's easier just to call them my dwarves."

"So does that make you Snow White?"

"Hardly." Although they had kind of adopted her when she first
began snooping around the forums, trying to pick up the skills
she needed to track King. "I'm more like the seventh dwarf."

"Happy," he said as if naming her. "You must be the one they
call Happy."

If only he knew the truth. Like that crazy fantasy he'd described,
nothing could be further from the reality of her life. Yet, he'd
painted such a vivid picture—a special world created for her and
Jesse alone, no fears, only hope and joy. A true perfectly perfect
day built for two. As if maybe someday they could actually share
a day like that. Together, outside, in the real world.

"I know you've been busy," he said. "Don't suppose you had a
chance to check on my dad."

She sighed. So much for fantasy. "About that. Are you positive he was headed to that job interview in Maryland?"

"Yes. The private investigators my mom hired said he never showed up."

"Where'd your mom find these PIs?"

"I don't know. I remember one was a retired policeman, so probably my uncle—he knows a lot of cops. Why? Did you find him?"

She hated the hope that brightened his voice. "No. But I called the company he was interviewing with. They said he was there—in fact, he got the job. Was supposed to start the following week but never showed up."

"So he ditched us and a job? Why would he head out with no money, only the clothes on his back, when he could have just taken the job and made some cash?"

"Maybe whatever happened, happened on his way home to you."

He sucked in his breath. "So maybe he didn't run out on us after all. Maybe he was hurt or kidnapped or hit on the head or—"

"Don't jump to conclusions. I'm running a variety of search parameters. So far no sign of him—dead or alive."

"But you'll keep looking?"

"Yes. Of course." At least as long as she was still alive. She glanced at her pillow, the journal nestled beneath it. If she was gone before her birthday—two days from now—King would have no reason to go after her parents; they'd be safe. She hoped. There were no guarantees he wouldn't still target them, but it was one hundred percent certain while she was alive that King would never stop.

But it would mean abandoning Jesse, breaking her promise to him. Maybe breaking more than that...She remembered the look in his eyes on the video that first night. That spark of defiance, yes. But also despair. If she took the easy way out, leaving him to face King and his uncle on his own...

For the first time, her determination wavered. For the past year, the only thing that had kept her alive was her hunt for King—and knowing she had a way out if she failed. That ticking clock counting down to her birthday had kept her focused, given her the strength she needed to face each day.

Could she sacrifice that for Jesse? If they failed to stop King before her birthday, what would King do to her? To her parents?

How could she risk it?

The sound of a car horn blasting came through the phone. "Can you hear me?" Jesse asked. "I'm passing the Tyrone exit, figured I'd say hello."

She ran to her window and opened it, glad for a diversion from her thoughts. "Do it again. We're not far from the highway."

He honked again. *Beep, beep.* Two times, like the Roadrunner. The sound was so faint through her window she wasn't sure it was even real. But she wanted it to be, wanted the connection however tenuous to the world beyond her room.

"I hear you!" She felt giddy, almost giggled. Stopped herself. Ariel giggled; Miranda didn't.

She turned away from the window, shoulders sagging, feet

dragging as she sat down at her desk once more. This time she focused on her second computer, the one that had no security, that she allowed the creeps into.

Since finding Jesse, she'd ignored it, but now, as soon as she clicked to her inbox, she saw dozens of alerts with Ariel's name on them. Links to chat rooms and forums where men still talked about Ariel. After King's repeated cybersmashing, sending not only Ariel's picture and private details but also information about her parents out into the world of cybertrolls, a rather noisy cult had grown around Ariel—cultivated by King.

Men posted her pictures on revenge porn sites, accompanied with links to her old social media, address, phone, school. Since the companies that ran the sites didn't post the material and their terms of use forbid underage photos, legally they were immune— despite the fact that they never enforced their own rules.

Those were bad enough—especially the comment threads that blossomed around each post. Men boasting about what they'd do to Ariel if they ever spotted her in real life, grading her on her "slut factor," talking about trying to hunt her down, like she was an animal for them to shoot and bring home as a trophy.

Worse were the "fan" sites that sprang up after her last birthday. Those were even more perverted. Filled with men fantasizing about her and her mom, would they kill her dad first or make him watch? Sick, twisted stories, as if her family's lives were meaningless.

Those scared her. Some were so intense, so detailed she knew their authors were doing more than writing about fantasies.

Obsessions were more like it, like the one guy who used King's photos of her and dressed them in wedding gowns and lingerie. He often posted updates about his search for her and her family. Thankfully, he'd never come close.

"Want me to come by and pick you up?" Jesse's voice startled her. She slammed a finger on the computer's power button—she'd find the strength to monitor King's pervs later.

"What?"

"If you're so close, do you want me to stop by?" he repeated. "It'd be nice to meet you. In person, I mean. And we could go together—you could make sure I picked up the right stuff, show me how to use it." His words emerged in a rush as if he were nervous, could barely get them out.

She pulled her knees up to her chest, wrapped her arms around them, making herself small, face down into the dark world she created with her body. "No."

There was a pause. "Oh. Okay. Guess I'm not exactly the kind of guy you'd like your parents to meet."

She didn't answer. She hated the disappointment in Jesse's voice—damn it, Griffin. He was Griffin. The whole reason she'd created the screen name for him was so she could divorce herself from him as a person.

Her breathing echoed in the small space as she squeezed her body tighter together, counting by threes in her head. Mom, Dad, Miranda. Three, a magical number, the best number, the only safe number.

She didn't have room for a fourth. For Jesse. Didn't have the luxury of time, not with her birthday and whatever horror King had planned for her family less than two days away.

Stick to the plan. Take down King. For the next thirty-six hours, that was her entire life. She couldn't let Jesse—*Griffin, Griffin*—distract her from that.

And if she was forced to, if it was the only way out, she'd betray Griffin, break every promise she made to him. Whatever it took to save her family.

"Miranda, are you still there?" his voice drilled into her brain.

Three, six, nine, twelve, fifteen…She freed a hand for a quick second to click the phone off, shutting Jesse—Griffin—out. Eighteen, twenty-one, twenty-four, twenty-seven…three, she could only save three, the plan was for three.

But if her new code worked, maybe she could save Jesse as well. *Wasn't that the point, changing her carefully mapped out plan so late in the game?* A rebellious voice whispered inside her head.

She rocked hard in the chair, balled herself up tighter, anxiety quivering through her nerves, her pulse drumming. Could she risk it?

She forced all thought away, squeezed her eyes shut so hard it hurt, and focused on the counting, the soothing numbers, three, three, three…

20

The phone goes dead. What did I expect? Practically inviting myself into her home—and after everything she'd done for me, staying up all night, coming up with a new plan so I don't have to face King in person, teaching herself all that stegno stuff.

I'm turning into a creep, just like King's clients or my uncle. I bang the steering wheel in frustration and disgust. It was so nice, having someone to talk to, someone I could be myself with, without hiding or lying.

Not just someone. Miranda.

I keep driving, barely noticing the landscape as I speed down I 99 toward Altoona. I have to make it up to her, show her I'm not a creep.

The best way to do that is catch King. I imagine the look on her face when King is led away in handcuffs. I have no clue what Miranda looks like—her voice is warm yet tough, like she knows exactly what she wants and how to get it. Images of actresses and cover models fill my vision, but none of them is right.

Miranda is different than all those fake glamour girls. She has real strength—she must, to have survived everything King has done to her.

Not to mention being brave enough to stand up to him in

the first place. And she was only a kid when she'd done that. Just thirteen.

"Idiot." The word collides against the windshield, hurls itself back at me. Not only have I just met Miranda, not only am I exactly the kind of guy you wouldn't want to invite to meet your parents, but I'd forgotten she's younger than me.

Creep. Perv. Idiot.

No wonder she hung up on me.

I debate calling her back, to apologize, but have no idea what to say. So I finish the drive in silence.

The address she gave me isn't to a Radio Shack like I'd expected. It's to a small storefront labeled "The Spy Shop" with a cartoon image of Sherlock Holmes holding an oversized magnifying glass. Personally, I would have gone with James Bond, but whatever.

Miranda still hasn't called. I sit in the truck and debate going in alone. It's not quite ten o'clock, and I realize the store is dark, doesn't look open, despite the fact that the sign in the door says open.

Maybe it's a spy thing. I climb out of the truck and try the door. Locked.

Just as I'm turning around to head back to the truck, the putt-putt of a Vespa sounds from the parking lot. A guy drives in, parks beside me. His bike is lime green and his helmet is lemon yellow. He has reflective stripes and a flashing LED lights covering his Windbreaker.

He gets off, glances at my F-150 in disdain, and takes off his helmet. "You're Miranda's friend."

It's not a question, but I nod anyway. "Hi. I'm Je—Griffin." I stand up straighter, like a guy named Griffin would. I channel my uncle—he's the most confident person I know. Everyone likes him as soon as they meet him. I thrust my hand out like my uncle does when he's meeting new people. "How ya doing?"

He looks from my face to my hand and back again. "Yeah. This way." He turns to the door, leaving my hand hanging. Guess I can't fake my uncle's charisma. No surprise there.

I follow him inside the small, cluttered shop. It's not exactly like Q's lab—definitely more like Sherlock Holmes's overcrowded apartment. And absolutely feels like something from a book or movie, not like reality.

Surveillance cameras stream my image onto screens lining the walls and part of the ceiling, following my progress as I move cautiously between two rows of display cases. The cases in the front are filled mostly with phones, walkie-talkies, and radios. But as I go farther into the store, the merchandise changes.

Instead of standard Bluetooth, there are tiny earbuds, surveillance equipment including cameras of every shape and size—including one in a tube of lipstick—GPS trackers, and then weapons. No guns, but Tasers, knives hidden in all sorts of objects, pepper spray, extendable batons, sword canes, even a walker that has something that looks like a potato gun built into its handle, designed to shoot a net over an intruder.

"We're strictly surveillance and nonlethal self-defense," the man says, sounding defensive. "No wet work."

I have no idea what he's talking about. The man   I still don't know his name, I realize—walks behind the rear counter and takes off his jacket. He's watching me as well. And not in a friendly shop owner–customer way. More like he thinks I'm here to steal something.

"How long have you've known Miranda?" he asks abruptly.

How much should I tell him? I pause at a display of bugs and cameras disguised as insects. They look really lifelike. Beside them, there's a microphone hidden in a wad of used chewing gum.

"Not long," I finally answer. When I look back up at him, he's leaning over the counter, palms pressed on it, obviously not happy. I think he's trying to intimidate me—hard to do when I have twenty pounds and four inches on him.

"She's a very special person. I wouldn't want to see anything happen to her."

I meet his gaze, not liking how possessive he sounds. "How long have you known her?"

"Going on two years. And this is the first time she's ever asked for my help." His gaze narrowed, making his face look a bit like one of the bugs beside me. "What kind of trouble are you getting her into?"

"She called me, asked me to help her."

He's not sure but relaxes a little. "Help her do what?"

"Find someone."

He shakes his head. "Miranda doesn't need anyone's help with that. It's her gift."

"Gift?"

"Some people are good with code, making machines do what

they want. Others, like me, are good at hiding things. Miranda, she's a natural finder—especially people. No one can stay hidden from her, not for long."

"Except one man. The Creep." I use Miranda's nickname for King, figure I'm not giving away anything too sensitive.

His chin comes up and his shoulders relax. "You're helping her find the Creep?"

"Not just find him. Finish him." I have no idea where the bravado comes from, but it feels good, saying the words out loud.

Finally he smiles. "Now that's something I'm happy to help with." He brushes his hands together and pulls a bag out from behind the counter. "Let me show you how this all works."

21

Half an hour later, I've mastered the art of slipping the pen recorder/camera into my pocket, positioning it at just the right angle, and turning it on without being too obvious. The damn thing looks like any other pen—even has teeth marks in the cap.

Clive, the shop owner, talks like he's the one on the run from bad guys, barely taking a breath as he also gives me a tutorial on lighting and acoustics.

My phone rings. Miranda. "How are you and Clive getting on?"

I'm relieved that she sounds like her normal self. "Just peachy."

"Can I talk with him for a minute?"

I hand Clive the phone. He listens, holds a hand up to me to wait, and hurries into the back room. He returns a minute later holding a folded sheet of paper. He sets it and the phone on the counter then hands me an earpiece—small, unobtrusive.

"I've synched it with your phone. You can talk and call hands free."

I realize the phone he's returned with is different than the old clunker Miranda sent me. This one is sleek, top of the line, a lot like the one King has me use. I take the phone from him, stare at it in distaste. I kind of liked the old one.

"Don't worry, I disabled the GPS. No one can track you."

"Thanks," I tell Clive, pocketing the phone. "What do I owe you?"

"Nothing. Miranda's helped me out too many times. This barely scratches the surface. Just"—he hesitates—"be careful. Watch out for our girl, will you?"

"Yes, sir." I turn to leave and he calls me back.

"Wait. This is for you as well. Miranda said to find a quiet spot and open it." He hands me the paper. "There's a Starbucks two doors down, if that helps."

I nod my thanks, slide the folded paper in my pocket, and head over to the Starbucks. It's just after eleven, and my stomach reminds me that it's been a long time since I've eaten, so I grab a chicken salad sandwich and milk.

The counter girl doesn't even question that I'm not in school, instead seems most concerned that I don't drink coffee. But with my constant heartburn, the last thing I need is to add caffeine to the acid churning in my belly.

I sit down, take a few bites to quiet my stomach, and call Miranda, trying out the new earpiece.

"Hey again." She sounds brighter, happy even. I'm glad my gaffe from this morning has been forgotten. I almost apologize for it but decide it's best just to leave things alone.

"Hey yourself. That Clive guy of yours is kinda weird." Whoa, now who sounds possessive? I soften my tone. "In a nice way, I mean."

"Yeah, he can be a bit intense, but his heart is in the right place. Did he give you the fax I sent?"

"Got it." I wipe my hands clean and grab the piece of paper Clive gave me. "What is it?"

"Do you recognize any of those screen names?" she asks. Her voice sounds intimate, the way it's so clear, right in my ear, thanks to the earbud. "Has King ever used any of them?"

Her handwriting is so precise, in control, that it's easier to read than something printed by a computer. I love the way she draws a diagonal slash through the zeroes to separate them from the letter O—it's always so confusing when they look alike. And she uses tiny dashes through the leg of her sevens, makes them look old-fashioned and dignified. Her fours have triangles, not squares missing their tops. And her eights are perfectly symmetrical; you can imagine a figure skater gliding around their edges, effortlessly flowing into each curve, into infinity.

"Griffin?" She's waiting.

I blink and the numbers and letters go from being Miranda to just lines on a piece of paper. I scan the list.

My eyes trail down the list of names, snagging onto the last one. I jerk my gaze away, bile burning my throat. I gag; my stomach rebels; I think I might puke. I stagger away from the table and into the bathroom. Thankfully it's a single seater. I lock the door behind me. It takes two tries my hands are trembling so hard. Sweat and heat and cold flood my body inside and out. I lean against the tile wall, fight to breathe. That's all. Just one breath.

It takes all my strength. I slide to the floor. If the wall weren't there, I'd have fallen and never noticed.

"You still there?" Miranda's voice in my ear is the only thing that feels real.

I swallow hard. My mouth tastes like fire started with kerosene and Styrofoam—a scorched taste that won't go away.

"The last one." My voice is small and trembly, a field mouse scrambling away from a firestorm.

"Phreak426?" Her voice is louder than ever, excited. "Really? Are you sure?"

Am I sure? I close my eyes, focus on her voice, trying to forget. It shouldn't be too hard—I've already blocked out most of that time. But the bits and pieces that remain, they're seared into my brain.

I used to think of him as the Phreak. I'd never seen it spelled that way before he used it, had no idea that it meant more than just being a pervert. Thinking of him as a freak, no matter how he spelled it, helped me feel like I wasn't the one who was screwed up; it gave me someone to blame other than myself.

Pathetic, I know. But this was in the beginning. I was only twelve, just a kid. And like any kid, I didn't have control. Instead of only thinking of him as the Phreak, one day I blurted it out when he was critiquing my performance. Called him "freak."

The next weekend, my uncle took me on a surprise camping trip—at least that's the story he told my mom. Early thirteenth birthday present. She was so happy he was including me, taking an interest.

We ended up in a slimy motel, middle of nowhere. He brought with him a bunch of kinky stuff as per the Phreak's orders. And the things he did to me that night…Even now, three years later, my insides drop out of me just thinking of it.

Couldn't walk after. Spent the next day on the floor of the

bathroom, naked except for a blanket, while my uncle watched football and fed me Gatorade. He knew enough about first aid and shit that there was no permanent damage—the Phreak wouldn't like that—and it was a long weekend. I can't remember, Veterans Day, Columbus Day…who knows? By the time school was back in session, I was pretty much okay.

When we got home, I unloaded the unused camping gear from the truck, moving slow because I was in so much pain. My uncle came out and cornered me against the side of the truck, out of sight from the house. I flattened against the door, scared, even made a whimpering noise as he raised his hand. I felt small and helpless—totally helpless.

My uncle didn't hit me. No. He smiled and ruffled my hair with his fingers, leaned down, and kissed the top of my head—the way Mom does when she says good night.

I just stood there, frozen solid, couldn't even feel my feet much less move them. My breath came in tiny little gasps so very fast, as if each might be my last.

"You're my good boy," he whispered.

Then he went back into the house. By the time I got inside, I overheard him telling Mom a story about how I fell while horsing around on some boulders with the other kids who'd gone camping and that's why I had a few bruises. Imaginary kids. But Mom didn't know that.

She wasn't upset at all. She was happy. Said how thankful she was that he'd taken me and I'd been able to make some friends.

My uncle said, "Sure, no problem. He's a good kid. Having

a rough time is all. We can hang together more if you think it'd help."

Just like that, Mom gave me to him. I can't really blame her—she had no idea what she was doing, thought it was part of my healing process after Dad walking out on us. Or maybe that it was good for a kid dealing with puberty and hormones and crap to have a grown man as a role model. Who knows what she thought?

All I know is that one slip of the tongue, using King's screen name, cost me everything.

The next week, I started my first fire. Almost killed my baby sister.

After that weekend, after that video went live, the Phreak was dead and the King was born. That night in the motel, me screaming but no one listening, no one caring, that session won him a bunch of awards from his fellow pervs. They proclaimed him their king.

He's been King ever since. Long live the King.

"Griffin? Are you okay?" Miranda's voice brings me back to the here and now. My eyes pop open—how long was I gone? Sometimes I fall into these gaping voids in my memory and next thing I know days have passed, forgotten in a sleepwalk haze.

"What?" It's a struggle to get the single word out. Pain and nightmare memories still grab at me. My mouth is dry, parched. I push myself to my feet and stagger to the sink, dunk my face under the water and drink.

"What's going on?"

"Nothing. I'm fine." I'm lying. From her pause, I know she knows it, but she's too nice to call me out. "That last screen name—"

"Phreak426."

Just hearing it makes me recoil. "Yeah. That's him. It was the first one he used."

"Griffin!" I've never heard her say my name like that. I've never heard anyone say my name like that, even if it's not really my name—happy, excited, like I'm the most important person in the world.

Electricity charges through me. I wish she would always say my name that way.

"You're amazing! We got him!"

22

Miranda practically knocked her laptop off the bed she was bouncing up and down so hard. The screen name Griffin recognized matched an old one used by one of Telenet's employees.

"You are so busted, Mr. Leonard Kerstater," she whispered, staring at the Creep's online company profile, complete with photo.

She settled down, sitting cross-legged, hugging her favorite stuffed animal, a calico cat, to her chest, feeling free and floaty and light and young...like she was a kid again. Like none of the past two years had actually happened.

Then she realized several minutes had passed without Griffin saying anything. She tapped the volume control, heard his ragged, panicked breathing.

"Griffin? Are you okay?" No answer. "Griffin? Jesse?"

When his voice came again, it sounded strangled tight. "Names. They don't mean anything. People just hide behind them. It doesn't mean you're anyone different than who you really are."

"You want me to stop calling you Griffin?" she asked, puzzled.

"I want to stop being Jesse. Stop being JohnBoy." There was a noise like a hand slapping something hard. "But that's never going to happen, is it? No matter what I call myself."

"I wish—" She wished she knew what to say. Lying would be

easy, but he deserved better. She borrowed from Dr. Patterson instead. "We can't change the past, Jesse. We can only work toward a better future."

"Future? You really think I'm ever going to have a future? We nail King—you know what that means? It means my mom and little sister and the kids at school and teachers and the guys at the fire station and, I don't know, Fox News and CNN and who knows who, they'll all know who I am. What I did. I'll be famous—not me, JohnBoy. Those pictures and videos, they'll go viral, end up on page one, flashed everywhere. What kind of future is that?"

She was silent. If anyone knew what that felt like, having your life ripped open, laid bare for the hyenas to feed on, it was her.

"I survived," she whispered, hoping he didn't hear the lie behind her words. Miranda had survived, been born out of the chaos and pain. Ariel hadn't. "I'll be with you," she promised, hoping it wasn't another lie. "Every step of the way."

"Maybe I'm not as strong as you. Maybe I'm not Griffin. I'm only Jesse, poor, pathetic Jesse who can't fix anything. Who couldn't say no. Maybe I can't go through with this."

She waited, the silence between them filled with a thousand possibilities. His voice returned, a tiny whisper piercing the airwaves. "You said you found King. Give me his address."

No. She wanted the Creep, King, to be exposed with as much public humiliation as what she'd suffered at his hands. She wanted him to face the scrutiny of hundreds of eyes on him, seeing him as he truly was: a wretched evil son of a bitch who preyed on the weak for profit and amusement.

She'd planned almost a year for this. Now that she'd found him, nothing was going to stop her. "No. Griffin, we need to stick to the plan."

"I don't give a shit about the plan. What if your file upload doesn't work? What if he's not there, at the arena, tomorrow? What if something goes wrong and he runs? No. We end this now. Tell me where he is."

"What are you going to do?" She almost didn't dare to ask, had a pretty good idea what he would say. He wanted King dead as much as she did. Maybe even more.

His breath rattled through the phone. "I have a gun."

23

I sit on the restroom floor, my butt going numb. The revolver feels heavy in my pocket, and I pull it out. Its chrome sparks in the overhead fluorescent light. Almost as shiny as my lighter.

I spin the wheel, liking the sound. Then I open it, remove all the bullets. Double-triple-check that the barrel is clear, and dry fire it, aiming at the lock on the door. I'm a good shot with pistols and rifles, shotguns too. My uncle likes guns—something besides fire, beer, and football that firefighters have in common. At least around here.

I pull the trigger again, timing it between breaths, my hand steady. Could I do it? Kill someone?

This isn't me. I've no idea who this is. Not Jesse. Not JohnBoy. Is this who Griffin is? A killer?

Miranda is speaking into my ear. I finally hear her over the roaring in my brain. "Griffin? Talk to me. Are you okay?"

"I'm here." I spin the wheel again. I can tell by her sudden silence that she can hear it.

"You're not going to hurt yourself, are you?"

"No. If it was that easy, I'd have done it long ago."

"Right. You're right." Funny, she's the one who sounds panicked.

"Killing yourself isn't the answer. Neither is that gun. Are you okay to drive?"

"I'm not drunk. Not high." I don't know what I am, can't explain how I feel. What comes after fury, after terror, after you've surrendered so much of your soul that you're empty inside, nothing left?

"I can't come to you. Will you come to me? Talk to me about this, about what we should do?"

"Are you going to tell me where he is? Who he is?"

"No." She pauses. "Not until we talk. Face-to-face." Her voice is a lifeline, crossing time and distance to guide me to safety.

What choice do I have? I grab on to the hope that is Miranda and use her strength to pull myself back onto solid ground.

Finally, I sigh. Rage simmers like a live wire in my veins, but it's a weary, frustrated rage that I can control.

I climb to my feet and shove the bullets into one pocket, the gun into another. I pull out my notebook and pencil. "Give me your address. I'm on my way."

———

Miranda had just hung up from talking with Griffin when her dad appeared in her open bedroom doorway. She jumped—Mom was at class and Dad was supposed to be at work.

"Dad, what are you doing here? You scared me." She closed her laptop, trying to look casual.

"Came home early." He leaned into the room, looking around. "I heard voices."

She jumped off the bed and gave him a quick hug before heading out into the hall. "I was Skyping with a classmate about our trig assignment. Let me fix you lunch."

Beyond the hallway she saw a bottle of wine and a bouquet of flowers on the kitchen counter.

"Why are you home early?" she called back over her shoulder, wishing he'd follow her. King's picture was still on the main screen of her laptop; she hadn't had a chance to clear it. Not to mention all the other tabs she had open, tracing her steps to get onto the Telenet site and find his personnel profile.

Nothing illegal—well, maybe, sorta, and definitely not exactly the kind of thing her dad would understand. Especially since after she'd left the hospital the last time, she'd promised her parents that she'd give up her obsession, stalking the Creep, and she'd leave it to the police. The first of so many lies she'd lost count.

"Dad? What do you want for lunch?" She turned to face him, the length of the hall separating them. Exactly the wrong length. Too close to hide, too far to reach out to him, guide him away from her secrets. From her lies.

He stared at her as if sighting down the barrel of his gun. His cop stare—very different from the soft, fuzzy expression she usually coaxed from him. His "don't even try to bullshit me" stare. As if she was some kind of criminal.

Well, technically she was. Kinda. A few bent privacy and cyber-security violations. All for a good cause.

At least it had been. But now she had Jesse out there with a gun. She'd grown used to thinking of him as Griffin, her imaginary hero, protector, avenger. But it wasn't Griffin who'd broken down. It wasn't Griffin who wanted to end things with King right now; it wasn't Griffin headed over here.

It was Jesse. Scared, desperate, and armed.

And her dad equally armed.

A buzzing filled her head. Her breath caught as possibilities collided. Her dad was trained to deal with emotionally distraught people—but if Jesse lost control here, in his own home, with his daughter present? Would he react as a police officer or a father?

Memories flooded over her: the thud of fists striking flesh, men hauling her dad off the men who'd attacked her mom, cuffing his hands behind him, treating him like a criminal. His eyes blazing with rage. She stared at the apartment's front door, turned, and looked at her father still in his uniform. Regret and fear throttled her.

What the hell had she done?

24

I make it back to my truck, not even sure how I get there. I set my notebook with Miranda's address on the dash. I think I know where I'm going, but I'm not one hundred percent certain. I could call her again, but I feel like I've let her down enough for one day already. I can find my way.

Almost immediately I have to pull the truck over when my phone rings. Not Miranda's. My real phone. The one my mom got me to "keep me safe." The one no one ever calls.

I grab it from the cup holder between the seats. "Hi, Mom." She and Janey are in Pittsburgh for the day at the cystic fibrosis clinic. "Everything okay?"

Wrong thing to say, I realize immediately. I glance at the clock, not quite one. I should be in biology, not answering my cell phone. Dumb, dumb, dumb.

"Where the hell are you?" she asks. Her voice isn't raised, not angry, more like bruised. "Mr. Walker called, said you never made it to school today. Said you were given detention yesterday and ran out of it. He's talking suspension, Jesse."

"Suspension? For what?"

"Said you knocked over a janitor. He's calling it assault."

"I never—" Wait, actually, I might have. I vaguely remember

a big yellow janitor's bucket standing between me and the door, skidding into it as I ran to save Janey. Had there been a person there as well? "It was an accident, Mom."

"And today?"

"I—I had to meet a friend. They're in trouble and need my help."

"I want you home right now."

"Yes, ma'am. What about Mr. Walker?"

"I told him you were running out because you were sick with that nasty stomach flu. Covered for you, said I'd forgot to call in this morning to let them know you were home still sick. Said I was too busy getting Janey ready for the trip to Children's."

I hated that she lied for me. Hated even more how easily it came to her—I always thought Mom was the one person I could count on to always be honest. "You didn't have to do that."

"Richey and I discussed it and decided it was best that we handle family problems here in the family." Richey is what she calls her little brother, my uncle. He's just as good at manipulating her as he is me. And she's oblivious, as always.

"I'm on my way home now, but I'm in Altoona." The noise of a hospital intercom mixes with a monitor's beeping in the background. "How's Janey?"

She blows out her breath in a sigh of frustration and worry. "Her pulmonary function tests are low and she's got a fever. They're keeping her here for IV antibiotics until they know what's going on. We're waiting on the X-rays now."

"Infection?" The nemesis of CF patients. All that thick gunk that collects in their airways and sinuses attracts germs. "She was fine yesterday." God, had I missed something, too busy worrying about King? I hit the steering wheel with my fist, squinching my eyes tight. Janey had to be okay; she just had to be.

"If it is, they've got it early. We'll know for sure once they get the tests back." Her voice is ragged, more than tired. "We won't be home for a few days and quite frankly, I'm not sure what to do with you, Jesse. I thought I could trust you, but—"

"You can." How can I prove that to her without telling her the truth? "I'm headed home right now."

"All right. Call me as soon as you get there—from the landline so I know you're really home. I'll see what your uncle wants to do."

"Yes, ma'am." I put the truck in gear and start driving.

I call Miranda to let her know I can't make it, but there's no answer. I try three more times before I reach my uncle's house.

Why isn't she picking up?

———

Her dad met Miranda's gaze, then pivoted, hand dropping to his gun. He entered her room as if it was enemy territory. She pushed back against the wall, holding her breath. He emerged a moment later carrying her laptop. Now open.

He didn't even glance at her as he passed her and headed to the kitchen table. He set the laptop down, settled into a chair, and waited.

Her mind spun with lies and excuses. How much to tell him?

Nothing was her first instinct, remembering what had happened last time she'd told the truth about King. That day in court when she'd testified. It'd felt like ripping out her guts, and what had come of it? Her dad hitting those guys, her mom in tears, Miranda back in the hospital…

She sidled into the kitchen and took the seat across from him, slouching until her chin was barely above the table. Eyes narrowed, she watched as he typed with two fingers, clicking the mouse keys, peering into her innermost life. Her real life.

"What are the flowers for?" she asked, hoping a diversion might buy her time to come up with a plan.

He looked up, startled, as if he'd forgotten the wine and roses. "We finally got an offer on the house back in Pittsburgh. Your mom can take more classes and I'll be able to quit my job at the arena."

The job she'd practically shoved him into. The job she needed him to keep—for a few more days at least. Just until the car show tomorrow.

"But you haven't quit yet, right? You'll be working there this weekend still?"

His gaze snapped from the computer screen to her. Too sharp, not easily fooled. She'd grown so used to the soft, teddy bear of a dad, the man who'd taken such gentle care of her when she'd come home from the hospital last year, she'd forgotten about the tough, street-smart cop.

"Why don't you start at the beginning?" he suggested. "And I'd appreciate it if you told the truth. I think you owe me that, don't you?"

His glance around the shabby, tiny apartment cemented her guilt. They'd had a nice house in Pittsburgh. A nice life. Before she screwed up.

She squinted at him, resenting that he'd chosen now to finally hold her accountable for her actions. Then she straightened, surprised as he lay his hand over hers.

"The truth," he urged. "It's the only way I can help you, Ariel."

"Miranda," she corrected automatically.

He winced at the name. She sat up, tall, proud, and met his gaze dead-on. He frowned and gave a small nod. More a jerk of the chin in acknowledgment that he'd heard her than actual acceptance. "Okay. Miranda. Who is this man?"

He turned the laptop so they could both see the screen. King's face in full color hovered between them. Miranda examined her cuticles, found a ragged edge and picked at it. Every time she looked at King, he appeared so normal, dull, the kind of guy who'd hold the door open for a stranger and you'd look right past him, never see or notice him.

Was that why he did what he did? Not just power...but attention?

She couldn't meet her father's eyes. Stared instead across the open bar into the living room at the front door. Jesse would be here soon. Maybe it was for the best, telling her father now, before Jesse arrived. Who knew what kind of state he'd be in? He'd sounded devastated over the phone, even after she'd calmed him down and got him to put the gun away.

"Who is he?" her father repeated, bringing her attention back to him.

"He's the one," she whispered, her voice tight and high-pitched like she was a little girl again. She blinked hard and fast. She couldn't believe she was fighting tears. This was her moment of triumph, what she'd worked so hard for all this year. But here she was falling apart, like she was a stupid little baby.

Her entire body shook. Her father noticed and moved to crouch beside her, hugging her tight.

"It's him, Daddy," she said, the words almost drowned out by tears. "I found him."

25

I take my time driving to my uncle's house. Focusing on the road helps me calm down. Imaging the look in Mom's and Janey's eyes is enough to make me realize I could never kill King. But I still want to hurt him, make him feel half the pain he's caused me and his other victims.

Even though it's supposed to be his day off, my uncle is covering the day shift for the chief while he and the state police arson investigators meet with the city commissioners and police. Hopefully he'll be gone until late, but you never know.

If Miranda's plan works, how will my uncle react once King is exposed?

It won't be pretty. He'll want answers from me, maybe even threaten Mom and Janey. Maybe I should tell the cops that I think he's the arsonist. Get him locked up and off the streets. But I've no idea if I have enough evidence—he might end up set free but even more pissed off.

I hate to even think about Janey being sick, but maybe it's good they'll be in Pittsburgh for a few days.

Now all I need to do is upload Miranda's photos with their hidden files to my computer, encourage King to take the bait, and wait for her to spring the trap.

I pull into my uncle's drive and jump out of the truck. The gun in my pocket knocks against my hip. Almost forgot about it. I should return it to my uncle's toolbox but decide it can wait until after all this is over and I know how my uncle reacts to losing his partner in crime.

Mom answers on the second ring when I call her from the house phone like she asked. "Really, Jesse, what am I going to do with you? I hope you have a good explanation for your actions."

"I told you—"

"You can tell me even more, including giving me your friend's name and contact info so I can discuss this with his parents as well. As soon as Janey's taken care of and I get home, you, me, and your uncle, we're going to discuss this and decide upon a suitable punishment. Do you understand me?"

Even though she can't see me, I look down at my boots. I feel awful distracting her from Janey. "Yes, ma'am."

"I just got off with Richey. He was called out to a fire, but he wants to talk with you tonight. In the meantime, you're grounded. No phone, no TV, no computer. You do your homework, clean your room, and think about your actions. I'll call and check on you when I can." She pauses but I don't know what to say. To my surprise, she continues, "I love you."

And she's gone. I hang up the phone, can't remember the last time I was home alone for longer than the twenty minutes between my school and Janey's bus—even then my uncle would be here most days. The house doesn't feel empty, though. Instead, it feels like it's holding its breath, waiting to see what I'm going to do next.

Easy. I'm going to set the trap for King. Last time I ever have to talk to him again.

I don't even bother taking my jacket off as I rush to my room. The computer is still shut, the way my uncle left it last night. I open it up.

Nothing. The screen is blank. But the power button is lit. Puzzled, I shut it all the way off, make sure it's plugged in, and reboot it. It whirls and whirls but nothing happens.

King's phone rings. I grab it from where I keep it stashed out of sight on its charger below the desk. The screen is filled with missed messages and calls, too many to count. Yesterday I would have marveled at how he knew I was home, but now, thanks to Miranda, I know it's his spyware using the phone's microphone and camera to monitor me.

The phone rings again, vibrating in my palm. I gather my breath, tap the recording pen so it's on, and answer, putting the call on speaker.

"What the hell you playing at?" King's voice thunders. "You don't shut me out, not ever. Do you understand me?"

"You said I had the weekend off to think about what you said, about looking for a kid for you to sell to your clients."

"Giving you time to think doesn't mean you're off the clock. I had to cancel two clients because you weren't answering your phone. Do you have any idea what that cost me?"

Actually I don't. But this is a good time to document it. "No. How much?"

He goes silent, surprised by my answer. So not JohnBoy.

Not Jesse, either. It's like I'm channeling an alternative personality. Griffin.

"What did you do to my computer?" I ask when he doesn't answer my question. "I can't perform for your clients without it."

"When you didn't answer I got worried that you were going to do something stupid, so I wiped the hard drive. But you're not going to tell anyone about us, are you, JohnBoy? Because you know I have just as much dirt on you as you have on me. More, even. I can make life hell for you and your mother and baby sister. So you better not even think of crossing me."

"Of course not." I force myself to sound like JohnBoy—scared, obedient. "I was out taking pictures of kids like you asked. Wanted your help in picking the right one. I don't know what to look for."

"Your uncle would be a better judge than I would." He sounds mollified, though. "It was time for a new computer anyway." He likes to switch them up, always worried about any traces of him on my hard drive. "I'll have a new one shipped out. You'll have it tomorrow."

That's when it hits me. No computer means no going through with Miranda's plan—at least not tonight. Now that she knows King's real name, she'll want me to meet him in person at the car show tomorrow.

Suddenly I feel like JohnBoy again—the part of myself that I hate. The sniveling coward who can't stand up to my uncle, to King, to King's clients. The only thing JohnBoy is good for is satisfying their twisted needs.

And protecting his family. I have to admit that. I hate it, but JohnBoy is the only thing keeping a roof over our heads.

"My uncle and I might go to the car show tomorrow," I tell King, hoping to draw him out. So far, our conversation implicates me as much as it does him. I doubt it's enough for the cops. "I can look for kids there."

"So you didn't need until Monday to make up your mind. I'm surprised." He sounds suspicious again. I hate it when he's like this. Sometimes his moods bounce around so fast that even when I'm trying to placate him, I end up triggering an outburst. Which always ends badly—for me.

"You shouldn't be. Not after you sent that man to hurt Janey. You know I'll do anything to keep her safe."

Another long pause as if he's dissecting my words and tone. "Don't you forget it."

He hangs up.

I stare at the phone. Did I screw up my one chance to get him on record? If he was suspicious enough to wipe the computer, he might decide to make a clean slate of everything, including me.

I'm going on two days without sleep and my mind is blurry. I need help figuring out what to do next. I leave King's phone in my room and go to the bathroom, turn the water on loud, and try to call Miranda, but she's still not answering. While I'm in there I wash my face, then I go back to my room, plug the phone onto its charger, and sit back.

All I can do is wait for my uncle.

I sit there, alone in the empty house, staring at a dead computer, imagining the worst. I remember the other kids who died because of King. Suicides supposedly. But what if they had help? Like from the man who came after Janey yesterday.

I wrap my hand around the gun in my pocket, quietly pull it out and load the bullets back in. I need answers. And my uncle is the only one who has them.

26

Her dad hugged her hard until his arms shook. Miranda abandoned all pretense at trying to act like an adult and bawled like a baby. Finally, after her tears had run dry and she'd stained his uniform shirt with snot, she sat up and rubbed her face with her palms.

"I'm pretty good with computers," she said, a hint of defiance in her voice.

He shook with laughter that was close to tears. "I know you are, sweetheart." He straightened, kissed the top of her head, and pulled his chair so they sat so close together that their legs touched, as if he couldn't stand to have any distance between them. "How'd you find him?"

"It was like piecing together a puzzle without knowing what the picture was," she tried to explain it in terms a nonhacker would understand. Details like ISPs and steganography would just muddy things. He frowned and she knew he was thinking of her promise that she'd give up her search for the Creep. She had to prove to him that her lies were worth it. "First, I was able to track some emails to Smithfield Telenet. It was the common denominator, so I started there."

"Telenet? The ones who own the arena. They're based in

Smithfield." He leaned forward, his gaze locking on hers. "It wasn't a coincidence that I got the job offer at Smithfield College after you got out of the hospital."

She shook her head. Easy peasy to find a job that suited him and do a little phishing, make it look like it came from the résumé site he'd signed up for. And who wouldn't want to hire him, with his qualifications and commendations?

"Want to tell me which jobs I missed out on?"

"Nothing you would have liked. Security guard at a West Virginia coal mine, stuff like that."

"But you wanted us to move near Smithfield. To be near Telenet."

"Convincing the doctors that a move would be good for me was easy," she admitted. "And Smithfield has classes so Mom wouldn't get too far behind. Plus, it's not very expensive to live here, so I thought it would help since we still had the hospital bills and the house back in Pittsburgh and—"

"You thought of everything." His gaze narrowed as he looked at King's image on the Telenet website. "You even got me to moonlight at the arena. Why? Because Telenet holds their events there? But how did that help when you didn't know who he was—"

"I knew I would. Someday." Her tone was grim. He hadn't figured out the rest and she hoped he never would. The part about her birthday and what she'd promised herself she'd do to end all this—one way or the other.

"What makes you sure this is him? This Leonard Kerstater?"

"I had a little help." There was no way around it, especially since Jesse would be here any minute now. She told Dad everything—except the part about the gun. She didn't want to get Jesse in trouble.

By the time she finished, he was standing, pacing the narrow space between the table and the counter. She stopped talking and he stopped walking, his expression going from concern to disappointment to anger.

"You were going to use this boy, this kid who's just as much a victim as you are, and have him confront Kerstater? What the hell were you thinking? Putting an innocent civilian into that kind of danger?" The table shook as his voice boomed through the room. "Why didn't you come to me? It's my job to take care of you. To stop men like this, this—" His face flushed as he fought for control.

Miranda didn't know what to say. Guilt flooded her. He was right. Her crazy plan had needlessly endangered Jesse, and she felt ashamed. "I didn't know what else to do. I don't have any concrete proof. But he's the only possibility. It has to be him."

He scowled at her, shaking his head sorrowfully. "I don't know you. I don't know what happened to my sweet baby girl, but she is not you. She was kind and gentle and she'd never betray us or anyone the way you have. You broke your promise to us. You acted recklessly." His glare was as painful as a slap. "You should have come to me—this is a job for the police, not two kids who are in over their heads."

Miranda lowered her face so her hair hid her from him. He was right, so very right, and yet, what else could she have done with the clock ticking down to her birthday and King's next attack?

"I understand your fears," he continued, pacing behind her. "For two years, your mother and I have been there, supported you every step of the way. But to use your disability as an excuse to draw this young man into—do you have any idea the danger you could have put him in?"

With his words, her fantasy of publicly humiliating the Creep, making a spectacle of his destruction just as he had done to her, crumbled. She closed her eyes. Her dad was right. It was childish and stupid and selfish and so many things…

She stood so fast the chair skidded into the countertop, ran to him, and hugged him hard. "I'm so sorry. I just needed—I wanted to make everything right again. I didn't know what else to do."

He stood rigid for a long moment. Then finally, he placed his arms around her. "What else to do? How about asking for help? How about letting your mom and me into your world? Don't you think we deserve that?"

She nodded, her face buried against his chest. "I was scared, afraid that if one more thing went wrong, if it was too hard—" Her voice trailed off, fear swallowing her words before they could make it past her lips.

He ran his fingers through her hair and lay his cheek on top of her head. It felt good. She felt good, solid, connected to the world in a way she'd hadn't in a long, long time.

"You never have to worry about us giving up on you," he whispered. "Never. You're our girl. We love you with all our hearts, your mom and I." He hugged her hard, kissed the top of her head, and straightened. "Speaking of your mom, I guess I should fill her in on what's going on, see if she can cut class early and come home."

"Why does she need to come home early?"

"So I can go check out this Leonard Kerstater for myself."

She clutched his arm. "No. Dad. It's too dangerous—what if he sees you? He knows who you are. Like I said, we have no real proof."

"Maybe not, but I want to get a look at him. And then we're going to have a long talk—you, me, your mom, and this friend of yours, Jesse. He needs help, and we need to make sure he's safe before we do anything else."

"Anything else? Like what?"

"Like take all these pieces of the puzzle you gathered to the computer crimes guys at the FBI. Maybe you don't have proof, not enough for a court of law, but you might have enough for them to find some."

She doubted it. King was too slick—two years of her tracking him and all she had were a few stray data points that added up to a name. No proof of any illegal activity. No proof of anything, really. Her stomach bottomed out as she realized the extent of her folly—drawing Jesse into this when it all added up to nothing. But without him, she would have never gotten the final clue to King's true identity.

Honestly, without Jesse, she might have taken the coward's way out and not waited for her birthday. She wished she was stronger than that, strong like Jesse was, but she knew the truth. It had been her hunt for the Creep that had kept her alive. Jesse answering her call for help had given her hope—funny how the word didn't seem so bad anymore.

While her dad called her mom, Miranda tried Jesse. She'd missed four calls from him—had something happened? He should have been here by now. But he didn't answer. The call went to voice mail.

"Where are you? It's me," she said. Who else would it be? She was the only one with this number. Still, she didn't want to say her name.

Her mouth went dry and the room wavered for a moment before she remembered to breathe. Her dad was right. Her plan was too risky; it would never work. As soon as he got here, she'd tell Jesse to forget it. They'd do things her dad's way.

"Your mom's on her way," Dad said, a hint of his old cop voice returning. It seemed like he stood straighter, was taller somehow. Now that he had an enemy to confront. "I'll call you—"

"No. Wait here for Mom and Jesse. Don't go see King—Kerstater, whatever."

"Don't worry. I'll be fine. He won't even know I'm there." He grabbed his jacket and opened the door.

Miranda stared out into the hall. Her dad paused, turned back. "Unless. Do you want to come with me?"

Yes. No. Yes, yes, yes. With all her heart. But no. Facing the Creep, even with her dad at her side, even hiding in the dark where he'd never see her...no, no, no.

Her hand clutched her throat, her pulse fluttering beneath

her fingertips like a hummingbird trapped in a net—desperate to escape.

"It's okay. Everything will be okay." He sounded excited by the chance to take action, regain control of his life—of their lives.

He gave her another quick kiss and left, walking hard and fast, radiating confidence. Like he used to, before King...

Miranda hugged herself, spinning in place, seeing the apartment as if for the first time. It was so tiny. Her world had grown so tiny. There was no space, not enough room for her to breathe. She ran to the door, yanked it open without even click-clacking the lock to a magic number, and took one step out into the hall, ready to yell to her father to stop, wait for her.

The fresh air hit her like a tsunami, the hall stretching out, out, out a warped tunnel lined with doors that hidden dangers lurked behind. Gasping for breath, her vision blurring red, she fell back against the wall, felt for the door back into her sanctuary, and collapsed inside. Panic roared through her, deafening, as she curled up on the floor and smothered her screams with her fists.

27

My uncle finally pulls up in his truck and hops out, surprised to see me standing inside the open garage, waiting for him.

He grabs his duffel. It must've been busy for a day shift. He still has soot smudges at the corner of his jaw. Right where the edge of his mask rubs. The first shower never totally erases those.

"Your mom tell you she won't be home tonight?" he asks. He blinks slowly, a smile growing. Not angry about me skipping school—what the hell would he care about that? Anticipating. And I know exactly what he wants.

"Yes," I say shyly, looking down at my boots. They're my steel-toed Timberlands. I'm hoping I won't need them.

The garage is filled with boxes, a real firetrap—boxes stacked on pieces of my grandparents' old furniture, boxes from my dad that Mom can't bring herself to throw out, boxes of old Christmas ornaments and books and clothes and half-empty paint cans and motor oil and dirty rags and clean rags and… well, right now, I'm not seeing them as boxes at all. I'm seeing them as tinder.

Because if this goes wrong, I'll need to get rid of the evidence.

"So," he says, drawing closer. "What should we do?"

"I was just thinking…" I pitch my voice low and he draws near. "I thought, maybe, we…you and me…"

He steps into the garage. The neighbor pulls up across the street. My uncle shuts the garage door behind him. No witnesses. Just the way he likes it.

Now it's just him and me and a single lightbulb crowding out the shadows. He places his hand on my shoulder. Lays it there, warm and heavy. Not reassuring. Not at all.

"You and me?" It's not quite a question, not the way his mouth twists into a smile as he says the words.

His eyes gleam in the reflection of the lightbulb over my head. He doesn't realize it, but I'm just as tall as him—he still thinks of me as a scrawny little kid. His hand slides down my shoulder. He squeezes my arm. "Nice. I knew someday you'd come around."

He tugs on my belt with his other hand, pulling me close enough that I smell the smoke and shampoo and steak and onions he had for dinner.

He leans in, his gaze on my lips, hungry for more than dinner. I slide the snub-nosed revolver from my back pocket and jam it under his chin, forcing his head back. Hard. Digging the barrel of the gun into his flesh.

His eyes flash with anger first. Then fear.

Funny, those two always seem to come in the reverse order for me. Maybe that's the difference between predator and prey. Or the difference between grownups and kids? Miranda will know. I file it away for later; it feels important.

"Jesse, stop," he stutters. "You don't want to do this."

Too late, he realizes that I am the same size as him, a grown man. Just as strong too. I'm not the little boy he made cry that first time. Right now I have no idea who or what I am, but I sure as shit don't feel like JohnBoy.

The thought brings with it strength—and the memory of Miranda's voice. "Griffin. The protector against evil," she whispers inside my head.

I force him back until he's pinned against the corner between the wall and the door. "You don't get to tell me what to do anymore."

My voice surprises me. It's not loud, but it's so big. Big enough to fill the garage, fill all the space between the boxes, space usually filled by shadows and cobwebs. Big enough to fill him with fear. I feel his body shrink away from me—not just the gun, but me. Not JohnBoy. Not Jesse. Me. Griffin.

"Wh-what do you want?"

"You're going to tell me. Everything. Every single damn thing you know about him." Even now I can't say King's name out loud. Not even for the recorder that's humming away in my pocket. Damning me as much as them, but I don't care. Not anymore. All I care about is ending King before he hurts someone I do care about.

He shakes his head—or tries to. I jam the gun up harder, and he makes a little squeaking noise like a rat with its leg caught in a trap. Tough choice. Chew your leg off or wait to see who comes to get you.

"I can't. He'll kill me."

"Think I won't?" I'm not sure of the answer myself, but he is. I can smell the fear coming off him in waves. "Tell me about King. Now."

28

At first he just glares at me. I do what I've wanted to do since I was twelve. I sucker-punch him. So hard he doubles over, gasping. That gives me time to handcuff him to the steel support for the garage door.

"Hey!" he says, surprised. I shove the gun back in his face and he shuts up. Fast.

I leave him there while I stroll over to the can of gasoline I use for the lawn mower. Bring it and some rags over to him. I open the can. Spill a bunch onto the floor. That's all.

He's rattling the handcuffs against the railing, realizes he can't break free. Glaring at me, he gives a jerk of his chin. Smart enough to know what damage gas fumes and a spark can do in a place like this.

"King." I sound like some tough guy from the movies. Power surges through me. I like it. It doesn't come from the gun—the gun isn't necessary anymore, so I pocket it. No, the power comes from me, from what I can do—things I can't even imagine. But he can.

"What do you want to know?"

"How did you meet?"

He laughed. "No one meets King. Ever. He finds you. Spots you in a chat room, spies you on video. Doesn't even have to be vid—dude has some kind of backstage pass into just about any webcam anywhere. Without you even knowing it, he's there, watching and recording everything in sight. People, especially kids, do a lot of stupid things in front of their computer, gives him all the ammunition he needs to get what he wants."

I think about Miranda, how King tried to blackmail her. "So that's what happened to you? He blackmailed you into, into," I stumble, trying to find the right word, "hurting me?"

He shakes his head. I don't like the smile on his face. It's as if he's rewinding every time he's touched me, some kind of warped highlight reel in his head. Like he's proud of it.

I slug him again. It's hard to stop with just one punch, but he pukes and I jump back to avoid it. He sinks down to the floor, not caring that he's sitting in his own vomit. Disgusting. How can anyone see him as a hero?

"Answer me," I shout.

He wipes his mouth on his shirt. Spits. "No. He didn't black-mail me. Didn't need to. You're mine, Jesse. You always were and you always will be. I've known since you were younger than Janey that we were going to happen one way or the other. Figured I might as well make some cash from it."

I step back. It's the only way to keep from beating him to death. "You—you went to him?"

"Sure. I ain't no victim. Word got around—you had a fantasy, he was the guy to find it for you. If he couldn't, he'd find someone to create it, custom-like. I knew if I couldn't resist you, there'd be others who'd also pay for the pleasure."

"You talk like you're ordering a freakin' pizza or something." And I was the pepperoni on top. Now I'm the one who feels like throwing up.

"That's all it is to King. Just business. Either you're making money or someone's making money off you." He looks up at me with a sneer. "Not like you ever turned down anything I bought you with his money. You liked those new soccer cleats and that trip we all took to the Outer Banks. Oh, and who did you think bought your mom that new car of hers? You're just as guilty as I am, JohnBoy."

The name does it. I lose it. Smash my foot into his face so hard his nose gushes blood like a truck running over a ketchup bottle. He screams and twists away in pain.

Shame floods over me hot and cold, so I'm shivering and sweating all at once. I'm disgusted with myself—but it also feels good. The power, the control. Almost as good as when I create my fires.

Fire. Perfect way to finish him and destroy any evidence. The whisper is seductive, dancing through my brain red and gold and purple. It would be so easy—so very, very easy.

No! I can't. Oh, but I *could*. I should. I'll hate myself if I don't.

Then I think: What would Miranda do? What would she think of me if I gave in to temptation and anger?

I step back, give him space to recuperate. It's easier to breathe when I'm not within striking range of him. "What's King's real name? Where's he live?"

He shakes his head, blood speckling the air, sniffs, and swallows, but his voice still comes out clogged with phlegm and blood. "No one knows King's real name."

Figures. Miranda said King was a genius at covering his tracks. Then I realize my uncle hasn't answered all of my questions. He's looking away, afraid to make eye contact. "Tell me. You know something, don't you?"

He doesn't answer right away. I take out my Zippo and flick it open, my hand hovering above the gas can, thumb on the striker.

"You're used to putting fires out," I say, my voice sounding like a stranger's. "Want to start one? I'll bet you'll light up like fireworks on the Fourth of July. Sorry I don't have a gag. You'll just have to listen to your own screams."

God, I sound evil. Where the hell did that come from? I hate myself, hate that someone that wicked lives inside me. But it works.

He shakes his head. "Don't. Just don't. I'll tell you everything."

I close the lighter but keep it in my hand.

"I don't know if he's still there, but since what we were doing is technically against the law, I wanted insurance."

His capacity for denial outrages me. *Technically* against the law?

Then I realize: My uncle is just as bad as King. Maybe not as manipulative or greedy. But neither man sees their victims as human. Hell, maybe they didn't see anyone as human. Maybe they don't—or can't—experience love or compassion or anything human. It's like they're cripples.

"What did you find?"

"It wasn't easy, but I tracked one of the cell phones he sent you to a store in Altoona. From there I got a name belonging to a guy who works for Smithfield Telenet. Figured it was the perfect place for him to work. And since it's right here in my own backyard, it was easy to track down where the guy lives."

"What's the name?"

"First, set me free."

"Not until I have the name and address." Once I reach Miranda, we can compare notes. It might even be enough proof for the police—without us ever having to face King ourselves. If I can keep him talking.

He stares at me. I stare back. Then I unclench my fist, dangle the lighter before his eyes.

"Okay, okay. But it's not him. Can't be, because the guy's in a coma—happened after being hit by a car while riding his bike. I figure King stole his identity, used it to set up his business, then once he got enough dough, bought however many new identities he needed to hide behind. After all, I'm not his only content provider. Guy must be rolling in dough by now."

Makes sense. "But when you first approached him, he was just starting out."

"Right. Which is what makes this name and address so valuable. It's the start of his trail." The sly look is back. He sees a way out of this. Or so he thinks. "Let me go and I'll give it to you. Hell, it's not that far away. I'll drive you over to meet him, see for yourself he can't be King."

I think about it. Wish I could reach Miranda—what if the name she found is the same dead end?

He rattles the cuffs, smiles up at me. Like he's trying to seduce me—does he actually believe I'd ever, ever want to be with him? I remember how easily I coaxed him into my trap and realize that's his secret desire: that I would want him as much as he's always wanted me. And I realize what he feels for me goes beyond sex, more like obsession.

My stomach rebels at the thought and I take another step back, revolted.

"C'mon, Jesse," he says. "I'll make it worth your while. All you need to do is unlock these cuffs and we'll forget this ever happened."

"You'd like that, wouldn't you?"

He misses the sarcasm in my voice. "I know how to make you like it."

Disgust roils through me and I can't trust myself not to hurt him, not to set the fire free and let it do what I so desperately want to. I pat my pocket with the recording pen. It'll have to be enough for the cops—at least enough for them to get him to talk. I'm finished here.

I make it to the door to the house, turn off the garage light, and leave him in the dark. I close the door behind me, listening to his shouts, shaking so bad it's all I can do to coax a flame from my lighter. I stare at the dancing light, my trembling breath making it flutter.

For once fire fails me. I don't feel in control. I don't feel powerful.

Instead, I feel sick and dirty and evil. Because I can't deny that it's taking all my strength to stand there instead of doing what I want to do: Turn around and throw the lighter into my uncle's lap. Light up the whole place, memories and all—especially the memories. Torch it, burn it, scorch it to barren earth.

Kill the son of a bitch.

29

Miranda still sat on the floor beside the apartment's door when her mother rushed in. She wasn't sure how much time had passed—she'd spent it in a dark haze, body curled up, back to the wall, rocking, rocking, face pressed down into the cavern she carved out with her arms wrapped around her knees, trying to find the right combination of numbers to lead her from the darkness.

"Are you okay?" Her mom's voice came to her from very far away. Slowly she realized Mom was there on the floor with her, had her arms wrapped tightly around her, face pressed against Miranda's head. "I broke every speed limit getting here. Your father told me what happened. He never should have left you alone."

Anger colored Mom's voice, sparking bright against the darkness surrounding Miranda. Dad. He was in trouble.

The thought and her mother's presence pushed through the veil of black. Miranda stopped rocking.

"I can't believe he did that," her mother continued, soothing Miranda's tangled curls with her fingers, like she had when Miranda was a baby—no, that wasn't Miranda, not back then. That was Ariel. Mom missed Ariel.

Sometimes so did Miranda.

"Talk to me, sweetie. Remember what Dr. Patterson said. Talk it out. What are you afraid of? Focus on me. I'm right here."

The numbers stopped their whirligig stampede through Miranda's brain. Suddenly it was quiet. Just her and her mom. Miranda painstakingly unlaced her clenched fingers. They ached from working to keep a grip on reality.

"It'll be all right. Everything will be all right." Her mother's voice coaxed Miranda's panic into submission. "Now, tell me what happened. Your dad said you found him? The man who—" Her voice faltered, crash-landed.

"Dad." Miranda jerked her head up. Feeling returned sharp and prickly to her face and mouth. "You have to stop him. He's gone to King's—"

"King? Is that the man's name?"

"One of them. Mom. You can't let Dad—what if he does something," Miranda faltered, choking back laughter that she was even thinking the word, "what if he does something crazy? Like in the courtroom when he tried to punch that guy?"

They couldn't lose her father, not because of her. How could she ever face her mother after that? Who would take care of her mother after Miranda was gone?

"It's okay, Miranda. He promised he was just going to see if the man was there."

Miranda shook her head, her curls bouncing wildly. Anxiety buzzed through her, stealing away any words to clearly explain her fears. "No, no. You don't understand. Please, call him. Make him come home."

"You have to trust us. We can take care of you. That includes making the right decisions about how to deal with this, man, King."

"Please," Miranda pleaded. "Just call him. Stay on the phone with him." Her mom could calm Dad down. Like Miranda had with Jesse. Where was Jesse? She glanced out the window—it was dark already. How much time had she lost?

Her mom pulled out her cell and put it on speaker. "It's us."

"Miranda," came her dad's voice. Normal. He sounded normal. Better than normal—he sounded like his old self: in charge, ready for anything. "Are you okay? I'm so sorry. I should never have left. I just needed—" He paused, made a small noise muffled by the airwaves. "It was a bad decision. I apologize."

"I'm fine," she assured him. "Please, come home."

"I'll be there soon. I've been doing some checking—things just don't add up. But don't worry. I'm fine."

"Don't do anything rash," her mom warned him. Funny, Miranda always thought of her mom as the emotional one of the pair—after all, she was the poet, the one who lived half her life in a dreamworld, interpreting ugly reality with a paintbrush of words.

Jesse would like her. Where was he? Was he in trouble?

———

I'm overwhelmed by disgust, shame, fury, frustration…feelings so tangled I can't begin to put a name to them. I run through the house, like I'm going to explode if I don't keep moving.

I don't care what my uncle says, don't even care that he's my mom's brother, family. What he did, what he and King did, it was wrong. Not just wrong. That sounds like an incorrect answer on a math test. There has to be a better word for it, but right now I can't think, can't see anything but a red haze that blazes through my body...

My palm strikes the hallway wall so hard it buckles the drywall. The force rattles through my bones and my hand stings. I bounce away, careening down the hall to my room. Not my room. Not really. Just a bedroom inside my uncle's house. Not my house, not my home.

I howl in frustration and yank my dad's jacket off, flinging it to the floor, not able to even admit to myself the real cause of my pain. The one who started it all: my father.

If he hadn't walked out, abandoned us, if he'd had the guts to stay or at least tried to take care of us, protect us, good God, give us a damn phone call to let us know he gave a shit...this time I hit the wall with my fist and it goes through. Just drywall. It hurts like hell, but as I flex and stretch my fingers I don't think I've broken anything.

I almost wish I had. I kick the desk chair across the room like a kid throwing a tantrum. Thanks to King's destroying my computer I have some privacy here, but it means nothing.

Not when I look at the bed and feel my uncle's body on top of mine, not when I see the chair in the corner where King would have me perform for his clients, not when nothing here really has anything to do with me at all...Lies, my entire life—empty, meaningless, lies.

As if he can read my mind, King's phone rings.

I hurl it across the room. It ricochets from the wall and slides under the bed, still ringing. The computer follows, making a more satisfying crash as it knocks over the lamp beside my bed.

I don't feel any better. I need to get out of here before I hurt someone—myself or my uncle.

Miranda's phone is finished charging. I grab it and start to leave. I turn back. Hesitate. As angry as I am, as much as I hate him right now, I can't leave behind the only piece of my dad that I have left. It's the only thing in the whole damn house that feels like it's also a piece of me. I grab my dad's jacket from the floor and run.

As I race out the front door, I think about calling Miranda. It feels good just holding her phone in my hand. Something she touched, a lifeline to sanity.

I can't call her, not like this. She'll think I've gone mad—I'm not even sure I can find the words to explain that I haven't, much less what I've done.

I need time. Just a few minutes. To calm down, regain control.

I glance at my truck but don't trust myself to drive without speeding headlong into a tree. Running now, it feels good: pumping my arms and legs, exorcising the emotions churning inside me. I pass the truck and race to the rear of the house, past the garden, past the barn, through the trees, to the abandoned trailer.

Fire. I need fire. Power. Control. A way to let the pain escape.

Then I can call Miranda. Together we can come up with a plan, maybe tell her father. He used to be a cop; he'll know what to do with my uncle.

But first, I need, I need…fire.

I bury Miranda's phone deep into my inside pocket and reach for my lighter. Feeling worse than a junkie craving a fix, I flick it, stare into the flame, center myself.

Slowly, the enormity of what I've done hits me. I look around the decrepit stink of a place that has become my sanctuary. No way can I ever return here, not after the police come for my uncle.

And me. I'd hit him. Hurt him. Made him bleed. I'd have to take responsibility for that. Stand up like a man.

I study the flame in my hand. It trembles as exhaustion overwhelms me. It's what happens after an adrenaline surge, I know, but I can't fight it.

I close the lighter without starting a fire. Fire can't help me gain control of my life. Never could. Just another damned lie. I feel empty inside, as if my emotions have burned to ashes, leaving nothing behind. Pretending not to feel for so long, I'm not even sure if there is anything left.

I don't even know who I really am.

The boy who let my uncle and King take possession of his soul? The kid who struck out in anger and hatred, beating an unarmed man, handcuffed and defenseless?

Am I Jesse or JohnBoy or Miranda's Griffin?

The trailer is pitch-black and cold. I sink to the floor, hugging my dad's jacket around me, huddled against a wall. Shivering and alone, I curl up in the dark and let exhaustion overtake me.

The last thing I sense before I drift away is Miranda's phone vibrating against my chest, right over my heart. I want to answer it but can't move, can barely even think the thought before my mind is swallowed by oblivion.

30

I wake to the smell of smoke. Not from my dreams, not from any fire I've started. And sirens. Lots of sirens. Something's wrong, something more than just the fire and sirens, but I can't stop to think about that. I run from the trailer into the night, make my way through the trees and brambles, burst onto my uncle's property.

The house is on fire.

All I can think is, *Thank God Janey and Mom are gone.* I know, I know. I'm a monster. Because it's not until I'm halfway across the meadow that I think of him. Trapped in the garage. Alone in the dark, chained like an animal. Unable to escape.

Wait. I don't know that. Maybe he did escape. Maybe he started the fire.

The smoke is black, thick, pouring through a shattered window in the back door leading into the garage. There are flames hanging upside down from my bedroom ceiling. I know the house is gone. Past saving.

But what about my uncle?

I run east, onto the neighbor's land, cut down the lane between their fields to the road. All the neighbors are outside, watching. The fire trucks, two cop cars, and an ambulance create a light show. The police are pushing people back—more people driving past are stopping. Everyone in Smithfield knows and loves my uncle. Women are sobbing and I wonder if they found a body.

I move closer but stay at the back of the crowd, the hood of my sweatshirt pulled up, so no one can see my face or ask questions. I listen as I watch the firemen do a rapid deployment. They're angry, arguing with the chief about going in. They know whose house this is, have been here for cookouts and parties.

The chief won't risk their lives. Not when it's obvious to anyone that no one can be alive inside. He orders an exterior attack only.

There's a small explosion—small to me and the firemen—but the crowd gasps and steps back. All but one man. Across the way from me, I realize there's one man not watching the blaze and the drama. He's scanning the crowd.

He senses me watching him and pivots, eyes only for me. He's tall, shaved head, narrow face, the kind of guy you'd never notice. Except for his eyes. Even with the flashing lights casting more shadows than illumination, I notice his eyes. Staring right at me.

My instinct for survival finally kicks in, but it's too late. He raises his hand, finger cocked like it's a gun, aims at me. I stumble back, my feet tangled as I want to run but also know better than to turn my back on a predator like him. He smiles, brings his index finger to his lips, kisses it, then lowers it like he's holstering a gun. *Bang, you're dead.*

I scuttle back, using the ambulance as cover to hide behind. Next time I dare to look, he's gone. Could it have been King? Or one of his minions—the man who came after Janey, maybe?

I edge around the crowd, hoping to get another glimpse of him, see where he goes, what kind of car he's driving. A dangerous man like that, I don't want him out of my sight—and I sure as hell don't want to be in his.

I can't find him, but I do spot a sheriff's deputy at the drainage ditch that runs alongside the road. He's found something. Waves another cop over as he shines his flashlight down into the ditch.

The second cop takes a photo with his phone. "Best secure it," he says, eyeing the crowd and chaos. I'm afraid to see what they discovered—it can't be my uncle, can it? No, they'd take a lot more photos, be calling the ambulance crew, making a big deal.

I stick my hands in my pockets and just as the deputy scrambles up out of the ditch holding something in his gloved hand, I realize what they've found. Now I know what felt wrong when I ran out of the trailer. Now I know why the stranger was smiling at me.

My jacket. The pockets are empty. The gun is gone.

———

Miranda and her mom dragged her mom's large whiteboards out to the living room and filled in all the data points Miranda had discovered over the past two years. Her mom colored the information with bright markers, drawing arrows back and forth, adding different colored stars alongside information, making connections that Miranda never realized before.

That was her mom for you. Miranda missed the old days back

in Pittsburgh when they'd have to eat in the kitchen because her mom's whiteboards had taken over the dining room. Mom would fill them with pictures and quotes that inspired her as she created her "word salads."

That's what Mom called them. Her professors at Pitt and the editors of the poetry reviews that published them called them "transcendent" and "illuminating" works of art.

Miranda sighed, regretting once again this murky, dismal wasteland she'd dragged her parents into. They didn't deserve this, living like this, fighting to just pay the bills when they had art to create and bad guys to put away and lives to live.

"Mom," she said from where she sat cross-legged on the floor, her laptop balanced on her knees.

"Yes, dear," her mom replied absently, darting from one corner of the board to put a big purple circle around a date and email address of one of King's cybersmash posts. She stood back, taking in the big picture.

"Thank you." Miranda realized she might never be able to tell her parents that enough, not even if she lived to be a hundred.

When she left Ariel behind, she'd given up on self-pity, on being a victim. But she'd also shut out gratitude: at being alive, at being blessed with parents as great as hers, at being able to do something instead of suffering in silence like Jesse had been forced to in order to protect his family.

Her mom turned around, looked down at Miranda with a smile, oblivious to the purple smudge the marker left on her cheek. "My only regret is that you didn't come to us sooner, sweetheart. I wish it hadn't come to this, this—" She shook her head, like she always did when the perfect word danced just beyond her grasp. Before she could wrestle it into focus, the door opened and Dad returned.

He didn't look happy.

"What happened?" Miranda asked, jumping to her feet. "Did you find him? Was he there? Do we have enough to take to the FBI?"

Dad just frowned and shook his head. He sank onto the couch, then got back up again when Mom glanced at his gun. She was okay with guns in the house, was a pretty good shot herself, but preferred them safely locked away from their somewhat crazy and suicidal daughter.

Miranda wanted to tell them it was okay—she was okay...but she couldn't lie to them. Not anymore.

Dad went to their bedroom to secure his weapon and returned wearing more comfortable jeans and a sweatshirt instead of his uniform.

"It wasn't him," he said before Miranda could ask.

She shook her head in disbelief. "No. It has to be."

"I'm telling you—it can't be him."

"How can you be so sure?"

"I met the man."

Her mom lasered in on that. "George. You didn't. Was that wise?"

He sank back onto the sofa. Mom joined Miranda on the floor, sitting cross-legged, chin resting on her palm.

"I just had to see him. For myself." He sounded as disappointed as Miranda felt. Kerstater had to be King; he just had to be. "So

I used a pretext to get inside. Said we were following up on a hit-and-skip fender bender on campus and had a partial plate that matched his."

"So you saw him?" Miranda persisted. "You actually met him? I don't understand—"

"His brother answered the door. Howard. Explained that the car is registered in Leonard's name, but Leonard can't drive anymore."

Miranda frowned, rocking in place. She didn't give a damn about registrations. Her mother wrapped her arms around her, squeezing tight to soothe her.

"George—" her mom said, a warning in her voice.

Dad rubbed his knuckles against his eyes and Miranda knew he was just as upset as she was. "It couldn't be Kerstater because he was in a coma, almost dead when you, when your event"—his euphemism for half-naked pictures of her being captured and distributed across the world—"occurred. Hit by a car while riding his bike at night. The guy's paralyzed, practically a vegetable."

"But, but—" Miranda's mind reeled in shock. It had to be him. Logic said…

Mom hugged her harder. Dad slid off the couch and joined them on the floor, wrapping his arms around both her and Mom. Her favorite kind of hug. What was she thinking, running away from all this? Pushing them away?

"It's okay, honey," he said. "We'll get him. But right now, don't you think the more important thing is that we help your friend, Jesse?"

She nodded. Of course, he was right. How could she be so selfish?

"Where is he?" Dad asked. "I thought you said he was coming over."

"He said he was. I haven't been able to reach him." She gathered in a breath, straightened, their arms falling away. "Let me try him again."

Mom stood gracefully, in one fluid motion, without using her hands. "It's too late to cook. I'll call for a pizza." She held a hand to Dad, helping him up from the floor.

His knees creaked, and he definitely wasn't as graceful as Mom. But it was good to see them working together—with their jobs and Mom's school and alternating shifts to watch over Miranda, they hardly ever saw each other anymore, much less ate together.

For a moment, they felt like a family again—all together, moving in the same direction. Miranda hadn't realized how much she'd missed that until now.

Then she opened her computer back up, ready to use the VOIP to call Jesse's home number. Saw a Google Alert with his uncle's name. Breaking news, from a local TV station.

She clicked on the video. Gasped. "Turn on the TV," she told her parents even as she frantically tried Jesse's cell. No answer.

"What's wrong?" her mom asked. Her father clicked the TV on. The local station had just started their evening news broadcast. The graphic behind the reporter was a house on fire.

Miranda stared at the image. She knew that house—had used

Google's Street View to look at it a hundred times before taking the risk of contacting Jesse. "That's his house. Jesse's house is on fire."

31

Don't run, don't run, don't run, I tell myself even as my feet slam the pavement and my body's leaning forward, wanting to sprint. I back into the crowd, trying hard not to make eye contact with anyone as I work my way to the outer edge, away from my uncle's fellow firefighters, away from the cops.

My truck is blocked in by fire apparatus and half-drowned by water from the hoses, so my only hope of escape is on foot. I have no idea where. All I know is that I need to find a safe place to hide.

Just as I think I'm clear, someone grabs my arm. I spin. It's the stranger, the one who knew about the gun.

The expression on his face, lit by the fire and the police lights, is like he's praying. Eyes wide, a weird smile. A kid who woke up on Christmas Day to find everything he wished for under the tree.

Except he's not a kid. He's old—older than my uncle or my mom, forty at least. Then I realize where I've seen that expression before: on King's clients' faces.

I jerk away. He reaches for my arm again, his eyes narrowing in anger. His other hand holds a knife. The same knife from the video yesterday.

He takes my hand and twists it back hard, stepping behind me, pulling my thumb with him. The pain is excruciating, lightning blazing up my arm. I have no choice but to lean over before my wrist and elbow break.

The only place I can look is down. And I see his shoes: black leather, tassels with tiny horseshoes.

This is the man who almost killed Janey.

"Who are you? What do you want?" I ask as he propels me forward, down the road, toward a dark-colored car.

He says nothing, only wrenches my thumb harder. I can't help it. I cry out in agony. He slows, and I can tell he's looking back, making sure no one heard me. He doesn't want to get caught.

I take advantage of his split second of distraction and pivot all my weight in the direction that will twist my hand free, getting one foot between his to trip him up and yelling as loud as I can the two words that will get the attention of any firefighter or police officer, "Man down!"

To my surprise it works. He drops his hand and I stumble free, tumbling into the pavement. I block my fall with one palm, push off again, and come up facing him.

His smile hasn't faded. But the knife has vanished. The hand he raises toward me is empty, just one finger pointing my direction.

"There he is," he shouts as he backs into the crowd. "He did it! That's Jesse Alexander. He killed his uncle!"

The crowd whirls almost as one. Cops shove their way through, all eyes on me. Bright lights hit me, pinning me in their glare: TV cameras.

I stand frozen for a heartbeat. Then my instinct for survival kicks in, and I take off, running.

———

They forgot about pizza. Miranda and her mom sat in front of the TV, Miranda's laptop on the coffee table between them, flipping channels, trying to stay updated, while her dad put his uniform back on and went to the scene to see if he could learn anything from the first responders.

"It's not good," he reported when he called an hour later. "The house is gone. And they found a body."

Miranda's mom reached a hand to grab the phone and take it off speaker but Miranda stopped her. "It's okay. Tell me everything. I'll find out sooner or later anyway."

Her mom nodded but wrapped her arm around Miranda. "Go ahead, George."

"They think it's his uncle. He's a firefighter, so everyone's pretty upset. Plus..." He trailed off as voices could be heard in the background. There was the sound of a car door slamming; then, it was quiet. "Plus the body was handcuffed. And they found a gun in a ditch in front of the house."

Miranda stiffened. Jesse said he had a gun. She should have found a way to stop him, to help him. She pounded a fist against her thigh, counting the blows. One two three...not enough... four five six seven eight nine... "They're sure? I mean, it couldn't be Jesse? Dead?"

The last word came out choked. Her mom hugged her tighter. Miranda wanted to run and hide, lock herself in her room, lock out the rest of the world, block out her dad's answer. It took all her strength to stay there, to wait and hope...*hope*, that nasty four-letter word.

If Jesse died because of her, how could she go on living?

"No," Dad's voice made it through the panic spiraling through her brain. "They don't think the body belongs to your friend." His words hung there and she knew there was more. "Honey, let me talk to your mom."

"No." She grabbed the receiver before her mom could reach it. "No. Tell me everything. Now."

"I'm on my way home. It can wait."

"Dad, whatever you have to say, it can't be worse than what I can imagine. They think Jesse did it, don't they? They think he killed his uncle?"

There was a long pause. "Yes. He was seen with his uncle at the house before the fire started, then afterward he was spotted running away."

"Is Jesse there? Did they arrest him?"

"No. But they have his truck. They found, they think...there's evidence that Jesse is the arsonist who started all those fires these past few months. They have city, county, and state police out searching for him and might soon involve ATF."

"Because of the arsons?" her mom asked.

"Yes. Honey, if you have a way to reach him, he needs to turn himself in. Because his uncle, he was a hero to these people, one of their family. I don't need to tell you how dangerous it could be for him."

"You mean, like shoot to kill or something?" Miranda broke free of her mom's arms and stood up, clutching the phone to her ear despite the fact that it was still on speaker and her dad's voice was plenty loud. "No. Dad, no. He didn't do it. I know he didn't."

"Then all the better that he turn himself in before things get worse. I'll help him any way I can, you know that, but—"

To her surprise, Miranda's mom took the phone from her and said, "Come home, George. We'll decide what we do next together." She arched an eyebrow at Miranda with a look that said she was taking a chance on Miranda doing the right thing. "As a family."

"I'm on my way." He hung up.

Miranda's mom set the phone down. Miranda gave her another hug. "Thanks, Mom. I won't let you down."

"It's not me you need to be worried about. It's Jesse."

32

If I ever have to retrace my steps, I couldn't tell you how I got here. I remember cutting through the woods across the street from my uncle's. Heading down the hill, staying off the road. There were dogs barking as I ran through the trailer park, babies crying behind curtains and TVs flickering. Then I was on Pine Street—not the nicest part of Smithfield with its condemned properties and crowded row houses, more bars than streetlights. I crossed the railroad tracks, hit the warehouses on Broad Avenue, and realized I'd reached the old bottling plant turned into student housing for the college.

That's when it hits me—I can't outrun the cops. Not forever. But I can hide in plain sight on campus, surrounded by a thousand other guys.

Smithfield College is an oasis of hope in an otherwise failing city. It sits between the warehouses along the railroad tracks and an old neighborhood with nice, big houses where most of the professors live, while the far edge of campus backs up to State Game Lands that lead up the mountain.

I need a place to hide, I need to call Miranda, and I need to get the recordings from the pen to her.

I stop running. There are classroom buildings across from me, windows dark. I jog between them, my stomach gnawing. A little food wouldn't hurt, either. The library is closed for the night, but the student union is open.

There's a guy and a girl heading inside it just as I arrive at the door. The guy gives me a nod, as if I belong there, even holds the door open long enough for me to reach it. Once inside, they go one way, toward a room with music coming from it. I stand tall and, ignoring the overhead TVs hanging at every corner, most filled with student events but a couple tuned to CNN and local news, saunter to the food court's vending machine area.

Five minutes later, I'm sitting in a shadowy corner, my back to the wall at the far row of computers, where I found one with its browser open, account still active. As I wolf down a microwaved cheeseburger and bottle of milk, I send Miranda an IM.

Griffin: Safe to call?

Miranda: You OK?

Before I can type an answer she calls the cell. "Jesse!" Her voice is breathless and hushed, like she's worried someone will hear.

I hate that she's calling me Jesse again. I prefer being her hero, Griffin.

"Are you okay? What happened?" she asks.

"First, I need to send you some video." Funny, now I'm the one with a plan. As she walks me through uploading the video from the pen's USB to an anonymous cloud account she has set up for us, I tell her everything. About King. My computer being wiped. My uncle. The fire. The gun.

And the man who tried to take me. "He's the same one King sent to hurt Janey," I finish. "I didn't know what else to do, so I just ran."

There's a long pause. I can almost feel her mind working on the problem. For the first time tonight, I feel like I might have a chance. Because Miranda's still on my side. She believes me, believes in me.

I take another bite of the cheeseburger and I can actually taste it. Wish I couldn't—the carton it came in would have more flavor, but that's okay. Miranda's still with me.

"Jesse," she says. I almost tell her to call me Griffin but don't. "You need to turn yourself in."

Disappointment pulls me down so hard I slump in the chair. The upload beeps that it's finished, and I put the recording pen back in my pocket. I have to try twice to clip it in place; my fingers have gone numb again. Sliding my lighter from my pocket, the reflection of the computer screen making it shimmer with color, I yearn for the comfort of fire.

Then I put it away. Fire's what got me into this mess.

I close down the computer, erasing my history like Miranda taught me, and grab the phone. Should I leave it? What's the point if she doesn't believe me?

Music and the voices of students edge my awareness. But really, I'm all alone.

"I believe you, Griffin." Her voice returns, solid, certain, lasering directly into my brain. "I do. But don't you see? That's why you need to turn yourself in. So the police can hear the truth."

Griffin. She called me Griffin again. I sit up in the chair, holding the phone tight against my chest. The fight-or-flight reflex starts to ebb—a little.

"I can't," I tell her. "There's no way to prove I'm innocent. My prints are on that gun. I'm the one who left him there. It's my fault he's dead."

Then I realize. She's right. If I ever want to be Griffin—to be the kind of man who stands up for what's right and takes responsibility for what goes wrong—then I have to surrender.

"The police think you're armed and dangerous," she says, sounding more scared than I am. "You can't let them chase you down—that's how people get hurt. The best way is for us to arrange for you to turn yourself in. My dad can help."

I blow out my breath, nodding even though she can't see me. "How? What do we do?"

"Are you safe now?"

"Yeah. I'm in the student union on campus."

"Smart. Hiding in plain sight. Last place they'd look for a deranged killer on the run." She's trying hard to be funny, but neither of us laugh.

A couple stumbles into the first row of computer stations. He spins her against the wall. They're kissing, his hand moving under her shirt. I look away.

"Maybe I should go. There are people here. What if they see me? I can hide in the woods, keep moving."

"If they catch you while you're running, they'll be more likely to shoot. Griffin, I got you into this. I can't let anything happen to you. Just stay there. We'll figure something out."

I can't stop watching the couple. They look like they're enjoying themselves and don't mind me at all. Or don't even know I'm here. Like I'm no one. Nothing.

Exactly how King makes me feel.

"I can't do this without you," I tell Miranda.

Suddenly the computer screen in front of me comes to life. I glance around the room. All the computers are turning on. Their monitors are filling with pictures of me—from the fire, when the TV cameras caught me.

I look like a monster, a madman. My eyes are wide, my mouth open like I'm screaming. I would shoot first, ask questions later myself after seeing that picture.

The TVs scattered around the lounge are all switching to the same image as well. What the hell? King, it has to be.

"Miranda," I gasp as I push my chair back and jog out past the oblivious couple to the main hall. Every TV there has my face on it, larger than life. "It's too late. He found me. King is here."

"Get out of there. Now."

I know better than to run, draw attention to myself. Instead, I join a crowd of kids leaving, chatting about an all-night dance club. Camouflaged in their midst, I walk outside with them just as two campus police cars pull up across the parking lot.

The kids keep going. The officers dash past them, guns drawn, into the building. The look on the officers' faces.

Miranda was right. They don't just want to arrest me—they want me dead.

As soon as the crowd is clear, I break away, edging into the shadows, then start running.

I need to find a place to hide. One where King can't find me.

33

I get across campus without too much trouble—more scaring myself every time I round a corner or cross an open space than anything else. I head past the sports complex and Telenet Arena.

The arena is a huge dome—think of a jelly-filled doughnut. Deep inside is the jelly, the center court on the ground floor of the arena where they hold the concerts and sporting events. Surrounding center court are three stories' worth of seating, tier upon tier climbing up. And the outermost layer, the thick doughy layer of the doughnut that surrounds the jelly, is the concourse, a twenty-foot-wide corridor that hosts vendors, exhibits, storage, and restrooms for the arena, and spirals around the outside all the way up to the dome, where the skyboxes and announcer's box are.

I almost decide to hide in the arena. My uncle took me there once on an inspection tour and I got to see all the tunnels and hidden areas off limits to normal people. It would take days for the police to search it, but my memories of it center on my uncle and I just can't bring myself to try to find a way in.

Besides, this time of night, there'd be guards and alarms and locked doors. I learned a lot from my uncle and the other firefighters, including how to break into buildings, but not how to do it without leaving a trace.

Instead, I keep going, out into the open countryside that used to be farmland but now is empty meadows gone to seed, sloping up into the forest that covers the mountainside. I skirt the edge of the trees that mark the start of the State Game Lands—I could spend the night on the mountain, but I'm already freezing and besides, I have a better idea. I follow the mountain's curve about a mile, to where the train tracks leave the valley. I'm way past city limits, in rural unincorporated land, where the only sign of civilization besides the train tracks and distant lights of Route 322 is Wilson's Salvage Yard.

It's one of those places that grownups call an "eyesore" and kids find irresistible. Old man Wilson, and his father and grandfather before him, turned acres of useless land into a sprawling junkyard. People haul old cars, appliances, heck, even busted-up mobile homes here and dump them. Wilson salvages the scrap metal, sells it, and leaves the rest to rot.

I came here a few times with my dad before he left us. He liked hunting for spare parts to the old cars he was always fixing up and selling. He and old man Wilson would spend hours prowling the lot for just the right parts, talking about cars, the weather, hunting season, the price of gas. Sometimes I got the feeling Dad came more to check on Mr. Wilson than anything else. He always said what a shame it was that the poor old guy wouldn't move to town to live with his son, who'd worked with Dad before they both got laid off.

Even though it's been years since I've been here, I feel safe. Plenty of places to hide, shelter from the night wind, and I can get some rest. I'm so exhausted after practically no sleep for going on three days and all the running and fear blasting through my system, that I'm about ready to fall down and never get up again.

I climb the rusted fence and drop down between a stack of old car batteries and a refrigerator missing its door. I make my way up the hill to an old Impala missing its wheels, sitting on the ground next to the fence. Perfect. I can get out of the wind and I'm high enough and far enough from the main entrance that if the cops come looking, I'll see and hear them before they can spot me.

It's not until I'm inside the car, starting a fire from stuffing torn from its front seat, that I realize I'm shivering so hard my teeth are clacking together. The fire thankfully warms me, but it does nothing to get at what's really wrong: how did King find me?

It had to be through the computer. Which meant Miranda might be in danger if he traced her via the files I uploaded to her cloud drive.

I hate to risk it, but I call her to check.

"Are you okay?" she answers.

"I was worried about you. King turned on all the computers in the student union—and he plastered my picture on all the TVs as well. I got out just as the cops were showing up."

"He controlled the computers and the TVs?" Somehow she doesn't sound as concerned about this as I am. Instead, she sounds excited.

"Yeah. I was worried he might trace the video upload back to you. Wanted to make sure you were okay."

"No worries there. I downloaded the video and closed that account while we were still talking. Your evidence is safe."

"But are you?" I try and fail to keep the worry from my voice.

"You really are Griffin. My protector against evil."

I smile at the warmth in her voice.

"Are we okay talking on this phone?" I hope so. I feel so alone out here I could really use the company. I could use sleep as well, but look what happened the last time I dared to sleep—my uncle ended up dead. "Can you stay awhile?"

"We should be fine. And of course I'll stay. As long as you like—or the battery lasts."

"It had a full charge." I glance at the screen, 98 percent. "We're good."

"I watched the video. You were so brave standing up to King when he called."

"You mean so stupid. King's totally on to us. On to me. But I'm sure he thinks I have help." I pause. "Maybe that's why he had my uncle killed?" Then it dawns on me. "You saw everything, didn't you? Me and my uncle?" Shame burns through me, hot and cold at the same time.

"You have nothing to be ashamed of. Jesse—Griffin..." Her voice trails off. She's just as confused about who I was when I beat up my uncle as I am. It was the bravest thing I've ever done—and the most vile, the most cowardly.

"They'll use it as evidence. They'll never believe I didn't kill him." I wrap my arms around my chest, my dad's old leather jacket creaking in the cold. "I'll spend the rest of my life in prison. If I thought my uncle was bad—" I can't finish.

Silence echoes between us as the tiny fire I built dies. I'm cold again but too scared and exhausted to rekindle it.

"We'll think of something," she promises. I try to hold on to that—she's never let me down, not yet. "I feel so bad," she continues. "This is all my fault."

"No. It's not. I knew what I was getting into." Kinda. "Are my mom and Janey okay?"

"My dad said the police are with your mom in Pittsburgh. She was on TV, asking for you to turn yourself in."

"She thinks I did it."

"They don't know the truth—they'll never know it until you tell them."

"What's the plan?"

"My dad's worried about how upset everyone is, thinks if we give them time to cool down, it will be safer for you to turn yourself in. But he'll come pick you up now, bring you back here where you'll be safe."

No way. I'm not putting her and her family in danger. "Not tonight. First thing in the morning."

"Okay. He'll take you to the police, stay with you, even get you a lawyer. He said you shouldn't say anything, just tell your lawyer the truth and let him handle it."

"Right. Some lawyer I can't pay is going to give a shit about what happens to me."

"My dad called one from Pittsburgh. Says he's the best. He said he can be here tomorrow—if you turn yourself in."

"When and where?"

"My dad will come get you. Just say where."

I give her directions to the salvage yard. "Will you be with him?"

The silence is so long I'm afraid I've lost her. I glance at the cell phone; still plenty of charge and three bars. "Miranda?"

"I never told you how King found me, did I?" she says instead of answering my question. "I was at a sleepover—my best friend since kindergarten. I was born on the third, Nina's birthday was on the fourth, so we took turns celebrating. That year when we turned thirteen, it was her turn. We decided just the two of us would have a sleepover the night before the big party at her house. Her older sister even snuck some rum from her parents, showed us how to mix it in our Cokes. We had so much fun, singing and dancing to music, her sister giving us makeovers, letting us borrow her clothes. Felt so grownup. Sexy." She makes the last word sound like a curse.

Silence again. Then, "I never even noticed her sister using her cell phone. Never dreamed she was taking pictures. And I was too drunk to have any idea how stupid we were being."

"Those were the pictures King found?"

"Yeah. That one night ruined my life."

Then I realize why she's telling me this. "You're still going after him. Alone? No, Miranda, you can't."

34

Miranda felt like laughing at Griffin's words warning her not to go after King alone. As if. As if she could leave this apartment without falling apart; as if she could look a stranger in the eye without becoming wrecked with panic; as if she had a tenth of the courage and strength he'd shown.

"You could have been killed," she finally said. "Because of me."

"We're in this together."

She bounced on her bed, pulling her quilt tighter around her, over her head, glad he couldn't see her hiding under the covers like a baby afraid of the bogeyman.

"No. We're not." The words came out sharper than she'd intended, sounding like a rebuke.

He didn't answer right away. "What do you mean?"

She didn't like the fear edging his voice—especially as it would soon turn to disgust at her betrayal. He couldn't be half as disgusted or ashamed of her actions as she was herself. Small comfort there. She wasn't the one running for her life.

"I owe you the truth," she said with a sigh. "I can't come with my dad to help you. I can't help you at all. I can't even leave this apartment."

He gasped. "You said King sent men to hurt your mom. Did he hurt you? Miranda—"

She closed her eyes, squeezed them tight against her shame. It would be so easy to let him think that. But he deserved to know everything. "No. No, that's not it. I just can't leave. That's all."

"I don't understand."

Neither did she. It wasn't something she could think about or analyze, despite the help of her parents and Dr. Patterson. "I have something called agoraphobia. It's Greek for 'fear of the market-place.' In my case, it's fear of everything and everyone outside my family and my apartment."

"What happens if you leave?"

"I can't. Not without having a panic attack—which usually leaves me curled up in a quivering ball on the floor, crying and slobbering. If King ever caught a picture of that, he'd love it."

"Don't talk like that," he snapped.

She jerked up so fast the quilt dropped from her shoulders, leaving her exposed. She didn't pull it back up—Griffin was more exposed than she was, safe here in her nice, warm bedroom.

"It's not your fault," he continued. "When did it start?"

She pulled in a deep breath. This part was the worst. "After the second time I tried to kill myself."

"You tried to kill yourself?" He didn't sound judgmental. More concerned.

"First time was after King sent those guys to hurt my mom. Second was after they went free and my dad almost got arrested. My folks, they'd lost everything because of me. I thought things would be better for everyone—"

"I told you not to talk like that. Miranda, you're the strongest person I've ever met."

"But you've never met me. You don't know me at all." Why was she arguing with him? She wasn't sure, but it seemed important that he understood the depth of her treachery.

She hauled in a breath and continued, "When I figured out King lived near Smithfield, I manipulated my parents so my dad would take a job here. I hunted King's victims in the hopes of finding one I could convince to confront King even though I'm too weak and cowardly to ever try myself. And then I found you. Jesse. Griffin. Both of you are stronger and more courageous and heroic than I can ever be. Standing up to your uncle the way you did—I'm so proud of you. And so very sorry that you're in this trouble because of me and how selfish I was."

"Selfish?"

"I don't want King to just be caught. I want him humiliated. I want him to suffer half as much as I have—as all his victims. I even"—she gulped, tears burning her throat—"I even fantasized that I could make you kill him. For me. How sick and twisted is that? I'm sorry, Jesse. You deserve so much better than me. I'm a pathetic, selfish bitch."

No stopping the tears now, she set the phone down long enough to wipe her face dry. He remained silent. Had she lost him?

Then his voice returned, a distant whisper. "I wanted to kill him too. Dreamed of it almost every night."

I hold my breath, hugging myself not so much against the cold but against the chance that I might never hear Miranda's voice again. Would she still believe I hadn't killed my uncle after hearing me confess my darkest secret?

Her laughter sounded strange. Not the full-on laughter that had made me smile earlier today. This was tight, a high-wire act between laughing and crying. "What a pair we are."

I blew my breath out in relief. "Do you think, I mean, when your father comes tomorrow—could I meet you? Before I turn myself in?"

Probably to spend the rest of my life in prison, I don't add. Seemed like a bit of a downer when this was the closest thing to a date with a girl I might ever have.

"Of course," she says. "I'd like that very much."

Cool. Great. I have no clue what to say that won't make me sound like an idiot. She can't see it, but I'm grinning. Stupid crazy for someone in my position, but I can't help it. That's Miranda's magic.

"We can still do it, you know," I tell her. "Out King. I still have the recorder pen."

"No. It's too dangerous. Besides…" She hesitates.

"What?"

"It's not the man I thought it was. Phreak426."

"Are you sure?"

"My dad went to see him. Turns out he did work for Telenet, but he got hit by a car and is paralyzed, had a severe brain injury. He was in the hospital on my birthday two years ago."

I'm disappointed but something nags at me. "Don't you think it's kind of weird that he works for Telenet and used a screen name that King used?"

"King probably stole it while the guy was in the hospital."

"No. That was the first one he used with me. It would have been the year before King found you."

There's silence, but it's the good kind. The kind that means Miranda's brain is churning through the possibilities. "What if Kerstater—that's the guy—discovered someone was using his screen name?"

"That someone being King. And then King—"

"Tried to kill him." Excitement makes her voice bounce. "I was right about the Telenet connection, I had to have been. That would explain how he found you tonight."

"Yeah. How did he do that? With the TVs and computers?"

"Telenet installed all the AV systems when the college updated everything. That's why the arena is named after them—the price for their corporate sponsorship was getting the telecommunications contract for the college."

"How do you know all this?"

"Are you kidding? I sit at home day and night obsessing about tracking the Creep down. Once I learned he was connected to Telenet, I learned everything I could about them."

"King isn't Kerstater, but someone else in Telenet's IT department using his screen name?"

"The upgrade happened three years ago. It could be someone working with Kerstater then, and they planted a Trojan horse in the software, letting them control all the computers—the TVs are really just computer monitors as well."

This was getting beyond my scope. "You found Kerstater. Can't you get back into Telenet's database and find anyone else who worked on the project?"

"I'm good, but I'm not that good. I found Kerstater through a LinkedIn profile that went to a public profile on the company's HR page. It just was never taken down or updated after he got hit by the car."

"Wait. My uncle said something about a guy hit by a car." I strain to remember, but exhaustion has my brain so foggy I'm not even sure I can remember my own name.

"Let me pull it up on the video," she says before I can admit that I'm not clear on the details. "Here it is. He said he tracked a phone number and address to a guy riding his bike and hit by a car. That's Kerstater. But why would King use his real-life address as well as his screen name? That's awfully lazy—and a sure way for a someone to find you sooner or later."

"So maybe that's how Kerstater found King. And it was when King was just starting out; he wasn't as good at covering his tracks as he is now." I can almost hear her frown, and I know there's more to the puzzle.

"My dad said something. Hang on, I need to check—" She gasps.

"What? What did you find?" Adrenaline charges through me and I'm fully awake.

"Dad said he lives with his brother who's his caretaker. Howard. Dad actually met him tonight—right before the fire at your house."

"My uncle's house," I correct her automatically. "So this brother is also a computer expert?"

"Let me see what I can find on him." The sound of computer keys clacking comes through the phone. I imagine her fingers flying over the keys like a magician casting a spell.

Finally she returns. "No, not IT or anything to do with computers. But Howard Kerstater does work for Telenet. In their human resource department."

I think about it. "Human resources? He hires and fires people. That sounds like King. Power, control over people's lives."

"Not only that. Wouldn't anyone in human resources also have access to credit reports and background checks, stuff like that? That would be perfect for King. He could decide which clients were vulnerable to his blackmail, who had the most money, know all their secrets."

"You think your dad's visit tipped him off? That's why he killed my uncle?"

"I'm sorry, Jesse. I didn't know." The sound of keys tapping. Fast. "I can't find anything else. If this guy is King, he's covered his tracks."

"Which means I'm the last loose end. What if he blackmails a cop or jail guard or someone to come after me after I turn myself in? What if he goes after Mom or Janey?" My voice sounds hollow as it echoes through the car. "I can't protect them if I'm sitting in a jail cell."

35

esse, you can't keep running. It's just as dangerous."

In my mind, I'm already gone. How far could I get? How long? I could go anywhere, do anything. For the first time in my life, the thought isn't frightening. It's liberating.

I think of the couple who wandered into the computer lab. That could be me. I could maybe find someone whose touch I invited, someone who wanted to be with me. Someone I could actually love…

My uncle is gone. I never again have to fear being touched, work hard to parse the meaning of every word and gesture, train my body and face to fake pleasure just to satisfy his warped needs. Could I learn to love? Could I ever be a normal guy, holding a girl's hand, kissing her lips, inviting her to touch me?

Free. It takes me a few moments to actually identify the feeling that makes me feel light-headed. I'm free.

If I can outrun King. "You said Mom and Jancy are safe?"

"Dad said they're in protective custody."

"Custody? They didn't arrest her, did they? She had nothing to do with this—"

"No. Jesse, they have cops protecting your mom and sister…" Her voice fades into the night.

Then I get it. "From me. They think I might hurt them."
Everything I've done for the past four years has been to protect
them, to save my family after my dad left. But now they're safer
without me. "So, if I keep running, they'll be protected from King."

"Yes. No. They'll be safe, but you won't." Urgency fills her
voice. "I have a plan."

"Yeah. One that leaves me behind bars and King out there
where he can hurt everyone I care about." Including Miranda, I
realize. She's trapped, will be at King's mercy if he ever finds her.

"No. A new plan." Her breath rustles through the phone,
louder than the wind seeping through the broken windows of the
car. "But it means not just exposing King to the world. It means
telling everyone what he did to us. Both of us. Everything—the
whole truth. Let the world see what a monster he is. That's our
best chance of stopping him and saving you."

The freedom I tasted a few seconds ago turns to ash in my
mouth. "My mom would know—"

"Everyone," she says firmly. "That's what will happen sooner or
later anyway. If they catch you and there's a trial, they'll want to
know why you wanted to kill your uncle."

"I can lie. Tell them I just snapped." Suddenly the car feels too
small. Despite the cold, I climb out, fill my lungs with fresh air.
The moon has set, leaving a shimmer of stars in its wake. I look
down the hill at the shadows cast by the assortment of abandoned
junk. I don't see cars and appliances and farm equipment. I see
dragons and winged horses and strange beasts…and griffins.

Could I do it? Tell the truth? Expose myself to the entire world?

It would kill my mom. I could never lead that normal life I fantasized about—not with every pervert out there knowing my face, seeing it all over the news. Who would ever want to be with me after that? Knowing what I let my uncle and King do to me?

"You could lie." Miranda's voice is a whisper of hope. "But then your uncle would win. All those perverts King sold your performances to, they'd win. King would win. And if they win, they'll never stop. They'll keep doing this to other kids. They'll think it's okay to ruin our lives, to hurt us like we're nothing more than dirt on the bottom of their shoes. Is that what you want?"

"No. Of course not. But my mom—"

"You think she'd feel better believing a lie? How does that help anyone? Wouldn't she want to know the truth? Not just about her brother but about the kind of son she has, someone willing to sacrifice everything for his family, someone brave enough to stand up and fight for what's right. Doesn't she deserve that son instead of a son who lies his way to jail for a crime he didn't commit and who lets the bad guys walk free?"

I stare at the stars. At the mythical beasts my imagination has conjured from the junk surrounding me. Disposable stuff. No good. Used, abused, and cast aside. Like me.

Like all the other kids King has tormented. How many of us are there? How many more will there be if I—if we—don't stop him?

"It's not that easy," I stammer, telling myself it's the cold that makes me shiver so hard my teeth knock together.

"I know. I'll be with you all the way."

"Right. From your safe little home with both your parents

there to protect you." I hate myself for saying the words, want to take them back, but I can't. If she wants the truth, maybe we need to start with each other.

"You're right. I'm sorry." Her voice sears my soul; it's filled with such sorrow and regret. "I can't be there with you. Maybe you should just run."

"No. Miranda—" I take a deep breath, air so cold it burns my lungs. "What's the plan?"

———

Miranda climbed off her bed and stood at her window. "Can you see the stars where you are?"

"Yes." Jesse paused. "The plan isn't for us to become astronauts and fly away to Mars, is it? Because I'm pretty sure you'd need to leave your home for all that weightlessness training and stuff."

His tone was both light and concerned at the same time, doubting her sanity. And he hadn't even heard her plan yet.

"Ha ha, already starting with the agoraphobia jokes." He had no idea how lucky he was. Even with everything that had happened, at least he had a choice: he could run or he could fight. The only way she could run was—her gaze darted to her journal—the ultimate escape.

Funny, after spending the day—even virtually—with Griffin, with Jesse, suicide just didn't have the appeal it once had.

"That thing you did this morning, when you imagined a perfect day for me."

"Yeah?" He sounded embarrassed by it.

"That was the nicest thing anyone has ever done for me. Listening to you, painting an entire world just for me with your words, it was…magical. I'll always treasure that. Always."

Awkward silence. He cleared his throat. "You're welcome."

She pressed her palm against the window, absorbing the cold. "I just wanted you to know that. No matter what happens."

"Why are you sounding like this is some kind of good-bye?"

"Not good-bye. I hope not. But if we go through with this, things might get pretty crazy."

"You haven't told me yet. What are we going through with?"

"We go public. Not just public. Viral. Use our stories to launch a massive social media campaign targeting King."

"Cybersmash him? Like he does his victims? Like what he did to you?"

"Worse than cybersmashing. Because we'll be telling the truth. Starting with the video you recorded."

"The video of me beating the crap out of my uncle? How's that going to help?"

"I'll edit it to stop before that. We'll just show him confessing. Talking about him and King and what they did to you."

Another long pause. "And you?"

"I have copies of everything King posted about me…I'll also tell people about what he did to my mom, tell them about how I tried to kill myself. About how I live now because of him, a prisoner of my own fear. How I plan to kill myself if he's not stopped."

She took a deep breath, pressed her palm against the window, but it was no good. She was trapped. Inside a cage of her own making. "How I *will* kill myself if he's not caught before my birthday, in twenty-four hours."

"No. Miranda you can't. You wouldn't—"

"I will. This is our chance to stop living a lie."

"They'll lock you up, just like they will me if I'm caught."

"But the truth about King, about your uncle, once that's out, they can't put the genie back in the bottle. The truth will spread. More of King's victims will come forward, tell the truth of what he did to them. We might not be able to save ourselves, but we can save others, stop King from stealing anyone else's life."

Silence. Dark and heavy. She bit her lip, counted by threes—a magic number, a safe number—until she became dizzy holding her breath and had to inhale. Her room was quiet, so very quiet.

Finally his voice returned. "Okay. Do it. But, Miranda—"

"Yes?" She could barely get the word out.

"Don't edit the video. If we're telling the truth, it should be all of it."

36

I hang up from Miranda and lean against the hood of the Impala. The junkyard shadows no longer look like mystical creatures. They look like junk, rusted and forgotten.

Wish I were one of them. My stomach clenches in a fist of pain. I try to blame it on the cheeseburger but know it's plain old fear. Helping Miranda get evidence on King, maybe needing to talk to a few cops, that was one thing. But her new plan—exposing ourselves to anyone on the planet with an Internet connection?

Insanity. Brilliant. Desperate. Brave.

After Miranda broadcasts her suicide countdown, they'll lock her away in some psych ward, dope her with drugs, give her shock treatment, who knows what?

I crane my neck, searching out the stars above, and zip up my dad's jacket, a thin barricade against the night chill. In a way, she's risking far more than I am.

After tonight, our lives will never be the same.

Mom and Janey are safe, I tell myself. That's what counts. Nothing else matters.

Except...I try to count the stars, turning fuzzy as mist rolls off the mountain behind me. I would have made a wish but there's...nothing. I think of the future, of anything I could hope or dream or wish for, and all I see is black emptiness. Stretching out forever.

My skin burns with the cold, and I climb back inside my makeshift shelter, curl up in a ball, trying to stay warm, and close my eyes. For the first time in years, my sleep is as empty as the rest of my life. No night terrors, no panicked jerking awake worried I'd missed a call from King, no dreams at all...except maybe one.

I'm not sure if it's a dream or a fantasy, but Miranda's with me, for one magic moment. We're in a field; I'm chasing after her; we're both laughing, and she turns and reaches her hand to me, letting me catch up. I can't see her face; she's wearing a pretty dress that floats in the breeze, but when our hands touch, I swear I feel it in every atom of my body.

Then it's gone, vanished along with the rest of my hopes and dreams.

Despite staying up all night, Miranda couldn't remember the last time she'd felt this energized. Not just energized—excited. Glad to be alive. The irony was intoxicating in its own warped way.

She uploaded Jesse's video and added her own story, including reading her suicide note and promising to go through with it if anything happened to Jesse. She debated naming Kerstater, finally decided to take a chance, trust in her gut instinct. Everything she'd found pointed to the man, and if she was wrong...Well, she just had to be right.

Finally, taking a lesson from King, she used the footage to create several teaser videos, all with countdowns to the flash mob.

The other dwarves were a huge help. Clive secreted the footage in several secure sites and set them to run automatically. She didn't tell him she wanted it that way so she couldn't chicken out at the last moment. Jesse was risking his life to help her; following through on her own promise was the least she could do for him.

Misscreant covered Clive's tracks so no one would be able to trace the video streams once they went live. Topaz would be monitoring the feeds so that if anyone blocked one, he could switch to another—a trick he'd learned from Syrian freedom fighters. The others were helping by reaching out to the white-hat cybercommunity as well as hitting all the local Facebook pages and message boards, recruiting members for the flash mob.

Miranda's fingers flew over the keyboard, one window after another opening and closing, typing furiously as she carried on five conversations at once. Over a hundred responses to the flash mob invite already. And the sun wasn't even up yet. More replies would follow after people woke up.

She'd timed the flash mob to coincide with the early-bird prize drawing at the car show, thinking if only a few kids showed up, that would still guarantee someone was there to see them, but the way things were going, she need not have worried. Seemed like everyone had had a brush with a cyberbully or knew someone else who'd been impacted—or maybe the clips of Jesse made them curious enough to want to come and see him arrested… She didn't really care; she just needed warm bodies as witnesses.

The more people watching, the less chance the cops would hurt Jesse when they arrested him.

Once her suicide countdown went live, the police would try to trace her, but it was a weekend, and she was counting on them not being able to get a warrant to commit her to a psych ward until it was too late. After Jesse was safe in custody and they arrested King, it didn't matter what they did to her.

Her dad had spoken with his FBI friend last night and gave him everything Miranda had found pointing to Kerstater, but it still wasn't enough evidence to go after him. And he'd told her dad the ATF had joined the manhunt to find Jesse. Which meant it was up to her to expose King.

Her parents would be furious, and she hated hiding anything from them—again—but if her plan saved Jesse from a murder charge, they'd understand. Although she might be grounded for life—not a terrible punishment for someone like her, who couldn't make it past her own front door.

Feeling giddy, she texted Jesse. She didn't want to wake him with a call; he was exhausted. Besides, it felt good doing this herself. She owed him that much.

A little lost sleep was small price to pay for taking her life back. Thanks to Jesse.

Needing a break, she stood and stretched, grabbed a quick shower, and changed into her favorite jeans and a crimson pullover she thought Jesse would like. She couldn't believe how nervous she was about meeting him—would he think she was too pale, too skinny? She tried to do something with her hair. It was long, past her shoulders, since she hadn't gone out for a real haircut in a year. She had her mom's bouncy curls, but Miranda's hair was lighter in color, less ebony, more a reddish brown that she wasn't sure was pretty or not.

She sank onto her bed, dropping her comb. She had no clue what pretty was. Not anymore. Hopefully not what she saw depicted on TV and in the movies. But not having been with other girls her own age for so long, she worried she was hopelessly out of style.

No time for a makeover now. She went out to the kitchen, thinking she'd surprise everyone by making pancakes. She imagined Jesse walking in with her dad, smiling as he smelled them cooking—he'd be hungry after everything that happened. Maybe he wouldn't notice her out-of-date clothes or too-long, frizzy curls.

She'd just gotten the ingredients lined up when her mom came out, still in her pajamas and bathrobe, yawning.

"Are they back yet?" Mom asked. Miranda's dad had left almost an hour ago to pick up Jesse.

"No." Miranda double-checked her recipe. It was simple enough, but she wanted them to come out perfect. "Aren't you going to get dressed?"

Mom ruffled her hair with her fingers, leaving it standing on end. "Your dad and I were up talking most of the night. We think we should call Dr. Patterson, ask her to come here for a session."

Miranda nodded without really listening. Where was the vanilla? She'd almost forgotten it. "After Jesse's safe."

There was a knock on the door. They both looked up. Mom frowned. Had something gone wrong? Dad wouldn't knock.

Mom walked to the door, checked out the peephole. Miranda watched, suddenly nervous. She reached for the phone, ready to call 911. "Who is it?" she whispered.

"There's no one there."

The phone rang. Miranda was so startled she almost dropped it. "Hello?"

"Good morning, Ariel. Tell your mom to open the door before someone gets hurt." It was a man's voice, one she recognized from Jesse's recording. *King.*

Miranda stood frozen, panic turning her blood to ice. She looked up at her mom, but before she could say anything, the door crashed open and a man with a gun burst in. He punched her mom so hard her body flew over the arm of the couch. Then he turned to Miranda.

"Do what I say and I won't kill her." He aimed the pistol at her mother, who was sitting up, holding her face in her hands. Blood and mucus poured from her nose.

Miranda dropped the phone. Her breath came fast. Whirling, she searched for a weapon, anything she could use to defend herself and her mom. She lunged for the knife rack but the man caught her in a bear hug, squeezing the breath from her.

Mom struggled to her feet, dazed. The man held the gun to Miranda's head, pulling her up to her tiptoes.

"We're going to take a little ride. Do anything stupid and you both die."

37

I wake feeling energized. Bang my knees on the front seat of the car before I remember where I am or why I'm here. My stomach's growling—it doesn't care about life or death; all it cares about is energy—but I ignore it.

There's a text waiting for me from Miranda. Well, two actually. The first is business: Dad will meet you 6:30, flash mob at Arena 9 a.m., woohoo!

The second is a photo of a colorful hot air balloon hovering over a field of wildflowers. The text says: Never forget! I erase the first and save the second.

It's almost six thirty. The sun has just made an appearance over the mountains to the east, but here in the valley, we're still in shadows. I climb over the fence and skirt the property line down the hill, until I make it to the road. Hiding in a cluster of sumac between the road and the railroad tracks, I hope Miranda's dad is bringing breakfast.

I spot a car coming from the east. Gray sedan, unremarkable. It slows slightly but doesn't stop. The driver is a man, about my mom's age, dark sunglasses hiding most of his face. He drives past me down to the entrance to the junkyard where he pulls in and makes a U-turn. Acting like just another driver lost on the back roads of central Pennsylvania.

He slowly backtracks toward me, his driver's side window rolled down despite the chilly air, looking at the bushes along the side of the road rather than the road itself. I stand up as he draws near, and he stops the car.

"Griffin?" he says. I relax. Only Miranda knows that name—and how cool is it that that's the name she gave her parents? Of course, with my real name blasted all over the TV they'd know the truth, but still, it makes me smile.

"Yes, sir. Are you Miranda's dad?"

He nods. "George Ryder. Hop in."

As I cross the road, my cell rings. Miranda is the only one with the number. "Hey, great timing," I say cheerfully.

"I thought so," comes a man's voice. "You've been a very bad boy, Jesse."

It's my uncle.

I stumble to the side of the car, bent over like I've been sucker punched. I feel like I'm going to hurl and fight for every breath.

"You're alive?" I gasp. "Wait, how'd you get this number?"

"How'd you think? From your pretty girlfriend. And her pretty mother."

Mr. Ryder realizes something is wrong and gets out of the car.

"What do you want?" I ask.

"You know the answer to that. You've always known."

"Let me talk to Miranda." I'm surprised by the steel in my voice. The rest of me can barely stand.

Mr. Ryder's eyes go flat as he takes the phone from my hand and holds it between us.

"Sorry, no can do. King has her and her mom tucked safely away. You come to us and they go free. It's that easy."

Nothing was ever that easy with King or my uncle. "Don't hurt them."

"I'm afraid it's a little late for that. But they're alive. For now. Where are you?"

Miranda's dad shakes his head, mouths a word.

"No. I want to meet somewhere public. So I can be sure they're safe." I think of Miranda's plan. Maybe her flash mob can help us. Plus, her father knows the arena. "The car show. Nine o'clock."

There's a pause. I know my uncle doesn't like me calling the shots, so I sweeten the pot. "Just don't hurt them. I'll do anything you want."

"Yes, you will." He chuckles. The phone warps the noise into a movie sound effect—the kind that comes right before the serial killer strikes. "Okay, the arena. Remember where the FD command center is? Be there at nine o'clock. Alone. Or they die."

I stand frozen after my uncle hangs up. He'll do it. I know he will. He'll kill Miranda and her mother just to show me who's in charge.

I can't let that happen.

Mr. Ryder takes the battery out of my cell phone. I remember what Miranda said about GPS tracking and how King can turn on a phone's microphone. Her dad's fingers shake the tiniest bit—the only obvious sign of emotion that I can see.

Until he speaks. "Who was that son of a bitch?"

"My uncle." I nod to his phone clipped to his belt. Right

beside a pistol. "King has Miranda's cell. That means he has your number as well. He could be listening to us now."

He dismantles his own cell and we get into the car. He guns the engine. *To hell with speed limits*, his driving says. He slides his sunglasses on as we head east.

"So your uncle's not dead."

I'm still absorbing that little tidbit myself. Then realize I'd never searched my uncle before leaving him in the garage. He must have called King and together they framed me for murder and the arsons. But whose body was in the garage? "He's working with King—you know who he is, right?"

A jerk of his chin. "My daughter calls him the Creep. Why the arena?"

I explain about the flash mob Miranda organized. "But the fire department command center is in the subbasement—no one can hear us down there."

"That's okay. We'll work it out." He glances at me. Same look my teachers give me when they can't figure out why I'm not doing better in school. "We have to go to the police. You going to give me a hard time about that?"

"No, sir. But how can we? They'll lock me up—then I can't meet my uncle and get Miranda back." He grimaces when I say her name. I guess if I were a father whose daughter was hanging out with a loser like me, I'd make a face as well. "Plus, if anyone sees me going to the police, if word gets out that I'm talking to them or that my uncle is alive, he and King will kill them both."

"He'll be monitoring the Smithfield police," he says, more to himself than to me. "My daughter says he can access any computer on campus?"

"Yes. He found me last night—I don't know how, exactly. Miranda thought some kind of monitoring program."

"That means he can access the campus security cameras. So I can't be with you."

He's a step ahead of me. Just like his daughter.

"Don't worry about me. I can take care of myself. As long as you get Miranda and her mother."

He nods at me. I wish he'd take off his sunglasses, so I can see if he's nodding because he believes me or just to humor me.

"Best way to do that will be if I get there first," he says. "Hide, out of sight of the cameras. I can borrow a maintenance uniform. He'll never know it's me."

I like how he treats me like I'm a partner, not a victim or, worse, the guy who put his daughter and wife in danger.

We've just hit the Smithfield city limits. He pulls the car over, driving behind a Sheetz and parking near the Dumpsters where we're out of sight of the road. "I'll buy a prepaid, make some calls."

"To who, sir?" I can't help but add the *sir*, not with him sitting there all calm and determined, hiding behind his sunglasses and a hard-edged scowl. I feel like I should be saluting but settle for sitting up straight and looking at him head-on, letting him know I'm ready for whatever it takes to save Miranda.

"When this first happened—" He glances out the window, checking the side mirrors, then back again. "When the Pittsburgh police couldn't track this guy, King, after he targeted Melody—my wife—I asked the FBI for help."

"Miranda said their computer task force didn't get anywhere."

"They couldn't trace him with what they had at the time, no. And they couldn't make him a priority, not with everything else on their plates."

I nod my understanding. I've read the newspaper articles about the FBI busting pedophile rings and child sex trafficking conspiracies. One cyberbully wouldn't even make the list of the Big Bads they fight—although I wish he had. Maybe they would have stopped King long ago…and my uncle.

"I've kept in touch with a special agent in the Pittsburgh Field Office. He's been trying to work the case when he can, and I've already sent him all the new info Miranda found. I'm going to call him and see if he can put us in touch with anyone in the Incident Command here."

"Incident Command?"

"What they call it when there's a multiagency case—something big enough to cross jurisdictions."

"Because this is a kidnapping?"

He shakes his head. "No. Because you're a fugitive wanted for murder and serial arsons. We've got the locals, the county sheriffs, the state police, the ATF, and the U.S. Marshals Fugitive Apprehension Strike Team all looking for you."

I swallow hard. I trust him, but I don't understand. "So, you're turning me in. Okay. If you think it's best. But how will that help Miranda and her mom? I can't miss the meeting with my uncle and King."

He claps me on the shoulder. "You'll be at the meeting. Don't you worry about that. But you won't be there alone."

Now I understand. "You're not turning me in. You're using me as bait."

"Want to back out? It's okay if you do. Even with help from the Feds, it's going to be dangerous."

"No, sir. I'll do it—I want to do it. As long as we can be absolutely certain there's no way King can find out. We can't risk Miranda or her mom."

His smile's more than a little scary. I'm glad I'm on his side. He opens the door and gets out of the car, then leans back inside, his face inches from mine. "My daughter said I could trust you. Said you were a good guy."

I'm not sure what to say to that. "Thank you. Sir."

"Just do me a favor and don't let her down, okay?"

"I won't." It's a promise we both know I can't be certain of keeping, but he nods his head and leaves. Alone in the car, I scrunch down in case anyone drives by. I take my lighter out and flick it, over and over and over…focusing on the flame is the only thing that keeps me from jumping out and running for my life.

How in hell am I going to face my uncle? Much less King?

38

"Don't make a noise or your mother dies," Jesse's uncle told Miranda as he directed her mother to the door and dragged Miranda with him.

Miranda couldn't feel her feet against the carpet—couldn't feel anything past the sight of blood on her mother's face. She'd done this, thought she could outsmart King. Instead she'd brought this madness, this pain, this...evil into their lives.

All her fault. And now her mother was going to pay the price.

"Please," her mother begged, her words choked with blood from her split lip and broken nose. "You don't understand. She can't leave. She has agoraphobia. Panic attacks."

Miranda flinched with each word as if they were blows. Her mother should just run. Why didn't she run, save herself? She opened her mouth to yell at her mother to leave her, but nothing came out except for a tiny mewing noise too weak to carry that far.

"Shut up and keep moving. Now." He jabbed the gun hard into Miranda's temple, forced her forward.

The doorway loomed, growing bigger and bigger, a monster's maw ready to swallow them. Her mom crossed through it, turned back, an arm out toward Miranda, stretching a mile or more to reach her as her mom's body grew smaller and smaller, fuzzy and blurred.

Run, please, just run. The words thundered through Miranda's mind but she couldn't force them past the panic that throttled her. *Mom, don't die. Not because of me. Please.*

The panic attack ripped through Miranda, squeezing her chest, making her heart pound with terror—somehow it was worse than the real terror of a gun to her head.

Only the fear that he might hurt her mom kept Miranda upright. As it was, she was breathing so hard and fast she couldn't feel her feet or hands or face. Jesse's uncle wrapped his arm around her throat and jabbed the gun in his other hand into her side as he shoved her out the door and into the hall.

All her fears crashed down on her. Fear of unknown people coming out of their apartments, seeing her. Where were they now, when they might actually help?

There was no one, not this early on a Saturday morning. No one but her mom backing down the hall, hands out as if ready to catch Miranda. Mom wouldn't leave her, wouldn't run to save herself.

Why not? Didn't she realize this was all Miranda's fault?

Miranda's vision darkened. She knew she had to slow her breathing, but she couldn't. She couldn't even think; the panic had taken over her brain.

Her mom was going to die. Because of her. Because she was weak and stupid and frightened and, and, and…a dozen recriminations swirled through her brain, the words turned into blows, pummeling Miranda's psyche.

Jesse's uncle's grip tightened on her as they started down the steps. Then they reached the front door to the building. The sun was up, the sky outside clear blue. But all Miranda could see was a bloodred haze.

No! She couldn't go out, couldn't go past those doors. She struggled, numb, useless fingers clawing at his face and arms, feet tripping as she tried to push him back away from the doors.

Run, Mom! But his arm tightened, choking the words before she could say them. Her mother didn't run, didn't leave her. Instead, she stepped closer, toward the danger.

Jesse's uncle pivoted, aiming the gun at Mom, who froze, hands held up, eyes locked on Miranda.

"Stop it or she dies," he ordered Miranda.

She gasped for breath, his words meaningless wisps in the fog of her panic. He cursed, the pressure on her neck growing from his choke hold. She saw her mother, the gun aimed at her face, fought as hard as she could to swallow the terror, to take control, to think of something brave and bold to save her mother, but then everything went from scarlet to black.

———

Mr. Ryder is back a few minutes later, talking on a phone with one hand and carrying a bag with the other. He tosses the bag to me: the aroma of eggs, sausage, and bacon almost makes me forget why we're here. As I chew, he's talking fast, at first looking frustrated then relieved. Finally he looks at me over the tops of his sunglasses and seems doubtful.

I wipe my face with my sleeve, worried I've got crumbs all over myself. It doesn't seem to help. But he nods and hangs up.

He gets back into the car and we continue heading down 322. I want to ask about the FBI but restrain myself. Not a whole lot I can do about it, sitting in a speeding vehicle, except trust him. I'm sure he's just as unhappy about being forced to trust me, a stranger, with his daughter's life.

We're almost to Smithfield when he turns to me and asks, "What is this Griffin business, anyway? Does it stand for anything? It's not a gang name, is it?"

"Miranda came up with it. She thought we should have screen names, make it harder for King to track us if he spotted us." It sounds stupid. Childish. But right now, heading over to the men who want to lock me up for crimes I didn't commit and then going on to negotiate for the lives of Miranda and her mom, I need all the Griffin I can muster.

He grunts. "Sounds like something she would come up with. Like her mom, that way. Always with her head in a book. So a griffin, that's like a winged monkey or something?"

He's smiling, sort of, so I know he's joking. "Something like that. They were mythical beasts who protected the innocent against evil."

"I'd say we need all the help we can get in that arena." He jerks his chin, decision made. We pull into the driveway of a small house just off campus. "The college owns this place, uses it for visiting professors, but it's vacant right now. And not in range of any security cameras." There are two black SUVs parked in front of us. It's a small house, made of fieldstone, with a sloped peaked roof, like something out of "Hansel and Gretel."

"These guys—" he starts.

"They're FBI?" I'm a little nervous. Regular cops are bad enough but the FBI?

"No. My friend at the FBI put me in contact with the US Deputy Marshal running the FAST team. I met the guy a few times when I was in Pittsburgh on the warrant squad. He's a bit of a cowboy, is going to want to test you," he says. "His butt is on the line here if anything goes wrong, so let him do—"

"Excuse me, sir," I interrupt. "But isn't it Miranda and Mrs. Ryder's lives on the line? I'm sorry, but I really don't give a damn about anyone else."

"Good man. But we need Oshiro and his team on board—otherwise, they'll just lock you up and we're shit out of luck." His hand is resting on his pistol as he says this, so I'm pretty sure he won't let it come to that. "Answer his questions honestly, like you have with me, and everything will be okay. Ready?"

"Yes, sir."

"Good. Because we're running out of time."

39

When Miranda came to, she was surrounded by darkness. They'd placed a pillowcase or something like it over her head. They hadn't done it to help her, but she was grateful for it. Because of it, she'd been able to breathe in the extra carbon dioxide she generated while hyperventilating, helping to end her panic attack. Plus, even though she knew she was lying on the floor of a car in motion, in the darkness she could imagine herself still safe inside her room, on her bed, hiding under her covers.

It even smelled of fabric softener—a tiny detail but powerful enough to ease the panic, enough that she could regain control. Of her body at least. Well, not even that. As feeling returned to her limbs, she realized her hands were duct taped behind her back and that she was lying on top of them. And she was barefoot—couldn't blame that on Jesse's uncle, she rarely wore shoes since she never went anywhere. But her feet were cold.

Not bound, though. She could run if she had the chance.

Her heart stumbled into a headlong whirl and her breath quickened with panic. She concentrated on slowing it. Right. How the hell could she run when the thought of the world beyond this nice, clean pillowcase was overwhelming?

She took a few more deep breaths. Finally the cobwebs clouding her brain cleared. *Mom!* She hauled in a lungful of air, ready to scream when a man's shoe planted itself on her chest, squeezing all the air out so she couldn't make a sound.

"Don't," he said. "It gives me a headache, and it won't do you a damn bit of good. Your mom is safe—as long as you do what I tell you to do. Do you understand, Ariel?"

She nodded but wasn't sure he could see with the pillowcase. He eased the pressure on her chest and she was able to gasp, "Yes."

Ariel. He'd called her Ariel. Jesse's uncle didn't know her by that name. And his voice was different—it was the man on the phone. King.

Her stomach twisted, and she had to swallow twice to keep from vomiting. She breathed through her nose, slow, deep, gulping in the fake flowers from the fabric softener. Mom. She had to find her mom.

Miranda swallowed, tasting lint. Fear edged aside, making room for anger. Her mom. They'd hit her mom, pointed a gun at her. They said they'd kill her mother.

Not. Going. To. Happen.

That one decision made, her heart slowed to a steady pace. Miranda might die today—a day sooner than she'd planned, but that was okay. As long as her mom was safe.

"Good girl," he said dismissively as she stopped struggling beneath his foot. As if she were a trained dog. In a way, she supposed he had trained her—but not the way he thought.

If he hurt her mom, she was going to kill him.

"Have you heard from Nina lately?" he asked in a casual tone, his foot still pressed against her chest.

Nina? That was her friend, the one whose house she was in when...it was Nina's big sister who'd taken the pictures King found two years ago. The ones that destroyed her life. A giddy drunk girl doing a silly striptease. Fake, for fun, not even taking everything off, but the camera caught enough, more than enough.

"No." She decided to stick with simple answers. Like her dad did when he had to testify. Dad? Were he and Jesse coming? Or did King have them as well?

"Poor, poor Nina." He sighed dramatically. "She's not doing so well. Failing school, acting out, fighting with her parents. Don't you want to know why?"

"Why?" she said. What did Nina have to do with her and Jesse? Shouldn't he be asking where Jesse was? What their plan was?

"Because of me. You see, your photos weren't the only ones I snagged that night."

She squeezed her eyes shut, guilt descending over her. She'd never seen any pictures of Nina, had assumed hers were the only ones, that she was King's only victim that night.

"You refused my offer," King continued. "Tried to fight back. As pitiful as that was, it was amusing. But Nina begged me to not publish her pictures said she'd do anything. So now she belongs to me."

He went silent. Lesson over: there was no winning with King.

Nina. Poor Nina. After Ariel was cybersmashed, her world crumbling around her, she'd been so angry at Nina's sister that she'd barely spoken to Nina except to yell at her.

Nina had said nothing. Not during the weeks they were still in school together, before the first time Miranda's parents transferred her to another school in another part of the city. Nina's life must have been even more hellish than Ariel's, but she'd never once asked for help.

"You used me to threaten Nina," she said, her anguish muffled by the pillowcase. Anger blossomed into something hard, enduring, tougher than any panic or phobia. She'd let Nina down. Had spent all that time and energy chasing after King's victims and hadn't even known her best friend needed help.

"Of course, dear. That's what I do. Oh, the money is nice, but the real joy comes from watching people destroy themselves." His foot jiggled and she could tell he was excited. Sick bastard. "I was going to take her viral—your birthday present, watching your friend's life come crashing down, all because of you. But this, finally getting to play with you in person, this is so much more fun, don't you think?"

She lay at his feet, tied up, blind, and she smiled. He thought he had Ariel—weak, meek Ariel—here. He thought he'd already won.

Wrong. She'd left Ariel far, far behind. She wasn't weak or meek. She wasn't about to lose; in fact, she had nothing left to lose. Her only choice was to win.

She was Miranda.

———

As soon as we step out of Mr. Ryder's car, there are two men with big, black machine guns, aiming at us from the doorway of the house. Another from beside the garage, putting us in a cross fire. Mr. Ryder doesn't seem to notice—or he pretends not to, because I see he's keeping his hands out to the side, away from his gun, as he walks up the front steps.

"Oshiro is expecting us," he says to the two guys at the door, nudging their machine guns aside as he walks past them. They're dressed all in black: cargo pants with holsters and small bags strapped to their thighs, gun belts, bulletproof vests under black Windbreakers. They glare at me as if expecting me to quiver and melt into a pool of jelly.

It feels good, disappointing them, following Mr. Ryder's nonchalant lead.

"Morning," is all I say as I pass through them.

Mr. Ryder leads the way into the front room, a dining room with a map spread out on the table and two more men bent over it. Their polos say *U.S. Marshal* above an embroidered star. There's another skinny guy wearing jeans and a polo shirt under a Windbreaker that has *ATF* stenciled on the back. He's the youngest of the group and doesn't seem to quite fit in with the rest.

And finally there's the leader, who must be Oshiro. The guy isn't tall, yet he's massive. Think sumo wrestler without the beer belly. Broad shoulders, no neck, big hands.

His glare stops me in my tracks. "This the kid? Where were you at 0620?"

"With me," Ryder answers, not at all taken back by Oshiro's abrupt question. "Why?"

"Because according to his life-support monitors, that's when someone killed Leonard Kerstater, the brother of the guy you said was one of our subjects." Oshiro planted both palms on the table. I swear the heavy oak groaned as he leaned forward. "So either you did it together, or—"

"I'm innocent." I can't believe I said it like that, daring him to not believe me, but I don't back down. Every instinct is telling me that showing fear or weakness to this man will get me eaten alive. "So can we stop wasting time?"

He jerks his head, dismissing me, and focuses on Mr. Ryder.

Mr. Ryder gives him a quick summary of everything that's happened.

"You disabled your cells? Both of you?" Oshiro frowns. "Good way to alert our subjects that you might be working together, get them suspicious."

I'm surprised at his tone. Like Mr. Ryder's an idiot or something. But Mr. Ryder shrugs it off, handing Oshiro his cell. "Didn't have much choice. This place would be on my patrol route, so if you want to put the battery back in and set it outside—"

"Got a better idea. Hey, junior G-man," he calls to the ATF agent, using the same dismissive tone. "Take this phone for a walk around campus. Do not speak to anyone, do not answer your own cell, turn your radio to mute."

He tosses the agent Mr. Ryder's phone. The agent catches it but looks confused. "For how long, sir?"

"Until I tell you to stop. Go." The younger agent leaves, and Oshiro turns to stare at me. Without saying a word, I hand him my cell and the battery. "This the phone our subject called on? Your not-so-dead, according to you, uncle?"

"I heard him as well," Mr. Ryder puts in.

"Yes, sir," I answer. "He called from Miranda's cell, so I'm not sure if it will help you—you're already tracing her number, right?"

"As soon as Ryder filled us in on what was going on. No help there. Seems our subject is also smart enough to remove a cell battery. Got any other bright ideas?"

Suddenly they're all staring at me like I have all the answers. I'm just a kid; they're the experts. But maybe this is the test.

"Yes, sir, I do."

He chuckles and raises an eyebrow in surprise. "Okay, then. Tell us, Mr. Jesse Alexander, how do we save our two damsels in distress without getting anyone killed?"

40

My plan is simple. Hopefully so simple nothing will go wrong and no one will get hurt.

"My uncle is expecting me to meet him at the arena's fire department control center. It's in the subbasement, room B28, right below the main arena entrance. I'll get him to tell me where Miranda is, then keep him there while you guys rescue Miranda and her mom."

Oshiro exchanges a look with Mr. Ryder. To my surprise, Mr. Ryder is leaning back on his heels, shoulders back, chest out. Like he's proud of me or something. My dad used to look at me like that.

"Kid's got cojones," Oshiro says. "It's a good start. I think we can improve on it."

"King controls the security system all over the campus," I protest. "We can't risk him seeing your men or any other cops."

"So we won't let him. The car show opens its doors at eight thirty. We go in with the crowd, plainclothes, fan out, cover the exits. The only trick will be getting backup downstairs to you—the subbasement isn't exactly open to the public."

"I can get down there," Mr. Ryder says. "I know all the camera blind spots. I'll dress like a janitor, push a mop. If I get in position before Jesse arrives, King will never see me."

Oshiro frowns again, a scowl that shifts his entire face into a grimace that would scare little kids into eating their broccoli. "Just one problem. How do we know he won't just kill Mr. Alexander here on the spot?"

I don't really care. But another thought occurs to me. "Make that two problems. How do we know he'll actually bring Miranda at all?"

"We need to make it worth their while to keep Jesse alive *and* set my daughter and wife free."

"You know they won't," Oshiro says.

"Of course. But they think Jesse's a naïve kid. All they need to do is convince him that they plan to free Miranda."

"If he has something to bargain with."

"How about a tape of my uncle confessing everything and implicating King?" I suggest. "Miranda has one ready to go live all over the web at nine o'clock when the flash mob hits." I leave out the part where the video also shows me beating my uncle bloody. Although I have a niggling suspicion Oshiro wouldn't have a problem with that. "I know my uncle would do anything to stop it getting out—so would King."

He nods slowly. "That'll work. They release Miranda and her mom, you stop the video from going live."

"You're going to wire him and give him a vest," Miranda's dad says.

"No vest," I tell them. "Nothing my uncle could find."

"No problem," Oshiro says. He beckons to the marshal he gave my phone to. The man hands me another phone. "Even if they turn this off or take the regular battery out, it will still record and broadcast to us. Every word within twenty feet, give or take."

I pocket the phone. "I won't be able to hear you?"

"Ryder will. You just keep your uncle talking and we'll take care of the rest." He snaps his finger as if he's forgotten something. "Almost forgot." He pushes a stack of papers across the table at me. "Jesse Alexander, I'm taking you into custody."

I bristle—the other agents, the guys with the guns, pick up on it, and suddenly all eyes are on me. I keep my hands out just like Mr. Ryder had earlier and focus on Oshiro. He's smiling—not a pretty sight, much more frightening than his frown—and holding a pen out to me.

"Just a formality. Sign here, here, and here. Says I read you your rights, you understand them, and waive them."

I glance at Mr. Ryder. He nods. I sign the papers.

"Good. Now you're official property of the U.S. Marshals." Oshiro beams at me. "Welcome aboard, Mr. Alexander."

"Enough, let's get started," I snap, irritated that this is just another job to them. I want them to care as much about Miranda and her mother as her dad and I do. I want them to leave nothing to chance and be willing to risk their lives to save them.

All I can hope is that it will be enough.

———

King went silent, leaving Miranda to her own thoughts, frightening territory that they were. Turned out Miranda was angrier than Ariel but still just as terrified and helpless. Who wouldn't be? You don't need to be agoraphobic to be frightened when you're tied up, blindfolded, being held at gunpoint by men who'd already killed and who would kill your mother if you made a single wrong move.

Dr. Patterson's voice infiltrated the storm of emotions threatening to overwhelm Miranda. *Think it through*, she'd say when they worked on her agoraphobia and OCD. *What's the absolute worst thing that would happen if you took action? What's the worst thing that would happen if you don't? Which path do you choose? You're in control, not your fears*, she'd say.

Miranda never believed her until now.

But when you're already facing your greatest fear, what have you got to lose?

The thought calmed her—better than numbers, better than any ritual. It was as if the blitzkrieg of panic brought about by her agoraphobia had cleansed her, stripped her naked but also free to act. Ariel could have never fought her way through the fear, but Miranda, living daily trapped by her own mind, had skills Ariel didn't.

In a warped way, the agoraphobia had prepared her for this moment. Miranda was glad King couldn't see her smile—he would not have liked it, not at all.

"I know about your video," King said. "I really don't care about it too much, but having it out there might make my exit inconveniently rushed. Last thing I need is to be on a no-fly list."

Miranda said nothing. She was too busy listening. The click of computer keys. King was typing—if he had a computer nearby and she could get to it, she could let the police know where she was…but what about her mom?

The car stopped. There was the sound of a car door slamming—the driver leaving.

"Where's my mother?" she asked.

"Nothing will happen to your mother as long as you do what I say."

"I'll do anything you want. After I see her."

"You'll do anything I want. Period." His foot ground down against her chest, making it impossible to breathe. Her vision went dark before he released the pressure. "I'm going to untie you. We're going inside the arena. You will not speak to anyone; you will not try to escape. If you do, your mother dies. Understand?"

Gasping for air, she nodded.

"Once we have Jesse secured, you will destroy the video. If any footage exposing me or Richard escapes, your mother will die and Jesse will die. You won't. You, I'll give to men with tastes far worse than anything Jesse's uncle ever did to him. Do you understand?"

She nodded again.

He yanked the pillowcase off, his face mere inches from hers as she squinted in the sudden bright light.

Howard Kerstater—she'd gotten it right. But he seemed an ordinary man. Shaved head, round face, bland even. Except the eyes. Plain brown but…soulless.

"Answer me, Ariel. Do you understand?"

She tried to swallow, but her mouth felt filled with cotton as if she'd swallowed the pillowcase. King raised an eyebrow, waiting. Finally she forced the word out. "Yes."

"Very good. Then we have a deal."

41

Miranda's father leaves to get into position and Oshiro's men plan vantage points and tactics while I sit and worry, watching the clock, waiting until it's time for me to leave. "I want to talk to my mom," I tell Oshiro.

He finishes giving orders to a state trooper and dismisses him. There's been a parade of uniforms in and out of the small house, but now it's just the two of us facing off over the dining room table. "Why?"

"I need to know my sister's okay." It's the truth but not all of it.

"She's safe. Still in the hospital."

"With my mom?" I want Mom as far away from everything happening today as possible, but I also need to tell her...It's overwhelming, the things I need to tell her. My stomach clenches and I realize facing her might be worse than facing King and my uncle.

"We brought your mother here. She's at the police station, being interviewed by the locals. A diversionary tactic in case King has any men on the Smithfield force."

As much as I don't like Oshiro using my mom, at least I know she's safe. "Can you bring her here?"

He raises an eyebrow, reminding me he can do any damn thing he pleases. "Why?"

"I need to talk to her." I gulp but there's nothing to swallow. Still, I square my shoulders and face him dead-on. "I don't want her to hear about my uncle from anyone else."

Something shifts in his face; there's maybe even a faint glimmer of humanity. Maybe. It's replaced by stone so fast I'm not sure. But he nods and ten minutes later one of his men is escorting my mother inside the house.

I watch from behind the kitchen door. I can't face her—not with that look on her face. It's more than fear; she's terrified. Of me.

Oshiro is a gracious host, welcoming Mom with much better manners than he showed me or Mr. Ryder. He sits her down at the table in the breakfast nook where we'll have some privacy, gets her coffee, then gestures for me to join her. He seems to understand my hesitation. "Want me to hang around, kid?"

Mom has said nothing since she got here. She just sits there, staring at the coffee Oshiro poured for her like she can't figure out if it's poisoned or not. Then for the first time, she raises her face and makes eye contact with me. Her face is a total blank. Even when Dad left, even the one time Janey got really sick and was in the ICU, I've never seen her like this. Utterly drained. Defeated.

And the worst is yet to come. This is going to be so much harder than I ever dreamed.

I glance at Oshiro, who's still standing beside me. I shake my head. He gives me one of those twisted things that pass for a smile and to my surprise claps a hand on my shoulder like I'm one of his men. "Okay, then. I'll be right here if you need anything."

He crosses through to the dining room where he can keep an eye on us without listening. I shift in my chair, trying to figure out how to start. "Janey's okay?" Talking about Janey is always safe ground.

Mom nods. "No more fever. They think it's probably just a virus. If her cultures are negative tomorrow, they'll let her come home." She gives a little jerk of panic, realizing we have no home for Janey to return to. A tiny noise escapes from her, and it breaks my heart.

Everything I've done, I've done to avoid exactly this moment. *Great job, there, Jesse.*

"I didn't kill anyone," I start, not sure how much the Feds have told her. "He's not dead."

She dips her face, talking into her coffee cup. "I know. The agent who drove me here told me. Said the dental records didn't match Richey's. But where is he? How did that man end up in our garage, dead? Why do they think you would ever kill your uncle?"

Suddenly it all pours out of me. I don't have the time or energy to be delicate, and honestly I'm so damn mad that this is the first time she's ever asked any real questions that I almost don't care how much the truth hurts. Almost.

I know how devastated she was when Dad left, understand the pressures of working two jobs and still not being able to keep a roof over our heads, not to mention how overwhelming it is to have a sick kid like Janey to take care of. But damn it, couldn't she have found a spare second, an ounce of energy to pay attention to me, to ask what was really going on in my life?

I worked hard to hide it, I know, but I was just a kid, not like I'm that great of an actor. Not if she really cared.

She's in tears now. They're dripping into the coffee that she refuses to let go of but isn't drinking. "No," she protests, not for the first time. "Richey saved us."

Finally I realize. It has nothing to do with how hard I worked to hide the truth…she never had a chance to see it. My uncle must have made tons of money from King, but he made sure we were always scraping by so she couldn't quit either of her jobs. Anytime she needed help, he was there, playing the hero, rearranging his shifts at work or taking me with him to the fire station so she could get Janey to a doctor's appointment or take care of her when she was sick.

He kept her hopes alive that my dad might still be out there somewhere, encouraging her to spend what little money and free time she had on searching for him. And when Dad wasn't anywhere to be found, he coaxed her into the depths of despair with hints that Dad had left because of her.

She was powerless against him, her own brother, someone she'd trust with her life. The man she'd trusted with my life.

Both of us victims.

Anger spins me out of my chair. Oshiro steps to the doorway, but I wave him off. Silence fills the space, sucking out the oxygen, leaving my chest tight.

I wait, fists at my side, bouncing on my toes. I know her next words will change everything. Will she believe my truth? Or cling to denial?

Mom chokes back her tears and finally relinquishes her hold on her coffee mug. She knuckles her eyes and wipes her face on her sleeve. She's still wearing her coat, hugs it around her as if she's freezing.

Finally she stands and faces me. Looks me straight in the eye. I brace myself—can feel Oshiro also tensing behind me.

"Jesse," she says my name like it's too heavy to hold on to. "Jesse. I'm so sorry. It's all my fault." She's blubbering now. I can barely make out her words as she rushes to take me in her arms. I tense, almost pull away, still furious. She only grips me tighter, despite the fact that I'm a foot taller than her and her arms barely fit around me anymore. "I'll make this right. I'm sorry. I never, I can't—"

I smother her words as I finally release my anger and hug her back. We hold each other, swaying as if we might both fall if one of us relaxes our grip, and I wipe my tears on her shoulder. Oshiro clears his throat and I know my time is running out. "Mom, I have to go now."

She clutches my arm, pulls me to her with strength I didn't realize she had. She wraps her arms around me tight. "I love you, Jesse. Please believe that."

I break away from her embrace and stand. I clear my throat, sucking in all the tears before Oshiro can see them. Then realize I really don't give a shit what he sees.

"No, Jesse. Please, don't go. I couldn't bear it, if anything happened…" she cries and I worry that this is too much, that she'll finally break.

But I can't carry that burden anymore. I can't protect her and still save Miranda. I lay my hand on her shoulder and squeeze. "Good-bye, Mom."

———

King—she couldn't bring herself to think of him as Howard Kerstater—tore the tape off Miranda's wrists and forced her inside the arena's rear entrance, away from the crowd. He kept a gun jammed into her back, hidden from view inside his coat pocket. They took a private elevator that he had the key code for up to the top level where the corporate skyboxes were situated.

The elevator was okay, but as soon as they exited, they were on the top level of the twenty-foot-wide concourse, curved windows revealing the sky as they arched overhead to form the arena's dome, the interior wall also with glass windows between the entrances to the skyboxes. Miranda hugged the interior wall, looking down over the huge expanse of the arena's seating area. On the main floor, far below the Jumbotron suspended from the center of the dome, exhibitors were already swarmed by eager car enthusiasts. Shiny new cars on rotating platforms gleamed in the harsh lights. They were so far away they looked like Matchbox toys.

Panic sped up Miranda's breathing and she fought to get it under control. Only one threat here that she needed to focus on: King. She forced herself to memorize the key codes as he entered them, tried to pay attention to any detail that might help her escape.

They didn't see anyone until he opened the door to the broadcast booth that housed the Jumbotron controls. There they found a man, young, he looked like a college kid, hunched over a large console filled with levers, buttons, and dials. He spun in his seat when he heard them.

Before Miranda could say anything, King shot him in the chest. The sound echoed like thunder as she stood, stunned, the acrid scent of gunpowder mixed with blood filling her nostrils. The man looked down in surprise, back up at King, his mouth opening, then he slumped off the stool and fell to the ground.

Dead, Miranda realized, her hand over her mouth, although she didn't think she could scream if she tried. Her throat was clamped tight. King had killed the stranger without blinking—had he done the same to her mom? Was she dead already?

"Just to let you know how serious I am," King said. He motioned Miranda to a chair, then kicked the body aside and took the man's seat at the controls. "Don't get any ideas about the cavalry coming. This booth is soundproof."

Miranda realized he spoke the truth when she spotted the microphone and cameras lining the desk along the glass wall at the front of the booth. Of course, they broadcast sports events from here.

A laptop was connected to the AV console. King used it to pull up the security camera feeds. "Now I can see everything."

If she stretched her foot out, she could have touched the man's body. She didn't stretch her foot out.

King watched as Jesse appeared on the laptop's screen. "Here's our boy, right on time."

42

I walk across campus, just another student out for a Saturday
morning stroll except for the armed U.S. Marshals and ATF
agents tailing me.

I don't bother with the front of the arena, instead head around
to the rear entrance my uncle used for his fire inspections. The
door is unlocked. I'm not surprised—if King can control any
camera on campus, there's no reason why he couldn't also control
the electronic locks.

There's a camera directly over the door. I look up and shrug,
arms wide, looking as meek and innocent as I can. No one here to
worry about, just Jesse/JohnBoy, the kid who never fights back.

The tunnels that run beneath the arena are brightly lit and smell
of exhaust fumes from the cars idling on the exhibition floor overhead. The noise is overwhelming: the pounding footsteps from the
crowd above echo in time with my pulse. I wish I wasn't frightened,
but all I can think about is what King might be doing to Miranda.

The path to the right leads onto the concourse, the twenty-
foot-wide concrete ramp that corkscrews around the arena,
hosting vendors, restrooms, and entrances to each seating area
as it climbs. At the top are the skyboxes and the broadcast booth
holding the Jumbotron controls.

Down here, at the bottom of the spiral, lies the infrastructure that keeps the arena working: electrical and mechanical, vents and pipes and conduits, and the fire department command center that controls the alarms, elevators, water pressure, and sprinklers.

I feel at home down here, out of sight. A lot like my real life. Now I just have one more role to play.

The FD command center is a room the size of a walk-in closet. It has cinderblock walls, a bunch of pipes, gauges, alarm indicators, access to the audio evacuation system, and a radio that can reach first responders or the building security staff. No one ever goes there except when there's a fire inspection, like when my uncle first brought me here.

The command center's solid metal door is shut when I arrive. I stand in front of it—I'm a few minutes early and wonder if I should wait.

The tunnel is empty except for me—and whoever's watching through the security cameras. No signs of Mr. Ryder, but I know he can't be far.

Before I can turn the knob, the door flies open, and I'm pulled inside so hard I'm jerked off my feet and careen into the opposite wall. I turn to face my attacker, hands held up, ready to fight. Until I remember the only way I can win this battle is to surrender.

I lower my hands and my gaze. Look up meekly. My uncle smiles at me. It's not the kind of smile you ever want to be on the receiving end of. With his black eyes and swollen nose and his teeth all showing, his smile is the kind of twisted grin you'd find on a Halloween monster mask.

"Jesse." He sighs my name with satisfaction. "I knew you'd come."

"Where's Miranda?"

"Not so fast." He spins me around, pushes me against the wall, one hand pressing his gun to the back of my neck, the other patting me down. He doesn't bother with the chewed-up pen in my pocket but does take my knife, cell phone, and my lighter.

I almost protest—the lighter has been my touchstone for so long…but then I remember. It was his to start with. It's always been his.

I'm glad to see it go.

He keeps me shoved against the concrete wall, leans in close. I realize he's hiding his face from the camera—from King. His voice drops. "We have a decision to make, you and I."

"What do you want?"

"What I've always wanted." I don't like the way his voice tightens with need. "You, Jesse. It's always been about you. King and I, we're headed off to one of those island paradises where no one can touch us. As long as he has a computer, he can rebuild his business."

"Then he doesn't need you. Why should he let you live? Why should he let either of us live?"

"Because I can supply the raw material for his business. We're partners."

Maybe I can turn him against King. "He can find his victims online. He doesn't need you or me."

He shoves me harder, my face smashes against the wall. Then

he steps back. Whatever decision he was making, it's made. I can't tell if that's good or bad.

I dare a sidelong glance over my shoulder. He's not looking at me; he's looking up at the security camera in the corner.

"King's watching us, isn't he?" I say for the benefit of Oshiro and his team. "He's in the security office."

I hope that's where Miranda is as well. All I need to do is stall my uncle long enough for Oshiro's men to reach her.

I notice the fire alarm control panel. Lights all red. Valves shut. No pressure in the system. The key's broken off in the lock so there's no way to reset it. "Why did you sabotage the fire suppression system?"

"What better diversion than to start a fire in the middle of that crowd upstairs?"

Shit. I hope Oshiro heard that and is calling the fire department. "Why do you need a diversion?"

"Maybe you're not so smart after all. We know about your video. Did you really think you could outsmart King?"

He takes a step back, his arm straight, the gun presses hard against my skull.

They already know about the video—does that mean Miranda is still alive, and told them? What did King do to her to get that information? It takes everything I have not to lash out at my uncle. But Miranda's only hope is for me to play the victim one last time. "I'll do anything you want. But first, I need to know that Miranda is safe, that you've let her go."

He senses a trap. Hesitates. I force myself to beg. "Please. Let me see Miranda."

That does it. He pulls his phone from his pocket. I crane my face around to see—and also to keep an eye on the door behind him. It's a picture of Miranda, looking panicked, lying against a dark background.

"No. That picture could have been taken anytime." He jerks the gun at my challenge. "Please. I need to see her go free." Inspiration hits me. It's almost nine. "Send her into the crowd, show me a video of her walking free—put it up on the Jumbotron if you don't want to stay too close. I'll go with you, stay with you. Just like you always wanted."

His eyes narrow. "Who are you to be giving us orders?"

He has no clue that I don't really care what he does—I'm just buying time for Oshiro's men. Surely they've found her by now.

He touches his earpiece, listening to King. Shakes his head sadly. "Sorry, Jesse. Guess there's been a change in plans. You're going to be found here, dead. After they sift through the ashes."

He's going to start the fire, with all these people? I push off the wall and spin to face him. He jumps back at the motion, gun pointed at my face. I raise my hands in surrender. "No. Stop. You don't need to do this. I'll go with you. I'll do whatever you want—"

There's a blur of motion behind him as Mr. Ryder rushes through the door and tackles him. I dive as the gun goes off, the shot hitting the wall beside me. They're struggling on the floor and it goes off again. Before I can do anything, my uncle leaps to his feet and runs out the door.

Mr. Ryder lies on the floor, blood staining the gray janitor's uniform along his left calf. I go to him, put pressure on the wound.

"Subject armed, on foot, heading up the tunnel toward the concourse," he shouts into his radio.

"Did they get Miranda?" I ask, my voice tight with adrenaline and fear. "Is she okay?"

He listens, then slumps back, shaking his head. "She wasn't in the security office. Neither was King. Oshiro killed the security feeds, though. King is blind."

I'm torn. My uncle knows where Miranda is—plus, I need to stop him before he can ignite whatever incendiary device he's planted. But there's a lot of blood coming from Miranda's dad.

"I'm fine," Mr. Ryder says, pushing my hands aside. More blood seeps out, but he grips his leg himself, slowing it. "Go stop him. Save Ariel."

"Ariel?"

"My daughter's real name. Hurry."

43

Miranda focused on examining the Jumbotron controls. The camera aimed at the inside of the booth was off now, but if she could turn it on, send the feed to the large screens…

"Now or never, young lady," King said, sliding the laptop in front of her. "Show me that you've killed that damn video or your friend is dead."

If Jesse was here, in the arena, then her dad must be as well. Hopefully with a plan. She needed to give them time.

"First, let my mother go." She prayed Jesse would forgive her. But she couldn't not try to save her mom.

King merely smiled and shook his head. "First, kill the video. Then we see how much your mother's life is worth to you."

Miranda frowned, trying to parse a path between his words. He'd never keep any deal he made—she and Jesse were as good as dead already. The best she could do was buy time for her dad to get here and find her mom. "You know as well as I do that nothing's ever truly lost on the Net."

"I know that. All I need is enough time to hop a plane. I need your little flash mob to fizzle and burn." He chuckled at the last.

"What do you mean?"

"Kill the video and I'll tell you."

She stood tall, faced him head-on. "I'm the only one who can kill the video, and you're the only one who can save my mom. If you want the video killed, I need to know she's safe."

Anger narrowed his eyes, but then he glanced at the clock. "Stubborn as ever, Ariel. Deal." He pulled a set of car keys from his pocket and set them on the console, out of her reach. "She's in the trunk of a car. Alive. Now your turn." He nudged her with his gun. "Don't try anything stupid or your friend is dead, followed by your mother."

He had no way of knowing that she no longer controlled the video's release. She made a big show of going to her own secured cloud drive and deleting the copy there. 8:58...she just needed to get Jesse out of here in the next two minutes before King realized he'd been conned.

"Done. Now let Jesse go."

King peered over her shoulder like a teacher double-checking her work. Nodded and spoke softly into his Bluetooth. She couldn't hear everything, something about things being taken care of. Then he turned back to her.

"Where's Jesse?" she demanded.

"Sad to say, your friend is already dead. As soon as you agreed to destroy the video, his uncle had orders to kill him."

Miranda leapt to her feet, almost tripping over the corpse of the Jumbotron operator. "No. You said—"

"I said I'd tell you what I have planned." He waved the pistol at her, and she backed up against the edge of the console. She could see the main Jumbotron screen over his shoulder, but King had his back to it. "Richard set a little surprise for everyone—one of his special fire starters. He's turned off the sprinklers and locked most of the doors. We'll be long gone before the panic starts." He raised the gun. "Well, I will be."

Her only weapon within reach was the laptop. Not bullet-proof, but heavy enough and sharp enough. All she needed was a distraction.

Right on cue the flash mob poured into the center of the arena and Miranda's video started on the Jumbotron. The kids in the mob cheered and raised signs—there hadn't been time to orga-nize anything more elaborate—as King's photo filled the screen.

"I'll be dead in twelve hours, and this man is the reason why," Miranda's voice echoed through the arena.

King whipped his head around, staring at his own image blown up larger than life. "You bitch—"

He raised his gun. Pointed it at her.

Miranda felt no panic. No numbers collided in her head, no urge to curl up and hide from the world. Instead, she felt calm. In control for the first time in two years.

There was no way she would win this battle. He was twice her size and had a gun.

As she saw King's face—his true identity—broadcast for the world to see, she realized she'd already won the war. With the most powerful weapon of all: the truth.

"Stop it!" he ordered, glancing at the Jumbotron controls. There were dozens of buttons and toggles with no obvious kill switch.

With his attention divided, Miranda saw her chance. She

swung the laptop with all her might, cracking it against the side of his head, driving him back, giving her the opening she needed.

———————

I race up the tunnel and push through the double doors leading onto the concourse. People are milling around, the car show in full swing. Noise echoes from the interior of the arena where the main events are, but the thick walls separating the seating area and this outer concourse deaden it.

The concourse is as wide as a two-lane highway, traveling up and around the outside of the arena. This is where they have the older cars on exhibit, cars lovingly restored by local amateur enthusiasts. Like what my dad used to do. Only he'd put all that love and care into a car, then sell it so we could have some extra cash.

My uncle is nowhere to be seen. I can't see Miranda or King or Oshiro or any of his men, either. All these damn people. I shove and push, trying to gain a vantage point. If King's ready to kill me, did that mean he's going to kill Miranda as well?

Maybe he already has, a tiny voice whispers inside me. I shake my head, forcing my fears aside.

There's a disturbance on the curve up ahead, someone pushing through the crowd. Has to be my uncle. But with all these people, there's no way I'll ever catch up to him. He's disabled the fire alarms, so that won't help. If I yell "fire!" all I'll do is start a stampede of panic.

A trio of giggling girls brush past me and I stumble into a British racing green Austin-Healey. I bark my shin against the fender and curse, moving past. Then I stop, tugged to a halt by a memory long buried.

I know this car. "Sprite," the carmaker called the model. My dad called it "Bug Eye" because of the way the headlights perched on the hood. It looks exactly like the last car we worked on together, the car my dad taught me to drive—well, how to start the engine and shift the gears as he tweaked things under the hood.

I stare at the little green car, knowing I'm wasting time. Miranda could be dying while I stand here; all these people could die because I'm not moving fast enough to stop my uncle, but… my mind fills with the scents of motor oil and Lava soap and sweat. My dad. The way he never hugged me without lifting me off my feet, as if he couldn't stand even a few inches separating us. The proud smile he gave me when we finished a car, wiping the final coat of Turtle Wax from its polished surface. Like we were in it together.

Suddenly, I feel as if he's here with me, like he's in the crowd pushing past me or in my head or…I don't know, but next thing I know, I'm beside the car, leaning over it. A glimmer of a plan is forming—it's crazy. Ridiculous. It will never work and everyone's going to die because I can't think of anything better, but it's all I have and I hang on to it with everything I am.

There's no outside door handle on the low-riding convertible. The keys dangle from the ignition. No owner in sight. I pop the door from the inside, slide into the driver's seat—on the wrong side, the right side—turn the key and am rewarded with a sputter of noise. Clutch and shift, I hear my dad's voice in my head. Oh yeah, don't forget the parking brake.

I lean on the horn—I'd almost forgotten about the lightning bolt on the steering column. As a kid, I'd loved that emblem, polished it to a shine. It feels good being behind this wheel, like it did working with my dad, as if somehow, he put this car here right when I needed it most.

The crowd parts, people pointing at me, others taking photos with their cell phones as I yell at them to get out of my way. The car jerks until I find second gear, then with the horn and people's shouts clearing my path, I speed up the ramp.

The other cars on exhibit don't leave a straight path for me, so it's a lot of wrenching of the wheel one way then the other. The Austin-Healey is so low slung all I can see are people's backs and legs until they jump out of my path, giving me little time to react. I can't even see my uncle, can only hope he hasn't ducked inside to the seating area where I'd never find him.

I steer clear of a candy-apple-red Cadillac convertible and almost hit a little girl. The car shudders as I jam the brakes. The girl's crying, her parents shouting, another guy running after me like he's going to try to hop in and stop me, and I clutch the wheel tighter, foot back on the gas pedal.

I feel crazy and giddy and totally out of any other options. The crowd parts for me, some of them laughing and pointing like this is some kind of joke. They think I'm crazy or stupid. But I shove all those thoughts aside.

Miranda. I have to save Miranda.

Finally, the crowd thins enough for me to spot my uncle. He's about fifty yards ahead, disappearing from sight around the curve in the building. I speed up, the engine begging me to change gears, but I don't dare risk stalling. As I round the curve, my uncle realizes something's going on, looks over his shoulder and sees me coming after him. The concourse ahead of him is empty; there's no way he can out run me now that I don't have to fight the crowd.

A rush of adrenaline excites me—I've done it! He speeds up, passing the restrooms. A mother and little boy are coming out, and he grabs the kid, pushes him into my path.

I spin the steering wheel, hit the brakes, stalling the car when I miss the clutch. The mother, screaming, rushes to save her child, forcing me to steer the other direction. Finally the car jerks to a stop, mother and kid are okay. I'm breathless with panic, and my uncle is nowhere in sight.

No way he could have run around the next curve that fast. I jump out of the car and stand, scanning the area, ignoring the mother yelling at me, clutching her boy to her. There's an unmarked door beyond the restrooms. With a sinking in my gut, I know that's where he went. He wasn't trying to outrun me; he was trying to buy time to set a fire. Create panic, disappear, and escape.

No way in hell. "Get out of here," I tell the mother. I race toward the unmarked door, expecting my uncle to come barging through it any second. I'm ready for him. No way is he going to get away this time. Unless there's another exit? Damn, he knows this place better than I do.

I open the door. A whoosh of flames roars through the air, slamming me backward. Rookie mistake—oxygen feeds a fire. My uncle knows that, set his trap so my following him would make things worse.

The people who've chased me up the ramp have finally caught up. Several cry out in alarm. A few run down toward the arena entrance; others open the doors to the interior and rush inside. There's something going on in the main area because I hear people stomping and shouting Miranda's name and "Truth changes everything."

Despite the noise, a new sound reaches me. My uncle's screams. He's trapped in the fire.

I inch as close as I can, wary that it's a trap. The room is a janitor's closet, narrow but long, filled with shelves of paper products and cleaning chemicals—plus whatever my uncle planted to start the fire. He's on the floor crawling toward the exit on the far wall, flames and debris covering his legs.

I'm not sure what went wrong but can guess. If he's used the same method as he did on the houses, the chlorine and petroleum, that mix creates a nice fireball. But it doesn't always give you time to escape first. In his rush to set the fire, he must have miscalculated, gotten trapped by the flames, unable to use his escape route out the other door.

There's a fire extinguisher a few feet away, beside the doors to the seating area. I break the glass, grab it, and return to the closet.

It's heavy in my arms, my lungs heaving with adrenaline. My uncle hasn't come out this door and I don't hear him anymore.

Black smoke fills my vision, and the heat is blistering even from several feet away. I pull my shirt and jacket up over my face, get down on all fours, and crawl inside. The flames are above me, dancing in delight as they find more fuel, hopping from shelf to shelf.

For a moment I'm mesmerized by their beauty and power. I'm tempted, so very tempted, to give them what they want, to let them feast. But my uncle is the only one who can tell me where King has taken Miranda.

I should be scared, but I'm not. I know fire. Know how to feed it, bring it to life. And how to kill it.

Stray sparks squirrel their way below my shirt collar, singeing my skin. Beside me, flames flick out, reaching for my arms, but Dad's jacket protects me. Aiming the extinguisher at the heart of the flames, I clear a path to my uncle.

My eyes sting with smoke and sparks rain down from overhead. He's slumped on the floor, not moving. Gagging on the foul air, straining to breathe, I pull him out to the concourse. Several men including a few security guards help me get him clear as they rush the fire, armed with more extinguishers.

We collapse together on the concrete floor. He's breathing, half his shirt is burned away, the flesh below black, with more burns on his legs as well. He opens his eyes.

"Where's Miranda?" I ask, coughing out the words.

He snorts and lies back, shaking his head at my foolishness. His gaze tells me to go to hell.

One of Oshiro's men arrives and I stagger to my feet, walk away—it's the only way I can keep from kicking the snot out of him again.

I lean against the open door to the main floor, gulping in air. My face is on the screen, but it's Miranda's voice talking about how she's going to kill herself if the police don't set me free. "Listen to Griffin," she tells the crowd. "Because truth changes everything."

I'm not sure what she said before this, but the people watching are totally riveted. A few are weeping. Suddenly the picture breaks up and a new image appears: it's the man who tried to kill Janey, head bleeding, face contorted in fury, charging at a girl...Miranda.

This isn't from the video. My heart lurches into my throat. This is live. King is trying to kill Miranda. Where are they?

I turn in a circle, my neck craned as I search the floors above me. There are lights on in the Jumbotron booth across the arena, on the top level, high overhead.

I race back out to the concourse. "They're in the control booth," I shout to Oshiro's man. I run back to the little car, shove it in gear, and ignoring his shouts, rev it up the twisting spiral leading to the skyboxes and broadcast booth.

Lucky for anyone else, there are no more exhibits—and thus no innocent bystanders for me to hit—this high up. The smell of rubber burning as I skid around the turns fills the air. It tastes like my fear. All I can see is Miranda; all I can imagine is her dead because I'm too late.

Finally, I spot the booth. The brakes squeal and I jump free of the car as soon as it stops. I yank the door to the booth open, rush inside. Miranda and King are struggling for a gun.

He's bigger than she is, but she's kicking and clawing and biting for all she's worth, refusing to yield her grip on his wrist, pushing the gun away from her so he can't get a shot. He grabs her long hair, tries to yank her off her feet. I tackle him from behind.

We go down in a heap, the gun flying across the floor to where it comes to rest against a man's body. Miranda scrambles for it, grabs it just as King heaves me off and gets to his feet.

Beyond the glass surrounding the booth everything we do unfolds on the Jumbotron. Miranda aims the gun directly at King. He stops, ready to pounce on her.

"Put it down," he shouts.

"No. I'm not taking orders from you. I want you to tell the world everything you've done." She fires the gun into the floor, inches away from his foot. Then she takes aim at his chest, center mass. The kill zone. "Tell them. Now."

The color drains from King's face as he stares at the gouge in the carpet, and I wonder if he's ever been threatened by anyone who can back it up. So very different than stalking little girls like Janey. He holds his hands up in surrender. "You can't shoot me. I'm unarmed."

Her aim doesn't waver. If anything her expression tightens with resolve. She's beautiful, I realize. Long, dark hair with curls that defy gravity, dark skin, dark eyes you could fall into. Eyes that are shiny with tears.

"I don't care," she says, her voice strong despite her tears. "They can send me to prison for the rest of my life. Killing you, I'd be doing the world a favor."

I take a step forward, unsure of what to do or say. She keeps the gun trained on King's chest. "Get out of here, Jesse. Before the cops come."

"No. I'm not leaving until you put the gun down."

She shakes her head, her finger sliding from the trigger guard onto the trigger.

"Miranda—Ariel!" I cry out. "You're not really going to kill him."

"Why not? He's taken everything from me!"

"No. He hasn't." I step between her and King. She pivots, shifting her aim around me. "Your mom and dad, you have them." I haul in a deep breath, stretch my arms wide. "And me, Miranda. You still have me."

King makes a sniffling noise behind me. Miranda's aim doesn't waver, but I can't give up on her.

"Put the gun down," I say, taking another step toward her. "For me, Miranda. For us."

Miranda jerks her gaze away from King. Looks me in the eye—not just at me, into me, like she's seeing my soul. Her expression softens. She drops the gun onto the console.

King lunges past me toward the door—only to run straight into Oshiro and his men. They shove him onto the floor and have him in handcuffs before I can blink. Miranda tosses Oshiro a set of car keys. "He said my mom is in the trunk."

Oshiro nods. "Don't worry. We're on it." They haul King out.

Miranda wavers, both hands clutching the edge of the control console as she leans back against it. I see the terror fill her face and I realize she's frozen in place, can't move. More than adrenaline—panic.

"Your mom will be fine." She's trembling now and I'm afraid her legs are going to give out. I cross the space between us and take her into my arms. Beyond her, our image fills the Jumbotron. The crowd goes wild. "I knew you wouldn't do it. Shoot King in cold blood."

"You know why I couldn't do it?" she whispers, circling me with her arms, letting me support her weight. "I thought of you. Of everything you've been through and how you never give up. I couldn't let you down."

The crowd is chanting, "Kiss, kiss, kiss." We ignore them, too busy touching and taking in each other. She's even more beautiful than I imagined.

"Ariel—" The cops are coming for me. We don't have long. There's so much to say and no time.

She shakes her head. "I hate that name. Silly mermaid."

"It's from Shakespeare. A spirit enslaved by an evil wizard who fights for freedom."

She laughs, tossing her hair as her entire body rocks with the magical sound. "*The Tempest*. Yes, I know. But I like Miranda better." She tilts her chin and wraps her arms around my neck. "Don't you?"

"I like you no matter what you call yourself." I sink into her embrace.

287

She hauls in her breath, searching for courage. "I have to face my parents."

I need to tell her about her dad getting shot, but I can't find the words. Somehow it was so much easier talking to her when I couldn't see her, smell her, feel her body against mine. All I want to do is stand here and hold her, make time stop rushing past us, an unstoppable current trying to force us apart.

"You'd better get going," she continues, her fingers stroking the back of my neck. "The police will be back for you any second."

I shake my head, not wanting to take the time to explain that the police—at least the Feds—are on my side. "You sticking around?"

She knows I mean much, much more than waiting for the police and courts to finish with me. "You want me to?"

"I'm done running and hiding."

Her smile turns into a grin that blinds me with its brilliance. "So am I."

Oshiro pokes his head inside the door. "We found your mom, Miranda. She's okay. They're bringing her in now."

I feel the relief surge through Miranda; we're that close. She squeezes me tight, bouncing on her tiptoes, as I hug her so hard I lift her off her feet.

Finally we can't avoid it any longer. Our lips touch. The kiss is better than anything I could ever dream of. The crowd is cheering and stomping their feet, rocking the floor beneath us. Or maybe that's Miranda rocking my world. I'm not sure, but it feels great.

EPILOGUE

O f course life isn't as easy as finding the girl of your dreams and solving all your problems with a kiss. Even if that kiss is earth-shattering.

I spend all day in custody, explaining everything to the cops, two lawyers (one for me, one from the DA's office), a child-protection worker, and then more cops, this time detectives and federal agents who listen and take notes as they go over everything again and again.

I ask for Miranda several times and they keep telling me she's fine, but I don't believe them, and it's starting to piss me off. I tell them she's only fourteen (they don't need to know she'll turn fifteen in just a few hours) and she has agoraphobia and they can't question her without her parents' and doctor's okay. I got that last from the lawyer Mr. Ryder got for me. I tell the lawyer I'll fire him if it means he can go be her attorney and watch out for her instead, and finally he goes to check on her, tells me not to say anything until he's back.

Another guy in a suit comes in, whispers something to one of the detectives, and suddenly they all leave. I wait by myself in the small room with no windows, not even the one-way mirror you see on TV. It's frustrating being kept out of the loop, but the only thing I'm worried about is Miranda.

Until the door opens again. Instead of my lawyer coming back, it's two guys in suits and my mom.

Her shoulders are slumped like an old woman's and she looks like her world has come crashing down around her, which of course it has. I know it's awful, but I just don't have the energy to care. Part of the reason why I'd insisted on talking without her present—I just can't handle worrying about how she'd take it, listening to the details.

"I told you," I snap when I see her, "I don't want her here." She's been hurt too much already and I'm so exhausted, I'm not sure I can protect her from everything I'm feeling.

The detective, I've forgotten his name already, pulls out a chair and helps my mom into it. The other guy, Mr. Ryder's FBI friend, a guy named Taylor who looks way too young to be an FBI agent but seems to know his stuff, sits down beside me. Now we four are gathered around the tiny table as if it's a family dinner.

"Things have changed," Taylor says, taking the lead. He doesn't look happy. "I need you both to hear this."

"What's changed?" I ask, on full alert. "Is King talking?"

"No. Not unless you count asking for a lawyer." They'd told me earlier that so far they had no concrete evidence against King. He'd destroyed it all in his preparation to leave the country. The scene at the arena he'd blamed on Miranda, said she'd been stalking him—even sent her father to harass him—that she was the one with the gun who'd forced him up to the control booth. According to his version of events, he'd tried to stop her, but she'd shot the man there. His word against hers.

Doesn't help that the only thing anyone at the arena saw was the two of them struggling for the gun and her threatening to shoot him, even though he was unarmed.

The cops also told me the recordings from my pen are circumstantial at best. Their only hope is my uncle, that he'll testify against King and lead them to the other men King worked with.

Suddenly I know exactly why they're here. "King's not talking but my uncle is, right? He wants a deal."

My mom looks stunned. She's still trying to deny the role my uncle played in all of this. I think it will be a long, long time before she can replace her version of the past with what really happened. I'm not looking forward to that day, not at all. When she realizes what she did, how she just gave me to him—how can a parent ever come back from that?

I can't deal with that now. I focus on the two men.

Taylor, the FBI agent, nods. "You have to understand, while the potential homicide and sexual assault charges are local, the cybercrimes are federal and so it's in the hands of the US Attorney. Given the extent of Kerstater's criminal activity—"

"You're going to do it. You're cutting him a deal."

Finally my mom gets it. She leans over the table. "You mean Richey isn't going to prison? Does that mean Jesse won't have to testify?" She says it like it's a good thing, as if the entire world doesn't already know what my uncle did—what I did. "Do we have a say in any of this? Can we recommend that you do that, give him what he wants?"

I know she thinks she's saving me—and her—the pain of testifying, but I can't help the flare of anger that she's willing to even discuss letting my uncle off the hook.

"I'm afraid not, ma'am. It's up to the US Attorney. I'm notifying you as a courtesy, that's all. He's asked for full immunity, and while one of my colleagues was taking his statement at the burn unit, something came to light that we thought you should know. This is all confidential, but—"

I jolt up straight as I finally understand what he's dancing around. I reach for Mom's hands across the table, take them both in mine, giving her something to hang on to. This is so much bigger than me and my anger issues. "He confessed," I choke on the words. "It's Dad. He confessed."

Mom's eyes go wide as Taylor continues, "A requirement for the plea bargain is that he confess any and all past criminal activity. Otherwise, his immunity deal is void." He turns to Mom. "I'm sorry, Mrs. Alexander. I truly am. As soon as we verify the identity of the remains found in your brother's house—"

For a second I think Mom's going to faint. The color drains from her face and her hands grip mine so tight my fingers go numb as Taylor tells us everything my uncle has confessed to.

How Dad went to my uncle, suspicious of the way he acted around me. Said I'd told him I didn't like it, didn't want to see my uncle anymore—I don't remember that, but I don't remember much about back then.

My uncle killed him. Then he let us get kicked out to the streets when Mom never heard back from Dad and we couldn't make the rent. Killing my dad was the perfect way for my uncle to get everything he wanted.

It was Dad's body they found in the fire. Dug up from where he'd been buried beneath my uncle's barn.

I thought Mom would break, hearing that. I know I almost did. Knowing he'd been so close all those years.

Dad stood up for me. He'd loved me that much. He hadn't abandoned me—us. He'd thought I was worth fighting for. He'd believed me, even though I was just a kid. He'd believed *in* me.

The rest of the night is a blur after that. Next thing I know, they decide there won't be any charges brought against me and I'm sitting with Mom in the front lobby of the police station when Miranda's folks come out from the detectives' area behind the desk. Mrs. Ryder has a black eye and split lip. Mr. Ryder is using a crutch. They both look scared. Miranda's not with them.

"Where's Miranda?" I jump to my feet. "What's wrong?"

Her dad answers, looking over his shoulder at the door behind the desk sergeant, as if expecting it to open and Miranda to appear. "Waiting inside. Our lawyer is still talking with the DA."

"Why?" I demand. "She didn't do anything wrong. She saved my life."

"They keep talking about attempted murder. Assault," her mom says in a dazed voice. "Federal computer crimes."

"It's bullshit. If she wanted to kill that scumbag, he'd be dead already." Her dad sounds more proud than upset.

"Is she okay?" I ask. "I mean, she told me about her panic attacks—"

Mrs. Ryder gives me a hug, the top of her head barely coming up to my chin. I can't believe she stopped the men who King sent to rape her; she's such a tiny thing. But definitely strong, just like her daughter. "Thanks for asking, Jesse. Her doctor says it can happen like this, flooding she calls it. The brain becomes so overwhelmed, there just isn't any more room for fear."

"So, she won't have to worry? It's not coming back?"

"Too soon to say," Mr. Ryder said. "But for now, she's doing all right."

"You know King's not talking—"

"Beyond trying to blame my daughter for the man he killed, yes, we know." Mr. Ryder's voice is flat, like he's trying to pretend he doesn't want to wrap his hands around King's throat and choke the life from him. But it's the fury that sparks in his wife's eyes that makes me take a step back.

I feel trapped, can't breathe, desperate for air, space to think. My lips go numb and I realize I'm hyperventilating. My chest is crushed so tight it takes me a moment to realize: this is what Miranda lives with every day. Yet, she's here, out of her safety zone, dealing with all this crap like the games King and my uncle are playing…because of me.

Feeling caged, I start pacing, fighting to find enough space, enough air.

"They aren't talking about—I mean, they can't actually arrest her, can they?" The room blurs around me I'm pacing so fast.

"No, of course not," Miranda's mom says. But I hear the doubt in her voice.

"They just need to get all the facts straight," Mr. Ryder adds.

He sounds certain, confident, but his arm tightens around his wife's shoulders and I know he's bluffing. He has no idea what will happen to Miranda. I think of all the stories about innocent people being falsely convicted of crimes they didn't commit, and I realize, as much as the cops helped us today, we can't always trust the law to do the right thing.

Case in point, the deal my uncle made. He's getting away with murder and the law is on his side.

After everything Miranda has done for me, I can't let there be the slightest chance that the cops lock her up. I have to help her, but I have no idea how. I stop my pacing and lean against the glass doors leading outside. The crowd from the arena has converged in front of the station. I'm stunned they're still here even though it's been hours and is now dark. *What do they want?* I wonder, tempted to put them in the same box as King's clients, voyeurs gorging on someone else's misery.

They're holding candles and signs, and there are speakers with bullhorns standing behind a police barricade. There are hundreds of them. Not just kids—moms and dads, as well.

It's weird. For so long one of my greatest fears was what the rest of the world would think of me if they ever learned the truth. I thought being branded a victim—or worse, people thinking I liked what my uncle did to me, that I wanted it—would be almost as bad as seeing Janey or Mom hurt because of me.

Now everyone knows the truth. And it doesn't matter. Sure, some might think badly of me. But I find I honestly don't care.

TV crews have set up on the steps of the station, filming the crowd and interviewing "experts" including Mr. Walker, my vice principal who started all this when he hung up on King. He's on the steps, talking to a pretty reporter from the local station, chest all puffed out.

Miranda said we could use the crowd. The power of the people, she'd called it. We need that power now.

If the crowd turns Miranda into a hero, there's no way they'll charge her. They wouldn't dare, not if they're letting scumbags like my uncle go free—and wouldn't the reporters just love to hear about that little deal?

I drag in a deep breath, my panic vanishing, and step through the doors.

The crowd sees me and goes wild. They hoist signs reading: *Take back the Net! Protect our Kids! Stop the Madness!*

Reporters crowd me. I'm blinded by the lights of their cameras. I don't know where to look or what to say, so I tell the truth.

"There's a girl, you know her as Miranda." The crowd roars so loud I'm disoriented for a moment and have to start again. "Miranda was cybersmashed because she dared to stand up to a bully. She was driven out of school, her family terrorized, and she tried to kill herself. Twice."

A gasp races through the crowd and they fall silent, listening.

"She's the bravest person I've ever known." I knuckle tears from my eyes, not caring how stupid I look. "She's been fighting predators, saving kids for years, and no one knew the price she paid. She almost died today saving my life."

Suddenly the crowd starts to cheer, drowning me out. There's a commotion behind me, and I turn to see Miranda rushing through the doors, running toward me. Straight into my arms. For another of those amazing kisses.

After that, I don't really care about much of anything else.

"We did it, Griffin!" she says when we come up for air. "They believe me. They're charging King!"

I keep my arms around her, don't want to ever let her go. "Jesse," I tell her. "Griffin is some made-up hero. I just want to be Jesse, a normal guy."

"As long as you never forget that you're my hero. Jesse," she says with a smile that makes me blink it's so blindingly bright. "I couldn't do this without you."

I pull her to me tightly. Lift her off her feet as pride surges through me.

For the first time in years, I'm proud to be Jesse Alexander. Son of James Alexander, a man who died protecting his family.

I wanted the truth and I got it, in all its painful glory. And the rest of the world now knows the truth about me. But the burning fear in my gut has vanished.

I can face tomorrow. I can face the world.

Miranda was right: truth changes everything.

ACKNOWLEDGMENTS

Thanks as always to my agent, Barbara Poelle, who believed in this story from the start; my critique partner, Toni McGee Causey, who wouldn't let me take the easy way out no matter how difficult it was to follow the truth; and to all the wonderful people at Sourcebooks who brought *Watched* to life.

NOTE TO READERS

The inspiration for this book came from clicking on a link my niece sent me. It led to the most heart-wrenching video I'd ever seen: Amanda Todd's suicide video.

Amanda was a victim of a capper and cyberstalker who succeeded in ruining her life. As a pediatrician, I've worked with a lot of victims—don't you hate that word? Victim? It immediately puts you on the losing side of a war you didn't even sign up for. It gives the bullies and the creeps the power.

You are not alone. We are all victims. We all lose when we let bullies and rapists and stalkers act like they've won, like they have the right to control any piece of our world, our lives.

We lose a piece of our own humanity every time someone like Amanda takes their own life. We lose the future she could have had, the world-changing ideas she might have come up with, the smiles and laughter and hugs she would have shared.

Watched deals with topics we usually relegate to the shadows, try our best to ignore, and pretend don't exist. I truly apologize for making you look into those dark recesses of the human soul. It wasn't an easy book to write—at times I felt nauseous, sick; other times I wept as I wrote, mainly because, as I told Jesse and Miranda's stories, I relived so many of the stories I heard from my patients.

My hope is that you found *Watched* empowering. Because we don't have to be victims or losers. We can stop the predators with the one weapon they have no power over: the truth.

The things happening to Jesse and Miranda in *Watched*, what happened to Amanda Todd, these things could happen in any country; they could happen in your city; they could be happening right now on the street where you live to someone you care about.

Here's what you need to do to help: tell the truth.

To a parent, a teacher, a doctor or nurse or police officer, a minister, rabbi, imam, or priest. Visit one of the links on the next page and tell the folks whose job it is to help. Tell the truth and don't stop until you find someone who not only listens but also helps.

It won't be easy. It will be the hardest damn thing you may ever have to do. But if we don't stand up, if we don't take back the power, if we accept our roles as victims, then what kind of world are we creating for ourselves?

This book started with a link to a video. I hope you click on one of the these sites and help put an end to stories like Jesse's and Miranda's.

Truth changes everything.

Thanks for reading,

CJ

WHERE TO FIND HELP

Rape, Abuse, and Incest National Network: www.RAINN.org
NetSmartz: www.netsmartz.org
Stop Bullying Now: www.stopbullying.gov
End Cyber Bullying: www.endcyberbullying.org

LOOKING FOR ANOTHER
HEART-POUNDING READ?

DON'T MISS
CJ LYONS'

BROKEN

1

If you want to get noticed fast, try starting high school three weeks late as the girl who almost died.

Unfortunately, attention is the last thing I crave. Give me anonymity anytime. Every time.

I just want to be a normal girl. No one special.

Saw a movie once, don't remember what channel, but it was in the dark hours of the night when it was just me and the TV. My favorite time of day.

It starred John Travolta back when he was young. The kid was so sick he lived in this plastic bubble and he was so excited when he got to leave it.

Me? When I saw the boy leave his bubble, I wanted it for myself. Coveted it.

God, how I'd die for a cozy little bubble to live my life in, safe from the outside world.

Only I'd paint my bubble black so no one could see me inside.

2

There are two metal detectors inside the main doors of Smithfield High and 337 students plus one trying to crowd through them. I'm the plus one. Not sure which line to stand in or if there's even a real line at all hidden somewhere in this mass of humanity. It's the largest crowd I've ever been in.

The school lobby echoes with voices and the stamping of feet. We're herded like a bunch of cows headed for slaughter. All that's missing are the cowboys and the branding irons.

No one else is nervous about this. They don't care about the metal detectors or what's in their bags or even the two guards manning the operation. They're not worried about being trampled or that there isn't enough oxygen or how many billions—no, trillions—of bacteria and viruses are wafting through the air, microscopic time bombs searching for a new home.

All they care about is me. The stranger in their midst. They shuffle around me uneasily, quickly sniffing out that I don't belong.

A girl with a pierced nose and heavy eyeliner looks at me like I'm a tacky rhinestone necklace on display at a pawnshop counter. She hides her mouth behind her hand as she whispers something to her friend with the purple streak in her hair.

A guy wearing a white and orange Smithfield Wildcats letter-man jacket trips over the backpack I wheel behind me, almost smashing into a wall before he catches himself. "Out of my way, loser."

His snarl is accompanied by a sneer. He stares down at me—he's huge, at least six feet tall, with shoulders that block my view. "I said, move it." I try to steer my backpack, but his feet get tangled as he zigs the same direction I'm zagging. "You don't want to piss me off. Understand?"

The crowd pushes him even closer so all I can hear is his voice. My heart booms in response, sending up its own distress call. His name is on his letterman jacket, embroidered above the wildcat with the long, sharp fangs. *Mitch Kowlaski. Football.* I shrink against the wall, making myself even smaller than my usual five feet two, and pull my backpack between my legs, giving him room to cut in front of me.

He joins a cluster of football players and continues to stare at me. His look is easy to read: what kind of loser brings a wheeled backpack to high school?

Not cool. Neither are my virgin-white, just out-of-the-box-this-morning sneakers that a guy in a pair of work boots stomps on. And why didn't I think to put on at least a little lip gloss this morning?

I scan the crowd, searching for the normal kids—and fail. Seems like being normal is out of style this season. You have to be "someone," create an alter ego: a jock, a church girl, a rebel, a loser.

Even I understand the danger of that last label.

I'm too skinny, too pale; my hair's all wrong; I should've tried to figure out makeup (as if Mom would ever let me!), shouldn't have worn this jacket (but I love my faded, soft, frayed denim jacket; my dad gave it to me). It's out of style and doesn't go with the new-blue of my jeans that everyone can tell are a last minute buy from K-Mart, because who needs clothes when you live in a hospital and—

An elbow nudges my back. My turn at the metal detector.

I roll my backpack—heavier than any other student's—over to the guard. He hefts it onto his examination table and zips it open. "What's this?"

"My AED." I try to sound hip and casual, like doesn't every kid carry their own advanced life support resuscitation equipment?

The guard snatches his hand away from my bag. "An IED?"

Now everyone is staring. At me.

"New kid has a bomb in there," Mitch, the guy I accidentally tripped earlier, shouts in mock dismay. His voice booms through the crowded space louder than a real IED going off.

Not everyone thinks it's a joke. A gasp goes up behind me, traveling down the line of waiting students faster than a roller coaster. I'm imagining that last part—I've never been on a roller coaster. Their stares push me forward.

"No. It's an AED." Sweat trickling down the back of my neck, I rush to explain before I'm branded a terrorist or, worse, a freak. Too late. Mitch and his group of football players are snickering and pointing at me. "Automated External Defibrillator. I need it for my heart."

Actually, I hope I never need it, but even though the school has an AED in the gym, Mom convinced the insurance company that I should have my own, smaller model to carry with me at all times. Just in case.

Story of my life in three words: Just In Case.

Just in case my heart does a backflip at the sight of a cute guy and lands on its ass, unable to spring back on its own.

Just in case the fire alarm goes off and startles me, releasing adrenaline, shocking my heart into quivering, cowardly surrender.

Just in case I'm too hot or too cold or eat the wrong thing or forget to take my meds and my heart decides today is the day to go galloping out of control, leaving me lying there on the floor for guys like Mitch Kowlaski to walk over while everyone else points and laughs at the girl who finally died...

Mom has a thousand and one Just In Cases. Like she keeps reminding me, if I were a cat, I'd already have used up more than nine lives.

Swallowing my pride and the chance that I'll ever be accepted here—who am I kidding? I never had a chance, only a hope—I pull my Philips HeartStart AED free from its case and show it to the guard.

He stares from the AED to me, taking in my way-too-skinny frame, paler-than-vampire complexion, sunken eyes, and brittle hair, and nods wordlessly. "Humor the girl-freak before she does something crazy" kind of nodding.

"See? Here's how you use it, it talks you through everything," I prattle on, trying desperately to sound nonchalant. Normal. I call the defibrillator Phil for short. The perfect accessory for any fifteen-year-old girl, right? The bright-blue plastic case matches my eyes, can't you see?

"Aw, look. Freakazoid has a broken heart," Mitch says. "Waiting for Dr. Frankenstein to shock some life into you, sweetheart? I got everything you need right here."

"Shut it, Kowlaski," the other guard yells at him. He turns to me. "You must be Scarlet Killian."

I now realize that the second line has also stopped to witness the end of my short career as a normal high school sophomore. Everyone now knows my name. Knows my heart is broken. Knows I'm a freak.

"Your mom told us to be on the lookout for you. Go ahead through."

Our hands collide as we both reach to return Phil to my pack. He jerks away. Reluctant to touch the complicated machine—or the girl whose life it's meant to save?

Why does everyone assume dying is contagious?

I shove Phil back in, zip the pack shut, slip through the metal detector without anything exploding, and bolt.

The football players, including Mitch, are crowded together on the other side, forcing me to push past them. "Must be tough having a heart ready to go tick, tick, boom!" Mitch laughs. His friends must think it's funny because they join in.

Totally embarrassed and certain everyone is staring, I keep my head down and walk away, hauling Phil behind me. My heart is beating so fast spots appear before my vision. Not a

Near Miss, just plain, old-fashioned, let-me-crawl-in-a-hole-and-die mortification.

Time spent in high school: three minutes, forty-two seconds. Time spent as a normal sophomore girl before being outed as the freak with the bum heart: fifty-five seconds.

Time remaining in my high school career as a freak: 5,183,718 seconds.

Maybe less if the doctors' predictions are right and I get lucky and drop dead.

ABOUT THE AUTHOR

Pediatric ER doctor turned *New York Times* bestselling thriller writer CJ Lyons has been a storyteller all her life—something that landed her in many time-outs as a kid. She writes her Thrillers with Heart for the same reason she became a doctor: because she believes we all have the power to change our world.

In the ER, she witnessed many acts of courage by her patients and their families, learning that heroes truly are born every day. When not writing, she can be found walking the beaches near her Lowcountry home, listening to the voices in her head, and plotting new and devious ways to create mayhem for her characters.

To learn more about her Thrillers with Heart go to www.CJLyons.net.